THE CHIRK CASTLE KILLINGS

A DI Ruth Hunter Crime Thriller #13

SIMON MCCLEAVE

STAMFORD
PUBLISHING

THE CHIRK CASTLE KILLINGS

By Simon McCleave

A DI Ruth Hunter Crime Thriller
Book 12

First published by Stamford Publishing Ltd in 2022

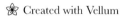 Created with Vellum

Your FREE book is waiting for you now!

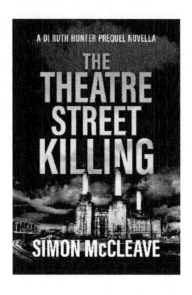

Get your FREE copy of the prequel to
the DI Ruth Hunter Series NOW
http://www.simonmccleave.com/vip-email-club
and join my VIP Email Club

For James, Barbara, Kitty and Vincent – and Rod x

Prologue

D *oncaster 2021*

IT WAS APPROACHING MIDNIGHT. OFFICERS FROM SOUTH Yorkshire Police moved into position beside a small bungalow on the outskirts of Doncaster. It had been four hours since Detective Inspector Ruth Hunter's partner Sarah Goddard had received a distressed phone call from her mother, Doreen. She was being held hostage. Sarah was going to give evidence in a murder, conspiracy and sex-trafficking trial. Taking Doreen hostage was a blatant attempt to scare Sarah into not testifying.

Having liaised with South Yorkshire Police, and explained the urgency of the situation, Ruth and Sarah had sped cross country to Doncaster from North Wales.

Ruth took a final drag on her cigarette, stubbed it out on the pavement and blew the smoke out into the cold night air. She was standing with Sarah behind the police line about fifty yards from the bungalow. They watched as four armed response officers - AROs - carrying Glock 9mm pistols and dressed in their black Nomex boots, gloves, and Kevlar helmets over balaclavas, moved purposefully to the front door awaiting instruction. Their presence was an eerie and ominous reminder of how much danger Doreen was in. No one knew if Vitali was armed or if there were others. Ruth hadn't said anything to Sarah but they didn't even know if Doreen was still alive.

The CID officers from Doncaster were also wearing bulletproof vests, and those with firearms training had handguns. They were taking no chances. DS James Foley of the South Yorkshire Police was in charge - he motioned for the CID officers and two AROs to head down the side of the bungalow. The unnatural silence that pervaded the scene added to the growing tension in the air.

DS Foley looked over and motioned for Ruth to join him close to the rickety, iron garden gate.

'I'd better go,' Ruth whispered to Sarah who was standing nervously behind the blue police tape, with about half a dozen *rubberneckers* – police slang for nosey members of the general public who were there just to see what was going on.

'Yeah, okay,' Sarah replied under an anxious breath. Her eyes were fixated on her mother's bungalow.

Ruth looked at her, reached out and squeezed her hand. It was cold. 'Don't worry. We're getting her out of there, safe and sound.'

'Thanks,' Sarah mumbled but she didn't look convinced. Her mother Doreen was suffering from lung cancer and she was frail and elderly.

Ruth flashed her warrant card to a uniformed officer, ducked under the *Police! Caution!* tape and walked over to join DS Foley on the pavement. Foley was in his 40s, awkward looking, with thinning straw-coloured hair and slightly buck teeth. He had a thick Yorkshire accent.

'You want to come in with us, ma'am?' he whispered. They might be in Yorkshire, but Ruth was still a DI and senior in rank.

Ruth nodded. 'The hostage, Doreen Goddard, is a family member. I want to make sure she's safe.'

'Of course,' Foley said with an understanding expression. He then walked over to a nearby squad car. He lifted the boot, pulled out a black Kevlar bulletproof vest, returned and handed it to her. 'Might be a bit big, ma'am, but I'm guessing you don't want to go charging in there without one?'

'Not really,' she replied as she took it and put it over her arms, 'especially as our intel suggests the suspect might have connections to Russian criminal gangs.'

Looking back over at Sarah, her beautiful chestnut eyes and blonde hair tucked behind her ears, it was hard to think over what they had been through in the past few months.

In November 2013, Ruth and Sarah had been living together as a couple in their flat in Crystal Palace, South-East London. Sarah boarded a train to London Victoria one morning and simply disappeared. No contact, no note, no clue as to where she had gone. As a copper, Ruth had made sure the CCTV footage from that day had been scoured. Every station on that line had been searched. There had been television appeals and articles in the press. There had been sightings of Sarah from all around the world. Ruth had even followed women who she thought looked like Sarah, but she had simply vanished.

Little did Ruth know that Sarah had become secretly embroiled in the seedy world of elite sex parties in London through a man named Jamie Parsons. A few days before

3

she had disappeared, Sarah had witnessed Lord David Weaver raping and then 'accidentally' killing a teenage girl in a bedroom at one of these *Secret Garden* sex parties. Lord Weaver was a life peer who had served as both Foreign Secretary and Chief Whip in the late 1980s. He was a very visible member of the House of Lords, often photographed with the great and the good, the rich and famous. His wife Olivia moved in social circles with lesser members of the royal family.

To make matters worse, Sarah's presence in the room had been spotted by Jamie Parsons and three others. Jurgen Kessler, a German banker and close friend of Parsons, who was wanted by Berlin Police for questioning in connection to the murder of two young women. Patrice Le Bon, the multi-millionaire owner of several Paris model agencies, who was under investigation for human trafficking. And Sergei Saratov, a Russian billionaire, who had gone underground when police investigated his extensive use of escorts and sex workers in hotels that he owned in an exclusive European ski resort. These men were very rich, very powerful – and therefore very dangerous. And Sarah was an eyewitness. She was taken away to France and was forced to move around Europe working as a high-class escort.

Ruth's first major breakthrough in her quest to find Sarah had occurred when she found CCTV which showed Sarah entering The Dorchester Hotel in London in 2015 with Sergei Saratov. It proved, for the first time, that Sarah hadn't been attacked or murdered on the train from Crystal Palace in November 2013. However, it posed a whole new set of questions. Saratov had been implicated in various trafficking crimes, as well as allegations of sexual assault. Ruth had no idea what Sarah's relationship to Saratov was.

With the help of Met Missing Persons Officer Stephen Flaherty, Ruth eventually tracked Sarah down to an elite escort agency, Global Escorts, in Paris. And that was where Ruth had her first glimpse of Sarah in over seven years during a FaceTime call. Before Sarah responded, the screen had gone blank, Ruth heard Sarah scream, and the call ended. Despite endless tracking by Ruth and then the Met Police Missing Persons Unit, the number couldn't be traced, and the Global Escorts website had been closed down.

It had now been just over three months since Ruth had flown to Paris and rescued Sarah from the clutches of Global Escorts. She, Nick and Sarah had nearly lost their lives.

It seemed likely the man calling himself Vitali, who had called Sarah earlier and had taken Doreen hostage, was working for Sergei Saratov.

'Right, let's get this show on the road then, shall we?' a voice said, breaking her train of thought. It was Foley.

Ruth nodded. She heard the thudding of her pulse in her ears and felt the grip of anxiety in her stomach. She adjusted the heavy ballistic vest.

God, this is bloody uncomfortable. I'd forgotten how heavy these bloody things are.

Foley was over 6ft tall, so it wasn't surprising his spare vest didn't fit her.

Ruth and Foley moved quietly along a paved, weed-strewn garden path and arrived outside the innocuous front door with a small wooden sign that read *Appleyard No. 23*. Ruth glanced up at the black night sky. An aeroplane, with its tiny red and white lights flashing, moved silently above them.

Foley beckoned to one of the AROs who then stepped forwards with a steel battering ram that would break down the door in one hit. Police officers often amusingly called it *the big red key*.

Here we go. Please God, let Doreen be okay.

'Gold Command from nine-zero. Officers in position at target location. Over.'

The radio crackled back. 'Nine-zero received. Gold Command order is GO.'

Ruth held her breath. It reminded her of all the armed raids she had led when she worked in Peckham, South London. Then she thought about what they might find once they gained access to the bungalow. Her instinct was that the Russian hitman – or whatever he was – would be long gone. This was Sergei Saratov's attempt to demonstrate to Sarah that he could get to her, or anyone in her family, any time he wanted. Ruth knew there would be contact of some kind in the next day or so warning Sarah to keep her mouth shut about the events of Friday 1st November, 2013. Of course, she knew that Doreen might have been taken from her home as a hostage. She might have been harmed – or she might have been killed.

Ruth took a long, deep breath. *Here we go.*

Foley nodded at the AROs and he and Ruth moved back a few paces.

Bang!

Ruth flinched as the door swung open with an almighty thud and the officers moved in, weapons trained in front of them.

'Armed police!' they bellowed as they stormed into the flat. 'Armed police! Everyone get down!'

Ruth followed Foley inside - her heart pounding hard against her chest.

The bungalow was tidy but smelled of damp, and stale cigarette smoke. A solitary coat and umbrella hung from the hooks in the hallway. A few pictures had been placed along the wall.

Where is she?

Moving swiftly, the AROs checked each room, shouting 'Clear!' as they went.

Ruth quickly manoeuvred herself down the hallway rechecking each room.

An ARO hurried down the hallway. 'Nothing, sir. No sign of anyone.'

'Shit,' Ruth muttered. *Please don't tell me that he's taken Doreen with him. This isn't good.*

Ruth frantically went from room to room again in the vain hope that Doreen was hidden somewhere. How was she going to go out there and tell Sarah that her mother had been taken hostage and they had no idea where she was?

Then, from inside the main bedroom, a noise and some movement.

What was that?

Ruth turned and walked over to where she thought the noise had come from – a narrow wooden cupboard that had been built into an alcove.

She stopped to listen and then heard the noise again.

Carefully opening the doors, she immediately saw a frail, elderly woman with brown gaffer tape over her mouth. Her hands were tied with a plastic tie. She cowered, looking utterly terrified.

Doreen! Thank God!

Doreen looked at her blankly, blinked, then shifted herself. She reached out and Ruth took her hand. Her bony, emaciated fingers were icy and still shaking with fear.

Ruth gave her a reassuring look. 'No one's going to hurt you, okay? We're going to look after you.'

Chapter 1

T wo weeks later

SARAH AND RUTH WERE UPSTAIRS IN THE HOUSE THAT HAD been provided to Sarah in North Wales by the UK Protected Person's Service – the UKPPS. It was close to the tiny village of Hanmer, but was actually in the middle of a wooded area and at least a mile to the nearest neighbour.

The house was small, tidy and had everything she needed. When Sarah had first moved in, everything seemed dated, antiquated, and from another age, probably the 70s. It even had an archetypal avocado bathroom suite. The walls had been marked with scuffs and flaking paint-work. There were roller blinds that looked like they had been stained with cigarette smoke.

Over a few weeks, she and Ruth had spent weekends and evenings giving the place a lick of paint. Old sofas had been covered with colourful throws and peppered with cushions. Woodwork had even been sanded and revarnished. The house now felt like home. The PPS had installed a series of discreet panic buttons throughout. They had also reinforced the door to the main bedroom and added a series of heavy-duty locks. The main bedroom was now effectively a panic room.

Sarah's mother Doreen had spent a few days in hospital after the incident at her home. The UKPPS had then agreed that Doreen could move from Doncaster over to North Wales to live with Sarah. It was the perfect solution and allowed Sarah to look after her mother properly.

Ruth padded across the landing, the soft carpet under her feet, holding a glass of iced water. For a moment, she looked at the framed Glastonbury poster that she had given Sarah as a moving-in poster – *Glastonbury 2003*. It's where they had first got together. Their first kiss had been as they watched *Radiohead* playing *Fake Plastic Trees* on the Pyramid Stage on the Saturday night. On the Sunday night, they had taken Ecstasy and danced to *Moby*. She could remember spinning and grinning as the song *Porcelain* played and the hairs on the back of her neck stood up in the intensity of that moment.

Ruth peered quietly into the spare bedroom where Doreen was resting.

'It's all right dear, I'm just having a bit of a rest,' Doreen said with a kind smile. She'd been to the University Hospital over in Llancastell for chemotherapy and it had knocked her for six. The wig that she usually wore to cover her hair loss had been replaced by a new orange patterned head scarf.

Doreen pointed to her head. 'What do you think?'

'The scarf?' Ruth said. 'I love it. Very colourful.'

'Yeah, well I saw that Nadiya who won *Bake Off*

wearing an orange scarf like this, so I went online and got myself one,' Doreen explained, clearly pleased with her choice.

Ruth smiled. 'Suits you, Doreen. Very stylish.'

'Thanks, love.'

A radio beside her bed was playing music. Ruth recognised the song as *Needles and Pins*.

'I love this song,' Ruth commented as she came over and put the water on Doreen's bedside table.

'*Needles and Pins*,' Doreen stated. 'But can you tell me the group?'

Ruth frowned. 'I can't. I want to say *Gerry and the Pacemakers* but I know that's wrong.'

'Close enough.' Doreen nodded. '*The Searchers.* I loved them. They were from Liverpool too, you know?'

'I didn't,' Ruth admitted. 'That whole *Merseybeat* thing.'

Doreen had a twinkle in her eye and whispered, 'Don't tell Sarah, but I had a bit of a dalliance with the guitarist John McNally one night.'

Ruth laughed. 'A *dalliance*?'

'Me and my friend Maggie went over to see *The Searchers* play at the ABC in Cleethorpes,' Doreen explained. 'Must have been about 1964. We went to get their autographs at the stage door and they asked us out for a drink. And you know, we went back to their hotel bar and one thing led to another, if you know what I mean?'

Doreen didn't need to fill in the blanks.

'Doreen, I never knew you were a groupie!' Ruth chortled. 'I'm shocked.'

'It was just the once, mind,' Doreen laughed, keen to let Ruth know that she didn't make a habit of that sort of behaviour.

'Of course,' Ruth reassured her with a smile as she

headed for the door. 'I'll leave you to your reminiscing. Let us know if you need anything.'

'Ruth?' Doreen said as she got to the door. She now had a more serious expression on her face.

'Yes?'

Doreen gave her a meaningful expression. 'Thank you. I'm so glad Sarah's got you, you do know that?'

Ruth smiled. 'Thank you. I'll come and check on you later, okay?'

Wandering down the landing, Ruth felt buoyed by Doreen's amusing story and her kind words.

She padded down the stairs and saw that Sarah was preparing the living room for the arrival of Maggie Pryce, who was her liaison officer at the PPS. Maggie wanted to debrief Sarah after what had happened in Doncaster, as well as update her on the progress of the investigation into Lord Weaver, Le Bon and Saratov.

Strolling into the living room, Ruth saw Sarah was plumping cushions and having a general tidy up.

'Mum okay?' Sarah asked as she scooped up newspapers and magazines.

'I should say so. She asked me not to tell you, but she just told me about a one-night stand she had with a member of *The Searchers*.'

Sarah gave her a look. 'John McNally?'

Ruth raised an eyebrow. 'Yeah. She told you?'

'About three times,' Sarah sighed with an amused smile. 'I think she's losing her memory, poor old bird. Wait 'til she tells you about the time she spent the night with Ringo Starr, when *The Beatles* played Scarborough in 1964.'

Ruth's eyes widened. 'Oh my God. I didn't know your mum was such a goer! Fair play, Doreen.'

Sarah shook her head. 'I know. We never really had the

whole mother/daughter conflict thing. I thought she was very cool.'

'She is very cool,' Ruth said.

There was a knock on the door and Sarah wandered out to go and answer it.

A few seconds later, she returned with Maggie. She was late 40s, smartly dressed with brown wavy hair and fashionable glasses. She spoke with the hint of a Scottish accent – maybe Glaswegian, Ruth thought.

Maggie had made her way over from Manchester, where she was based. The UKPPS had recently become more centralised under the leadership of the NCA – the National Crime Agency.

'Maggie, this is my better half, Ruth,' Sarah explained as they came in.

'Nice to meet you.' Maggie shook Ruth's hand. 'Detective Inspector, isn't it?'

'At work, yes,' Ruth said with a nod as they all sat down.

'How's your mum doing?' Maggie enquired with genuine concern as she settled in the armchair.

'She's getting there but still a bit shaken up,' Sarah replied.

'I'm not surprised.' Maggie shook her head. 'I can't imagine how scared she must have been. Especially at her age and I know she's not been well.'

'I'm so glad you've allowed her to come and live here,' Sarah admitted.

'Yes.' Maggie reached for some folders in her briefcase.

'Do you want some tea or coffee?' Ruth asked.

'You know what, I've just had a coffee in the car, so I'm fine thanks,' Maggie replied with a smile. She then looked at a folder. 'As far as we know, the location of this house hasn't been compromised.' She took out a photo of a man with a shaved head in his 40s. 'We believe this is the man who took your mum hostage. Vitali Lenkov. He's ex-Russian *Spetsnaz*, which is their special forces. Now he's effectively a mercenary – a gun for hire.'

Sarah looked over. 'And he works for Saratov?'

'We can't establish a direct link yet,' Maggie admitted, 'but that's our guess. You haven't had any contact from anyone since then, have you?'

Sarah shook her head. 'No, nothing.'

Ruth sat forward on the sofa. 'My experience is limited on hostage situations, but I am surprised that Sarah hasn't been contacted to explicitly warn her not to give evidence.'

Maggie shrugged. 'Maybe they felt that what they did to your mum was obvious enough?'

'What about the investigation?' Sarah enquired.

'There is good news on that front,' Maggie explained. 'The police believe that they have a location where they think Gabriella Cardoso's body might be buried.'

Ruth looked at Sarah. It was very significant news.

Gabriella Cardoso was the seventeen-year-old Portuguese au pair that Sarah had seen Lord Weaver strangle in November 2013. She had told the family she worked for that she was going out with friends in Notting Hill on Friday November 1st 2013, but never came home. There was a police investigation but there was a suggestion that she might have travelled to Australia to meet up with backpacker friends from Portugal out there. There is no record of her travelling out of the country in the days after her disappearance. It wasn't until Sarah's testimony that there had been any suggestion of foul play in Gabriella's disappearance.

'Oh my God,' Sarah said with a shocked expression.

'Clearly this is a major breakthrough for the police investigation,' Maggie stated. 'The police will let us know as soon as they have any news. They're starting to search the area tomorrow.'

Ruth looked at Sarah. If the police could find Gabriella's remains, then it wouldn't just be Sarah's testimony that the CPS were relying on in court.

Sarah bit her lip as a tear rolled down her face. 'Sorry …'

Ruth reached out and put her hand on her shoulder. 'Hey …'

Sarah blinked and then looked at them. 'I just remember the look on her face. In that room. She looked so scared. I should have helped her.'

Maggie shook her head. 'You mustn't blame yourself, Sarah. It all happened so fast. You're not responsible for what happened to Gabriella.'

Sarah nodded. 'I just hope we can get those bastards put away and they can rot in jail for the rest of their lives.'

Chapter 2

March 15ᵗʰ 2021

THE VW CAMPERVAN HURTLED AROUND THE DARK BEND. IT was about 11pm and pitch black outside except for the blazing headlights from the car that was following them.

They were being chased.

Daniel found himself thrown across the inside and banged his head against a low cupboard.

Ow, that hurt!

'Dad!' he shouted as he winced from the blow to his temple.

'Hold onto something, Daniel,' his dad yelled. He sounded scared. His dad never sounded scared.

Oh God, what's happening?

Ten minutes earlier, Daniel had been sleeping in the back of the orange VW campervan that he lived in with his dad, Vince. They never seemed to settle anywhere very long. In fact, Daniel couldn't remember the last time he'd been to school for more than a term or two. His dad said that traditional education was a waste of time. Exams were just a memory test. Daniel would learn a lot more on the road, travelling the country.

Once in a while, they would rent a flat somewhere when his dad decided they needed a break from being on the road. Daniel would be enrolled in a local primary school which he hated. It meant he was permanently *the new boy* and when he tried to explain that he and his dad travelled around a lot, the inevitable comments about them being *pikeys* or *Gypsy scum* would start. After a while, teachers would begin to ask questions and try to contact previous schools. The Educational Welfare Officer would start to ring and sometimes social workers would knock at the door.

His dad would give him that familiar look and say, *Looks like we're back on the road, old son.* And off they would go in the middle of the night.

Daniel loved being on the road. They would stop at castles, beaches or the odd museum along the way. His dad said that he was giving him a proper education. A couple of times they even stayed overnight at a hotel. It had been amazing. There was even a telly on the wall.

When the teachers or other kids asked him what his dad did for a living, he would make something up. *Tell them I'm a sales rep and that's why we have to travel around the country so much,* his dad advised him. Even though Daniel was ten years old, he wasn't stupid. He knew his dad made money selling *wacky backy*. He heard other people call it lots of other names – *grass, pot, ganja, bud.* He hated the smell of it but his dad only smoked it once in a while. Whenever they parked up there would be a few phone calls, or a trip to the local pub, where his dad would sell the stuff. If he ever

asked about it, his dad would tell him that it was *medicinal.*
He said that people who were in pain, or had certain
diseases, smoked weed or had it in cakes or cookies to
make their pain go away. He told Daniel that it wasn't even
illegal in most of America now. It was just the British
Government who were being bloody old fashioned and
stupid. He said it wasn't surprising as they all went to
public schools and Oxford and Cambridge. Apparently
they were all *out of touch.*

Suddenly, Daniel felt the tyres at the back of the van
skid and lose their grip on the road. His stomach was tight
and his heart was beating hard against his chest.

Why are they chasing us?

Reaching out to grab onto a handle, he looked out of
the back of the van. He squinted at the dazzling headlights
of the car that seemed to be hunting them down.

'You okay, mate?' his dad shouted back, trying to sound
calm.

Daniel didn't answer. Of course he wasn't all right.
They were being chased and he'd banged his head hard.

'Fuck this,' Vince growled as he pulled the van over to
the side of the road.

What the hell is he doing? Daniel wondered as he took a
gulp. His breathing was quick and shallow.

'Dad!' Daniel cried. 'Why are you stopping?'

Leaning down, Vince pulled a baseball bat from where
it rested under the passenger seat.

'Don't worry,' Vince replied. 'I'm gonna sort this out.
Once and for all.'

'Dad,' Daniel whimpered.

Vince turned and looked at him. 'Listen to me, mate.
I'm sure this is just a misunderstanding. But if anything
happens to me, I want you to get out and run and hide.
Okay?'

Daniel nodded but he now felt physically sick. What did he mean? What was going to happen to him?

'Good lad,' his dad reassured him with a forced smile.

Glancing back, Daniel could see that the car which had been pursuing them had pulled over and was parked about thirty yards behind them. The car's full beam headlights still glared out angrily into the darkness. It was one of those big cars. The Americans called them SUVs didn't they?

Vince opened the van door, got out and marched purposefully towards the car as two figures got out of the car behind.

Daniel squinted. He couldn't see anything in the fierce brightness of the headlights. His stomach was in knots.

Putting his hand to the window, he could see he was trembling.

What's going on? What's going to happen?

For a moment, there was an eerie silence outside that was then broken by the sound of shouting and arguing.

Daniel could see the shadow of his dad holding the baseball bat aggressively.

BANG!

The air exploded with a gunshot.

He saw a momentary flash of bright light over by the passenger door of the car.

What was that?

His eyes darted to see his dad crumple to his knees and then fall to the ground.

No! Dad! Please, no.

Daniel could hardly breathe. He wanted to run to his dad and make sure he was okay.

Then he saw the two figures moving slowly towards their campervan.

Grabbing the sliding panelled door, Daniel clicked back the handle and pulled it open as quietly as he could.

His heart felt as if it was going to burst through his chest.

Stepping down, he gulped, took a deep breath and sprinted into the woodland that bordered the road.

Sticks and leaves crunched under his feet, making a noise.

They're going to hear me. Then they're going to catch and kill me.

The moon and the beams from the car meant that he could see roughly where he was running. He zig-zagged through trees, pushing small branches out of the way as he went.

He didn't even know where he was. All he knew was that they were somewhere in North Wales and they had planned to visit Chirk Castle the following morning.

Turning for a moment, Daniel could hear the shouts of the men behind him.

They're chasing me!

He ran again, this time up a wooded incline. A branch scratched his face as he went.

Breathless, shivering, he only had socks on his feet. The rough, uneven ground was painful on the soles of his feet. He fell into a shallow, muddy ditch. Disorientated, he clambered out of its dankness and struggled on again.

Come on, you can't let them find you.

Teeth chattering, he tried to think. Hide. *I need to find somewhere to hide and then just stay there until they're gone.*

His feet were now bleeding. The sludge between his toes was cold. At the top of the ridge, he found a huge tree. Resting his hand against the rough, uneven bark, he gazed for a moment up at the black sky - it felt endless and all-consuming. As he squinted, he could see the trees became less dense.

He ran on and came out of the trees into a small winding track and clearing. Up ahead a towering medieval castle above him on a mound. It had huge walls and turrets. Like something from a Gothic film.

Daniel ran towards it, glancing back to see if the men were still chasing him. He needed to find somewhere to hide.

Please God, don't let them find me.

Chapter 3

'What do we know?' Ruth asked as she and Nick sped out of Llancastell and headed west.

It was 12am and a uniformed patrol had come across a man's body at the side of the road. They thought he had been shot.

'Uniform called it in just after eleven. A man lying dead with gunshot wounds,' Nick explained. 'There was an abandoned VW campervan nearby.'

'And where was this?'

'Stone's throw from Chirk Castle.'

For a moment, Ruth was taken back to the afternoons she had spent wandering around Chirk Castle with her late partner Sian. It had been a while since she had thought of Sian, who had died nearly two years ago in a police operation at Solace Farm. Ruth felt a twinge of grief.

'You okay, boss?' Nick enquired. He had clearly picked up on her change of mood.

'Yeah,' she said quietly. 'Me and Sian spent a lot of time at Chirk Castle, that's all.'

Nick nodded with a sad expression. 'Amanda and I took flowers up to her grave a month or two ago. You can see the castle from the graveyard.'

Ruth took a breath. 'I never go up there.'

'No?'

'I can't,' Ruth admitted. 'I know that's a terrible thing to admit.'

'Not really,' Nick said. 'If it's too much for you to go to her grave, no one's going to judge you for that.'

Ruth shrugged. 'Except me.'

For a few seconds, there was silence in the car as they both thought about their former colleague.

Hearing the faint burble of music, Ruth decided it was time to change the uncomfortable mood. 'What are we listening to this morning?'

She and Nick had decided long ago that whoever was driving got to choose the music in the car. As Nick did 99% of the driving, she was subjected to whatever new album he had purchased. Ruth was purely an 80s pop and 90s vocal house girl. Nick's taste was far more indie and guitar-based. But a deal was a deal.

Nick gave a boyish grin. 'Hey, we're going old school this week.'

'Oh God,' Ruth sighed. 'It's not *Aerosmith's Greatest Hits* again is it? That really was a low point, Nick.'

'This week we will be mainly listening to *U2's The Joshua Tree*.'

Ruth eyes widened. 'Classic. I saw the tour.'

Nick looked at her with a dubious expression. 'You went to a U2 concert? I thought you were a strictly Whamette type of girl in the 80s?'

'Nope,' Ruth replied. 'Well, actually I went with my then boyfriend Ian. He was mad into U2. Wembley Stadium. I'm guessing the summer of 1987.'

'You guessed correct,' Nick nodded.

'That bloke who sang that *Walk on the Wild Side* song.'

Nick snorted incredulously. 'You've seen Lou Reed live?'

Ruth laughed. 'You do know that you've now crossed the line of being patronising?'

As they came around a bend, they saw that the road had been cordoned off by uniformed officers. Patrol cars were pulled across the road and their blue lights flashed rhythmically in the darkness.

'Here we go,' Nick said as he pulled over.

Getting out of the car, Ruth felt the chill of the night in her bones. She buttoned up her coat and thrust her hands in her pockets as she and Nick walked over to a uniformed officer who was standing by the blue police evidence tape. Beyond that, she could see an old orange VW campervan which had been pulled over to one side of the road. About twenty yards behind the van lay a body covered with a blanket.

Taking out her warrant card, Ruth showed it to the young officer. 'DI Hunter and DS Evans, Llancastell CID. What have we got Constable?'

'A passing motorist saw the victim lying by the road and pulled over,' the officer explained and looked down at his notepad. 'Charles Winner. Local farmer. He's over there.' The officer pointed to a navy Land Rover that was parked up further down the road. 'Mr Winner said that he went over to the victim but he wasn't breathing. Then he called us.'

Ruth nodded. 'Cause of death?'

'Gunshot wound,' the officer replied. 'From the looks of the size and pattern of the wound, I would have said that someone shot him in the stomach with a shotgun. I guess he just bled to death.'

Ruth looked at him. 'Thanks, Constable.' She knew the type. Smart, keen and eager to impress officers from CID. It wouldn't be long before he was looking to transfer over to CID as a DC. He had that confidence that could quite easily spill over into arrogance.

'Can you start a crime scene log for us?' Nick asked. 'No one comes in or out without talking to you.'

'Any sign of SOCOs?' Ruth enquired.

'No, ma'am. Not yet,' the constable replied. 'My sarge is over there by the campervan if you want to talk to him?'

'Okay, thank you Constable,' Ruth said as she and Nick turned and made their way towards the van and the body.

On the other side of the van, there was thick woodland that seemed to rise up into the darkness.

'So, where's Chirk Castle from here then?' Ruth asked, trying to get her bearings.

Nick pointed. 'Through that wood and then up the hill.'

As they approached the body, Nick took out his Maglite.

Ruth crouched, carefully took the blanket and lowered it to see the victim's face. The man was in his 30s, bearded, with several earrings and a distinctive oriental tattoo on his neck. His eyes were still open but the hazy grey film of death had formed over them. They looked like opaque pebbles that you might find on a beach.

Continuing to pull the blanket down, she could see that he was wearing a silver cross necklace and camouflaged jacket. His stomach was a dark, sticky bloody mess but Ruth instantly recognised the spread-out pattern of the wounds.

'Yeah, this is definitely a shotgun wound,' she said. Given that thousands of people in North Wales owned shotgun licences, it wasn't particularly helpful in narrowing down the murder weapon.

Nick crouched beside her and turned the torch over to the ground where the body was lying. It was covered in blood. 'Looks like he just bled out here.'

A uniformed sergeant approached. He was in his 50s, portly with a ruddy face. 'Sergeant Jarvis, Chirk Police.' He had a thick North Wales accent.

'DI Hunter and DS Evans, Llancastell CID,' Ruth explained, spotting that Jarvis had something in his hand.

'Found something, Sergeant?' she asked.

He nodded. 'Victim's wallet was in the glove compart-ment.' He then opened the wallet and pulled out a driving licence. 'Vince Thompson. Date of birth, 3rd November 1988. There's an address here in Cheshire but the licence is dated 2017 so it might be out of date now.'

'Okay, well that's a start.' Nick pulled an evidence bag from his pocket and allowed Jarvis to drop it inside.

Ruth scanned the area. On one side of the road were fields, on the other was thick woodland. There wasn't a house or even a building in sight. 'Doesn't look like we're going to get any eyewitnesses around here.'

Nick gestured over to the farmer, Charles Winner. 'Maybe we should have a word, boss?'

Ruth nodded and they walked over to where Winner was standing beside his muddy Land Rover.

She showed her warrant card. 'Mr Winner?'

'Aye,' he replied. If he was shocked by what he had found, he wasn't showing it. He was in his 40s, thick set with a mop of blond hair. 'Am I gonna be here long? I've got to get my herd in for milking by five,' he asked impa-tiently.

Ruth knew that farmers were a tough breed, but

Winner seemed very blasé that he had just found a man murdered at the roadside.

Nick gave Ruth a knowing look as if to say *Christ, he's a piece of work, isn't he?*'

'Just a few questions, sir,' Nick reassured him as he pulled out his notebook and pen. 'And then we can let you get on your way.'

Ruth looked over at him. 'Can you tell us exactly what happened, Mr Winner?'

'I was driving home,' he explained. 'I came around that bend when I seen that fella lying by the road.'

'Where were you coming from?' Nick enquired.

'My brother's place,' he replied. 'He lives down in Dudley. He's not well, so I drove down to see how he's doing.'

Ruth nodded. 'Can you tell us what time you left your brother's house in Dudley?'

Winner frowned and looked decidedly grumpy. 'What difference does that make?' he snapped.

Nick gave him a mollifying look. 'Just routine questions, that's all, sir.'

Winner scratched his chin and sighed. 'Suppose it was nine by the time I left.'

'And what time do you think you stopped?' Ruth asked. She knew the 999 call had been logged at just after 11pm but she wanted to check that his story tallied.

'I guess it was about eleven,' he replied.

'You mentioned a herd,' Ruth said. 'Is your farm near here?'

Winner pointed north. 'Out towards Llandegla.'

Ruth nodded. 'And you saw this man lying by the road and pulled over?'

'Aye, that's right.'

'Did you see anyone else?' Nick enquired.

Winner shook his head emphatically. 'No, not a bloody soul.'

Nick stopped writing and looked at him. 'And you went over to where he was lying?'

'Yeah,' Winner nodded. 'Wasn't much point. I could see he was dead. His chest wasn't moving. Someone had done him with a shotgun. Pretty close by the looks of it.'

Ruth frowned. 'You sound like an expert, Mr Winner?'

Winner snorted. 'I've been around shotguns all me life. I know what a shotgun wound looks like.'

'And then you called us?' Nick asked to clarify.

'Aye,' Winner replied. 'I called your lot and then waited with him. Poor bugger. Do you know who he is?'

'I'm afraid I can't discuss that with you at the moment, Mr Winner,' Ruth replied. 'But thank you for your help. Do we have your address and phone number?'

Winner pointed over to the young police officer that was manning the cordon whom they had first spoken to. 'That young chap over there's got all my details. Do I have to go to court or something?'

'We're not sure yet,' Ruth said, 'but we'll let you know if we need to speak to you again.'

'Right, so I can get off now can I?' he enquired, pointing to his Land Rover.

'Yes, that's fine.' Ruth and Nick turned and headed back towards the crime scene.

'Well, Mr Winner was a very touchy-feely kind of bloke, wasn't he?' Nick joked.

Ruth smiled. 'Either he was in shock or maybe he just finds dead people by the road every day,' she said sarcastically.

As they got to the campervan, Ruth glanced over at Jarvis. 'Sergeant, have you looked through the back of this campervan?'

Jarvis shook his head. 'Not yet, ma'am. Thought I'd better wait for you guys to get here. I just looked through the windows to check there was no one else inside.'

Ruth nodded. 'Anything else?'

Jarvis pointed to the area where Vince's body was lying. 'I did notice significant tyre tracks over there, ma'am. I'm not an expert, but I'm pretty sure they don't belong to a campervan.'

Nick nodded. 'We'll get SOCOs to look at that.'

'Okay, thanks,' Ruth said to Jarvis as she took her blue forensic gloves from her pocket and snapped them on. She took the handle of the sliding panel door, clicked it back and slid it open. Then she looked across to see that the panel door on the opposite side of the van was wide open. Maybe Jarvis hadn't seen it in the darkness.

'Sergeant?' Ruth called over. 'The sliding door on the far side is open. I'm just checking that none of your officers have touched this part of the van since you arrived on the scene?'

Jarvis shook his head. 'No, ma'am. I'm sorry I missed that.'

She gave him a reassuring smile. 'Don't worry. It's hard to see something like that in the dark.'

Nick had manoeuvred himself inside the back of the van, using a torch and a pen to search through the contents. 'I think Vince Thompson was living in this van.'

As Ruth poked her head inside, she got the distinct smell of dirty washing and stale food. 'Certainly looks and smells that way.'

Opening a small cupboard, Nick shone his torch inside. He then turned to look at her. 'Boss, you might want to come and have a look at this.'

Standing up, Ruth trod carefully to where Nick was standing – there wasn't much room.

'What have we got?' she enquired as she peered inside. Then she saw what he was talking about. Five large bags of marijuana.

'Now we know how he was making his money,' Nick said. 'That's about five grand's worth of weed.'

Ruth looked at him. 'And maybe that's why someone shot him?' As she turned to go towards the back of the van, she spotted something on the floor. A pair of Nike trainers. But they were small.

Crouching down, she inspected them. They were children's.

'Size 4 trainers,' Ruth said. 'They definitely don't belong to our victim.'

Nick rummaged through a pile of clothes, pulling out a small t-shirt and a pair of boy's jeans. 'Neither do these.'

Ruth frowned as she clicked on her phone light and continued to search the van. Towards the back was a small pile of books and exercise books. She picked one up and read the front out loud, 'Daniel Thompson, Year 6, Maths.'

'You think there was a child living in here too?' Nick asked.

Ruth looked around. 'Maybe.'

Nick pointed to the sliding door that they had found open when they got in. 'Boss, this door was open when we arrived. But we're assuming that Vince was driving this van when he pulled over.'

'Yeah,' Ruth agreed.

'If Vince had a son, Daniel, that was living with him, where is he now?'

Ruth looked at the open door again. It was a good point. 'Maybe Daniel saw his

father get out of the van, shot and killed. He then slid open this door and ran for his life.' She pointed to the woods. 'Maybe he's just hiding out there somewhere?'

Nick gave her a dark look. 'I hope not. It's bloody freezing for starters.' He then went to the open door, jumped down and used his torch to look at the ground.

'Anything?'

Nick turned to her. 'Yeah. We've got small footprints in the mud here. Must be a kid's. And they lead in there.' He pointed to the woods.

Chapter 4

It was an hour later and Ruth had managed to commandeer every spare uniformed patrol in the area to carry out a search of the woods. She was hoping to get the police helicopter with its searchlight across but it was being used for a major accident on the A5.

As she and Nick made their way slowly through the wood, leaves and twigs crunched under their feet. The air was damp and thick with the scent of rotting mulch. Glancing left, she could see an array of torch beams that zipped in varying directions as uniformed officers moved north in a parallel line.

'Daniel?' came the shouts of various male officers.

Ruth knew that if there was a ten-year-old boy hiding out in these woods, they needed to find him soon. It was freezing and the temperature was still dropping. In his terror, she assumed that Daniel would not have thought to grab a coat or anything warm to wear. He would also be petrified, hiding somewhere, and might not make himself known to police officers.

Ruth clicked her Tetra radio. 'Three six to all units. Please make your identity as police officers known. Daniel might well be hiding, over.'

The terrain began to get steeper as they trudged on slowly.

'Don't understand it, do you?' Nick moved his Maglite to and fro.

Ruth frowned. 'What's that?'

'Living with your son in a campervan,' he replied. 'It's not the best environment to bring a kid up in, is it?'

'Depends, doesn't it?'

'Does it?'

'A child could be living in a mansion. But if they're subjected to violence, bullying or emotional abuse, they're going to be damaged. Maybe Vince Thompson was just doing the best he could,' Ruth suggested, thinking out loud.

Nick shrugged. 'Maybe. Although I'm not sure dealing weed is *doing his best.*'

Before they could continue their debate, she saw that the woods stopped about fifty yards ahead. There was a clearing beyond that, but it was hard to make out much more.

'Daniel? We're police officers,' Nick shouted. 'We're here to help you.'

'Bloody hell, he could be anywhere,' Ruth sighed.

As they came out from the edge of the woods, the uneven ground rose up dramatically to a large hill. On top of that loomed a large, 13th century medieval castle with cylindrical Gothic towers.

Chirk Castle.

Even though Ruth had been there many times, she had never seen it at night. With the silver hue of moonlight giving the grey stone an almost luminous glow, it seemed far more sinister and unsettling in the dark. A thick cloud slid deliberately over the moon, cutting out the light in an instant, like a shadowy hand placed menacingly over a face. The castle seemed more desolate, soulless, even haunting in the strange shift of light. As if it could now allow whispers from its past. A daunting stone tomb to those who had fallen in the sieges and battles nearly eight hundred years earlier.

From out of nowhere, the night sky exploded with a thundering sound. The air seemed to swirl and move violently around them as autumnal leaves scattered frantically. Pushing her hair back, Ruth looked skywards as the whole area was lit in a clean white blazing light from above. A black and yellow EC135 police helicopter hovered over them and moved slowly towards the castle.

'I hope that doesn't scare him even more,' Nick yelled.

Ruth could feel her whole body shudder with the deep, rumbling noise of the helicopter's powerful Rolls-Royce M250 turboshaft engine.

'There!' Nick shouted over the din, pointing to a figure in the distance running away from them across a field that led downhill towards the castle's car park.

It had to be Daniel.

It seemed that the helicopter's arrival had spooked him and flushed him out from wherever he had been hiding.

They turned and broke into a sprint after him.

The helicopter rose up and followed his run, using its enormous searchlight to illuminate the area around him.

God, he must be terrified! Ruth thought to herself as she and Nick threw themselves over a wooden fence and ran at full pelt after him. The ground was uneven and bumpy. Losing her footing, she slipped but managed not to fall.

'Daniel! We're police officers. We're here to help you!' Ruth shouted at the top of her voice.

Suddenly, Daniel seemed to just collapse to the ground about a hundred yards ahead of them. He lay completely still where he had fallen.

Oh God!

The searchlight illuminated the patch of ground where he lay.

A few seconds later, Ruth arrived, hit the ground and felt his neck for a pulse – it was weak. Daniel was only wearing a t-shirt with a gaming logo on it. The skin on his arms was icy cold but flushed red.

Ruth looked up at Nick as she took off her coat. 'I'm pretty sure he's got hyperthermia.'

'Shit!' Nick took off his coat too, handed it to her and then waved up at the helicopter, signalling for them to land. They needed to get Daniel over to University Hospital in Llancastell as soon as possible.

'Daniel?' Ruth wrapped him tightly in their coats. He looked so young and vulnerable. And he'd been through so much in the past few hours.

The noise of the helicopter intensified as it lowered itself onto the ground about fifty yards away. Ruth squinted as leaves and debris blew violently around her – she brushed the hair and dirt from Daniel's face.

A few seconds later, one of the officers from the helicopter came sprinting across.

'We think he's got hyperthermia,' Ruth yelled over the din of the helicopter's engine.

The officer nodded and scooped Daniel up from the ground. 'Okay, we'll take it from here. We've got foil blankets on board.'

'His name's Daniel. Daniel Thompson,' she told him.

Ruth and Nick gave each other a meaningful look as the officer jogged away with Daniel in his arms.

God, please let him be okay.

Chapter 5

R uth and Nick were sat quietly in the waiting area of the trauma unit in the University Hospital in Llancastell. They had explained to a nurse who they were, why they were there, and she had gone to see if she could find a doctor who could update them on Daniel's condition.

They were both deep in thought. Ruth knew how dangerous hyperthermia could be, especially for someone as young as Daniel. The fact that he had lost consciousness was worrying.

'Are we thinking Vince Thompson's shooting is drug related?' Nick asked after a long silence.

'That would be my first instinct,' Ruth said quietly as she checked her watch. It was 2am.

'Do you want a coffee while we're waiting?' Nick enquired, gesturing to the coffee machine down the busy corridor.

Ruth pulled a face. 'Have you tasted the coffee in this place?'

'Only once.' Nick smiled. 'Yeah, let's give coffee a miss, eh? How's Doreen doing?'

'Not great, if I'm honest,' Ruth replied with a sad expression. Sarah's mother hadn't responded to the chemotherapy as well as the doctors had hoped. Even though they had suggested radiotherapy, they had warned Sarah that it was unlikely to be effective.

'Sorry to hear that,' Nick said. 'I remember how ill Amanda's dad became with cancer. It's horrible.'

Before they could continue, a young female doctor came towards them. 'Are you the officers that were enquiring about Daniel Thompson?'

'Yes.' Ruth nodded. 'DI Hunter and DS Evans from Llancastell CID. How's he doing?'

'He's conscious and he's stable,' the doctor explained with a serious expression.

Thank God, Ruth thought.

The doctor continued. 'We've managed to stabilise his temperature, which is the main thing. We're keeping him under observation.'

'Any idea when we can speak to him?' Ruth enquired. 'We believe that he's a witness to a murder.'

'He needs to rest,' the doctor stated, sounding a little annoyed at her question. It wasn't that Ruth wasn't concerned about Daniel. Far from it. But the sooner they spoke to him and got some idea of what had happened, the sooner they could find whoever had brutally killed Vince Thompson.

'In the morning?' Nick asked.

The doctor thought for a moment and then nodded. 'Let's see how he is overnight. But if he's up to it, then yes.'

Chapter 6

Getting out of the car, Nick pulled up his collar against the icy wind. He would probably only get 4-5 hours' sleep before having to head back into Llancastell CID again. That's how it worked with major incidents such as murder. He was used to it.

Spotting that Amanda had put out the green garden waste bins, Nick got a sudden glimpse of what his life had been like just over four years ago. Instead of coming home to his beautiful wife and daughter, he had been in the darkness of active alcoholism. That meant blackouts, bed wetting, shakes and sweating – and vodka for breakfast. And the very green bin that he now looked at had been where he kept all the empty bottles – away from the prying eyes of his neighbours. It was a living hell.

With the help of Alcoholics Anonymous, a sponsor and a twelve-step programme, Nick had been sober for over four years. And that was a bloody miracle. It was in moments like this that he could be overwhelmed by incredible gratitude. Had he not got sober and into recovery, he might well now be dead or in prison. When he first joined

AA, there had been the promise of *a life beyond his wildest dreams* in recovery. In the *bad old days*, that would have meant a mansion, a red Ferrari, a million pounds, and a string of one-night stands with beautiful models. Now, with his new-found sobriety, coming home to his family after a decent day of helping others was more than he could have ever hoped for.

As he opened the front door, he saw that there was a sliver of vanilla light coming from the living room.

Home sweet home.

Amanda's eighteen-year-old daughter, Fran, had been staying with them while her adoptive parents went on holiday. It had been several months since Amanda had revealed to Nick that she had had an unwanted pregnancy when she was only a teenager. She had given that baby up for adoption. Having turned eighteen, Fran had decided to track down her birth mother, Amanda, and make contact. Although he was shocked, Nick supported Amanda's reconnection with her daughter. After all that Nick had done in the dark, twisted journey of his life, he was in no position to judge her. Fran was a smart, thoughtful and kind young woman and it had been a pleasure to get to know her in recent months. Megan, Nick and Amanda's toddler daughter, had been delighted to learn that she now had *a big sister*.

Pushing the door open quietly, he saw that it was Amanda who was sitting on the sofa.

That's weird.

Nick frowned. 'Everything okay? What are you doing up?'

Amanda looked concerned. 'I was waiting up for Fran.'

Nick thought for a moment. 'She's not back yet?'

'No.' Amanda shook her head. 'I know she's eighteen

but she said she was only going for a quick drink after work with some friends.'

'Have you called her?' Nick asked. It wasn't like Fran to be out late or not contact them to say where she was.

'Yes,' Amanda nodded. 'And I've sent a couple of texts.'

Nick began to feel a little uneasy. 'Do you know where she was going after work?'

Amanda shook her head as she sat nervously forward on the sofa. 'No. I thought she'd be home by nine or ten.'

'Do you want me to drive back into town to look for her?' Nick suggested. It was only a fifteen-minute drive. 'Or I can contact uniformed patrols to see if anyone has seen anything.'

Amanda nodded at his suggestion. 'Yeah, if you don't mind?'

There was a noise from the front door – a key in the lock.

Amanda looked at Nick and sighed – 'Thank God for that!'

'Don't go mad at her,' Nick said gently.

'Thanks,' Amanda whispered sharply.

Fran appeared at the door. She had been crying and she looked terrible.

Getting up from the sofa, Amanda immediately went to her. 'Fran. Are you okay?'

'Not really.' Fran dissolved in a fit of tears.

Amanda took her in her arms. 'Oh no. What's happened?'

Fran wept and couldn't get her breath. Amanda led her over to the sofa where they sat down. 'Hey, what's happened?'

Fran blinked as she took a deep breath. 'I went out

after work. We went to a few bars in town. And I drank too much. Eventually, it was just me and Paul left.'

'Paul?'

'He's my manager at work,' she explained as she sniffed and wiped her face. 'He asked me to go back to his place. He said I could get a taxi from there. But I said I'd get one up on the high street.'

'Okay.' Nick started to feel uneasy.

'And then ...' Fran began to sob.

Amanda reached over and took her hands. 'It's all right. You're safe now.'

'Then he tried to kiss me but I told him I wasn't interested,' Fran explained. 'He insisted that he walk me up to the taxi office. And then we went down that little cut through by the Nat West bank and he ...' Fran took a deep breath and blew out to try and calm herself. 'He pushed me against the wall, kissed me and put his hand up my skirt and ... I tried to push him off but I couldn't.'

Nick could feel the anger twist inside his stomach.

'Oh God, I'm so sorry.' Amanda hugged her. 'You poor thing.'

'I shouted out and then some people came down there so he let me go,' Fran said in a virtual whisper. 'And then I ran to the taxi office.'

'Did he follow you?' Nick asked, trying to control his rage.

Fran shook her head. 'No. But I had to wait ages for a cab ... I was so scared.'

Amanda looked at her. 'Why didn't you call us? I could have picked you up.'

'My phone ran out of charge,' Fran explained. 'I'm such an idiot.'

'You're not an idiot,' Amanda reassured her. 'I'm so sorry that's happened to you.'

'What's his surname?' Nick enquired, trying to hide the fact that he wanted to go and kill him.

'Thurrock,' Fran muttered.

'Paul Thurrock,' Nick said quietly. 'I'll get a uniformed patrol to go and pick him up.'

'No.' Fran's eyes were wide with fear. 'You can't do that.'

Nick frowned. 'He assaulted you, Fran!'

'No. I don't want you to arrest him,' Fran insisted, rubbing more tears from her face. 'Please.'

'Why not?' Amanda asked in an understanding tone.

'I love my job,' she explained. 'He's my manager.'

'He needs to go to prison, Fran,' Nick stated a little too forcefully.

Amanda gave him a look as if to say '*Calm down.*'

'You know what it's like,' Fran said. 'It's my word against his. I'd been drinking all night. We were on our own. He's not going to be convicted of anything. I've seen all the statistics.'

Even though Nick hated to admit it, what Fran was saying was probably true.

'Maybe you should get some sleep.' Amanda put her hand to Fran's face. 'You might feel differently in the morning. You can sleep with me tonight, okay?'

Fran nodded but she was still shaking.

Nick leaned forward. 'I'm really sorry to say this, but there's forensic evidence that needs to be taken right now. Otherwise … it really is your word against his.'

Fran shook her head. 'No. I'm not doing any of that. I'm going to have a shower. I'm not going to spend hours writing statements. I just want to forget it ever happened.'

'Sorry.' Nick felt guilty for having mentioned it.

Amanda nodded. 'You need to do what's best for you, Fran. We can't tell you what to do.'

'Thank you,' Fran said.

Amanda gestured to the hallway. 'Why don't you come upstairs with me and I'll run you a bath?'

Fran nodded as they got up and headed out.

Nick watched them go, knowing that he would have to do something about it – he just hadn't worked out what yet.

Chapter 7

I t was 7am by the time Ruth got to the children's ward at the University Hospital at Llancastell. As she marched along the corridor, the air smelled of stewed tea, breakfast and disinfectant. An earlier phone call had revealed that Daniel had regained consciousness, was no longer in danger and had been moved to a single room on the children's ward on the third floor. The nurse did mention that Daniel hadn't said a word since he'd regained consciousness but given the trauma of the previous evening, that wasn't a surprise.

Approaching the nurses' station, Ruth got out her warrant card. 'Morning. DI Hunter, Llancastell CID. I spoke to the Ward Sister about thirty minutes ago about Daniel Thompson?'

A large, buxom woman in her late 40s with dip-dyed hair that was scraped back off her face caught her eye. 'That was me.' She then gestured down the corridor. 'Do you want me to show you where he is?'

'Please.' Ruth smiled at her. 'Has he said anything since we spoke?'

'No, poor little thing. And he's hardly touched his breakfast.' The Ward Sister shook her head as she walked down a dimly-lit corridor. 'One of your officers told us what happened last night.'

'I assume you have a paediatric psychiatrist who can take a look at him?' Ruth asked.

'I'll talk to the consultant,' the Ward Sister said. 'But I'm guessing that's what she'll recommend … I gave him some colouring pens and paper in case he wanted to do some colouring in.'

Even though Ruth had an enormous amount of sympathy for what Daniel had been through in the last twenty-four hours, she also knew it was likely that he was the eyewitness to who had shot his father.

Opening the door gently, the Ward Sister took a step into the small single room. Daniel looked up at them. He had a red crayon in his hand.

'I'll be down at the nurses' station if you need me,' the Ward Sister informed her as she left.

Ruth closed the door and went very slowly over to a chair bedside the bed. She waited for a few seconds and watched as Daniel returned to his colouring.

'Daniel, my name is Ruth,' she explained gently. 'And I'm a police officer.'

For a moment, he stopped colouring as his eyes roamed around the picture he was drawing. Then he started to sketch again.

She looked at him. 'I'm here to help find out who hurt your dad.'

There was no response.

'I'm so sorry that you had to go through all that last night,' she whispered. 'You must have been so scared.'

Daniel stopped drawing again, blinked as if he was deep in thought and then reached for a blue crayon.

'And you know what, Daniel?' she said. 'It's all right to feel scared and confused. I just want to help you, is that okay?'

For a second, Daniel glanced at her as if he was sizing her up.

Getting up from the chair, Ruth moved the narrow table on wheels. She peered over at what Daniel was drawing. Her first response was one of surprise at the incredible quality and detail of Daniel's picture. It wasn't what she had expected from a ten-year-old boy. It was beautiful.

He had drawn a footballer in mid-air heading the ball towards a goal. He was dressed in a blue strip with white shorts. She recognised the badge on the shirt.

'You like Chelsea?' she asked.

Daniel looked up at her, slightly incredulous that she had recognised the football strip. He nodded slowly.

'Yeah, that's my team. Chelsea,' Ruth explained with a smile. 'I'm originally from South London, you see. And where I lived as a kid, you could see the floodlights at Stamford Bridge across the Thames when there was an evening game. It was only about two miles from our flat.'

Daniel's eyes roamed around the room again and then he went back to his drawing.

'Do you play football then, Daniel?' she enquired. From what they had gathered from the campervan, it didn't seem that they were ever in one place long enough for him to have ever joined a local team. Maybe he and his dad just had a kick around every once in a while.

Without pausing, Daniel nodded.

'My dad was very good at football,' Ruth said. 'In fact, he had trials with Chelsea in the 1960s.'

'Did he?' Daniel whispered.

Even though it was barely audible, Daniel had spoken.

Wow. I never thought talking about my old dad would have that effect!

'That's what he told us.' Ruth smiled as he looked up at her. Something about his expression had changed. The blank, slightly glazed look in his eyes had been replaced by a brighter, more connected appearance.

'Did he play for the proper Chelsea though?' Daniel enquired quietly.

'No,' Ruth replied. 'But I did see him play a few times over at Battersea Park when I was very young. He was a centre forward … What position do you play?'

'CDM,' he said without thinking.

CD what?

'Central Defensive Midfielder,' he explained. 'You know, like N'Golo Kanté?'

N'Golo who?

'Oh, okay,' Ruth nodded. 'I know.' She pointed to the picture he had drawn. 'And that's him, is it?'

'No.' Daniel gave her a look of disbelief. 'This is Mason Mount.'

Yeah, I've heard of him.

'You're very good at drawing, aren't you? Is that your favourite subject at school?' she enquired, trying to move the conversation very slowly to where she could ask about Daniel's father.

'Yeah.'

'What's the name of your school, Daniel?'

He frowned as he started to draw again. She sensed he was feeling uncomfortable. 'I dunno … I can't remember.'

Ruth smiled at him again as she went and sat down. 'You know what, you've been doing something that I've always wanted to do, you know that?'

He stopped drawing and frowned at her.

'Travelling around in that campervan,' she explained

and then waited for a few seconds. 'I've always wanted to do that. The freedom of being out on the open road. Stopping wherever you want. No one telling you what you should do.'

'That's what my dad said,' Daniel explained. Then his expression changed as if the realisation of what happened to his father had suddenly hit him.

'You and your dad must have been very close?' Ruth said quietly. 'Just the two of you on the road together in that van.'

Daniel nodded slowly. Then he just stared into space, biting his lip. His distress was clear.

Ruth's heart went out to him. Reaching out, she put her hand gently on his arm. 'It's okay, Daniel. I promise you that I'm going to find the men who hurt your dad, okay?'

He didn't say anything. His eyes glazed over a little and his chest rose and fell rapidly.

Maybe that's enough for this morning, she thought to herself.

'Okay, I tell you what I'm going to do. I'm going to let you get on with your drawing for a bit. But is it okay if I come back and see you later on?'

He gave an almost imperceptible nod and blinked.

'I'm going to see if I can find you a football magazine. Would you like that? And maybe some sweets? Or crisps? How does that sound?'

It seemed that Daniel had retreated somewhere inside his head. Ruth had seen it before with victims of trauma, especially if they were young. He just needed time and lots of TLC.

Getting up from her chair, Ruth patted his arm gently and smiled at him. 'I'm going to go now, okay? And I'll see you this afternoon.'

She turned and made her way to the door.

48

'They weren't just men,' Daniel said.

'Sorry?' Ruth stopped in her tracks and turned to look at him. 'They weren't just men? Do you mean the people who hurt your dad?'

He nodded and whispered, 'Yeah. There was a woman. She was driving the car.'

'Okay.' Ruth gave him a quizzical look. 'And you're sure about that?'

'Yeah,' he replied as he went back to drawing.

'Did you see what the woman or the man looked like?'

He shook his head. 'It was too dark.'

'What about the car they were driving?'

'It was big.'

Ruth took a step back and looked at him. 'Do you mean big like a van?'

Daniel shook his head. 'No. It was a big car. My dad says that down south they call them *Chelsea Tractors*. I didn't know what he meant.'

Ruth knew exactly what he meant as she reached for her phone. She searched for a photo of a Range Rover, went over and showed him. 'Did the car look like this?

He nodded. 'Yeah. That's it.'

'Can you remember what colour it was?'

He shook his head.

Ruth gave him a kind smile. 'Okay, thanks Daniel. That's very helpful.'

Chapter 8

Striding into Incident Room 1 at Llancastell nick, Ruth could see that her CID team had moved computers, desks and chairs over from the CID office. They only used the Incident Rooms when there was a major crime like a murder. At the far end of the room, two scene boards had been set up. At the centre was a photo of Vince Thompson that had been copied from his passport. Besides that, the basics of what they knew had been written in blue ink –

March 15th 2021

Vince Thompson

Date of birth, 3rd November 1988

C.O.D – Gunshot wound - shotgun

'OKAY EVERYONE, LET'S SETTLE DOWN,' SHE SAID AND THEN took a long swig of her coffee. She'd managed to grab a couple of hours' sleep and needed as much caffeine as she could get. Approaching the scene boards, she pointed to the photograph. 'Just to bring everyone up to speed. This is our victim. Vince Thompson, aged 32. Born in Dagenham. He was travelling in an orange campervan with his ten-year-old son, Daniel, when they pulled off the road in Chirk. Tyre tracks show that another vehicle pulled in behind them. Vince was then shot and killed. It looks likely that the murder weapon was a shotgun.' She went to the map. 'Daniel fled the scene, heading north through these woods up to Chirk Castle. Nick and I found him and he was taken to the University Hospital suffering from hyperthermia. Nick?'

Getting to his feet, Nick approached and pointed to some of the photos that SOCOs had taken inside the van. 'It appears that Vince and Daniel were living in this campervan, possibly moving around the country. We also discovered five large bags of marijuana with a street value of about five thousand pounds. Next to that was two thousand pounds in cash. It seems likely that Vince was dealing drugs.'

'Do we think that's the motive for the shooting?' enquired Detective Constable Georgina Wild. Blonde, attractive and very ambitious, she was one of the junior members of Llancastell CID. Even though she was an excellent copper with a sharp, insightful mind, Ruth also knew that she wasn't a team player.

'That would be my first instinct,' Ruth replied.

'How's the son doing?' DC Jim Garrow asked. Garrow was university-educated and from a middle-class background. What he lacked in being streetwise, he more than made up for in his ability to logically analyse evidence.

'He's conscious and out of danger, thank God,' Ruth replied. 'I spoke to him this morning. Obviously he is still very traumatised by what happened last night. However, he told me that his father's killers were in a 4x4 car, probably a Range Rover. He says that there was a woman driving that car and a man in the passenger seat.'

'Could he describe either of them?' Georgie enquired.

Ruth shook her head. 'No. But he's still in a state of shock. I'm hoping some of the details might come back to him.'

'Boss, I rang the DVLA,' DC Dan French replied. 'Seems that Vince's driving licence is legitimate.'

'Even though Daniel identified the vehicle he saw as being something like a Range Rover, let's get forensics to analyse the tyre tracks that the SOCOs found,' Ruth said, thinking out loud. 'Can they confirm they belong to a Range Rover? If they do, can they narrow it down by model?'

'I ran an initial PNC check, boss,' French stated. 'Vince has three prior convictions for drugs offences. One for possession, and two for intent to supply. He served a year of a two-year sentence in 2011.'

'Where did he serve his sentence?' Nick enquired.

'HMP Rhoswen,' French answered. HMP Rhoswen was the huge new *'Super Prison'* that had been built in North Wales.

'Okay,' Ruth said. 'Maybe Vince was trying to deal on someone else's patch and they didn't like it?'

French pointed to his notes. 'There is a note that in his teens, Vince was connected to several gangs in Essex and the East End of London. His dad, Patrick Thompson, was a known associate of Jack Whomes and Michael Steele.'

Ruth raised her eyebrow. She knew their names.

Nick looked at her. 'Is that significant?'

'It might be,' Ruth replied. 'Jack Whomes and Michael Steele were convicted in the late 90s of the murder of three rival drug dealers. They were all shot dead in a Range Rover on a farm track out in Essex. It became quite a famous case at the time. I think they even made a film about it.'

'*Rise of the Footsoldier*,' French informed her. 'Terrible film.'

Ruth frowned. 'I can't see the connection. But the MO is similar. Car pulled over in the middle of nowhere. Rival drug dealers shot dead with a shotgun.'

'We need to find out who is Vince's next of kin. Check if he had any bank accounts or credit cards,' Ruth said. 'It looks unlikely, but had he paid any taxes? What about housing benefit or universal credit?'

Georgie looked over. 'Looks like the mobile phone he had in his pocket was a *burner*.' A *burner phone* was a prepaid mobile phone which criminals often used because it was hard to trace, could conceal their identity and could be easily discarded.

French looked over as he put down the phone. 'Boss, Professor Amis is carrying out the preliminary PM in about an hour.'

'Okay thanks.' Ruth looked out at the CID team. 'Listen up. This was a man who was murdered in cold blood in front of his ten-year-old son. Vince deserves our best work. And his son Daniel deserves to see his father's killers brought to justice, so let's get cracking on this, shall we?'

There were nods and a few murmurs of agreement.

Ruth then looked over at Nick. 'Shall we see what Professor Amis can tell us?'

Nick raised an eyebrow. 'Can't wait.'

Chapter 9

R uth and Nick approached the dark blue double doors that led to the Llancastell University Hospital mortuary. As they entered, Professor Tony Amis gave them a cheery wave and got up. Ruth could see Vince Thompson's body laid out on the metal gurney at the far side of the room.

Amis had milky skin and ginger hair that was now greying. He pulled down his mask and smiled. His teeth were a little crooked.

'Morning, Tony,' Ruth said. Although Ruth knew that Amis was good at his job, he could go off on frustrating tangents. This was a constant source of amusement for Nick.

'Here they are again,' Amis quipped in his usual jovial manner.

'Anything you can tell us?' she enquired, trying not to sound too impatient. She had a murder investigation to get on with.

'Llancastell's answer to Rick and Ilsa,' he joked.

Nick frowned. 'That's even too obscure for me, Tony.'

'Come on. *Casablanca*. Here's looking at you, kid. We'll always have Paris,' Amis waffled on.

'We know what *Casablanca* is, Tony,' Ruth sighed. 'It's just that it's not a very good parallel for me and DS Evans, is it?'

'Starsky and Hutch?' Amis suggested with a wry smile.

'Tony!' Ruth exclaimed in a tone of mock annoyance, although there was part of her that didn't want to have to go through the whole *song and dance* routine every time they entered the mortuary.

'Okay, come over here.' Amis beckoned them as he put down his mug of tea that had *'Please don't confuse your Google search with my Medical Degree'* emblazoned across it.

Ruth and Nick turned and followed Amis to look at Vince's colourless body that glared under the harsh post-mortem lights.

'Cause of death was the shotgun wound?' Ruth asked.

'Yes,' Amis agreed. 'Huge amount of internal bleeding. He would have been dead within a minute or two.'

'Anything else you can tell us?' Nick enquired.

'Your victim had a kidney transplant in the last two years.' Amis pointed to the internal organs. 'I ran some tests and it turns out this man was suffering from something known as Alport Syndrome.'

Ruth shrugged. She had never heard of it.

'It's a hereditary disease. There's a mutation of collagen in the body which affects the structure and function of the ears and sometimes the eyes,' Amis explained.

Ruth remembered thinking that there might have been something wrong with Daniel's hearing. She wondered if the two were linked. However, it didn't really help with the investigation in any way.

'There is something that I noticed,' Amis said moving up to Vince's head and pointing to his face. 'Might be a long shot.'

'Come on, Tony,' Ruth said. 'How long have we been working together? There isn't such a thing as a long shot. You give us the evidence and let us rule it out.'

'Your victim has a scratch or an abrasion to his face,' Amis explained, pointing to an inch long mark on Vince's right cheek. 'Just there.' Amis pulled down the overhead light to illuminate it and make it clearer.

'Looks like a fingernail scratch to me,' Ruth stated instantly.

Amis smiled and nodded. 'Good, because that's exactly what I thought.'

Nick shrugged. 'Maybe Vince got into a struggle before his killers shot him?'

'That was the theory I was going on,' Amis replied and then approached Ruth.

What's he doing?

'DI Hunter, if you can face me please,' Amis said.

Ruth rolled her eyes. 'Tony, I haven't got time for this.'

'If I swing my arm to strike your face like this,' Amis said slowly swinging his hand towards her, 'what do you notice about where I strike you.'

Ruth frowned.

'It's her left cheek,' Nick observed.

'Exactly,' Amis stated with a winning smile. 'Except your victim was struck from the opposite side.'

Ruth nodded. 'So, it's likely that they were left-handed?'

'Exactly. Got it.' Amis nodded like a proud teacher who had just explained a complicated maths theorem to a student.

Nick frowned. 'Isn't all that *we're looking for a left-handed killer* the stuff you see on all those terrible cop shows on the telly?'

Amis shrugged. 'It's just a theory, DS Evans. Take it or leave it. And you'd be surprised how accurate some of those shows are now these days. Not like in our day, DI Hunter? Remember *Z-cars*?'

'Bloody hell, Tony. *Z-cars*? I was born in 1969,' Ruth said. She was a little offended. 'How old do you think I am?'

Amis pulled a face. 'Erm, no comment?'

RUTH AND NICK WALKED AWAY FROM THE MORTUARY AND headed down the corridor to the lifts.

'Isn't it time Tony Amis retired?' Ruth grumbled.

Nick laughed. 'He really annoys you, doesn't he?'

'He's what my dad would call *a right wally*,' Ruth replied. 'Harmless but bloody irritating.'

'I actually think he's funny,' Nick admitted.

'Good for you.' Ruth checked her phone as they waited for the lift to arrive. She frowned.

'Everything all right?' Nick asked.

'I'm just checking the news,' Ruth explained gesturing to her phone. She looked around to make sure no one was in earshot. 'This thing that Sarah is mixed up in. Met police think they've located an area where that young Portuguese girl might be buried.'

Nick raised an eyebrow. 'Right. That would be a massive breakthrough in the case, wouldn't it?'

'Huge,' Ruth admitted. 'There might be forensics or DNA on her remains. And that would mean that the

Crown Prosecution's case wouldn't be relying so heavily on Sarah's testimony.'

Nick nodded. 'And that could put her in less danger.'

'Possibly,' Ruth agreed as the lift arrived and they stepped inside.

The doors to the hospital lift shut with a metallic clunk. Ruth reached over and pressed the button for the third floor. She wanted to speak to Daniel again and see if he remembered any more details. She had also bought him a copy of the *FourFourTwo* football magazine and two bags of Haribo.

Nick ran his hand over his beard. He had seemed slightly distracted ever since arriving in CID earlier. Ruth knew him well enough now to know when something was on his mind.

'You okay?' Ruth asked.

'Not really.' Nick took a moment and then looked at her. 'I was going to tell you earlier. Amanda's daughter, Fran, was sexually assaulted last night.'

'Oh no,' Ruth said. 'That's awful. What happened?'

'She went out for drinks with the people she works with. Eventually it was just her and her boss Paul left. He tried to persuade her to go back to his flat. When she refused, he pushed her against a wall and sexually assaulted her.'

'Did she report it?' Ruth enquired.

Nick shook his head. 'She doesn't want to.'

Ruth frowned. 'Why not?'

'She says that she was drunk. She thinks it was partially her fault. I told her that it wasn't but she doesn't want to take it any further.'

'Poor her,' Ruth said. 'What a prick.'

The lift reached the third floor and stopped with a jolt. The doors opened and they stepped out.

'I said that I'd go and talk to him, but she thinks that will just make things difficult at work,' Nick explained. 'She loves working there and she doesn't want to have to leave.'

Ruth shook her head. 'How is she going to work for someone who attacked her?'

'I don't know.' Nick shrugged. 'What I really want to do is to go and beat the shit out of him.'

Ruth looked at him. 'Yeah, well you can't do that.'

'I know,' Nick said. 'But he's going to think he got away with it and he'll end up doing it to someone else.'

'Have you run a check on him?' Ruth asked as they arrived at the children's ward.

'PNC shows that he's got a couple of fines for drunk and disorderly but nothing like this.'

'If Fran won't press charges, then there's nothing we can do.' Ruth shrugged. 'You know what it's like.'

Nick sighed. 'Yeah, unfortunately.'

As they entered the ward, Ruth saw the Ward Sister she'd seen the day before.

'How's he doing?' she enquired.

'Good.' The Ward Sister gave a half smile. 'Whatever you said to him, it's worked. We've had a long conversation about *Minecraft* this morning.'

Ruth nodded. 'How long will he be here for?'

'He's recovering really well,' the Ward Sister explained. 'The doctors think he can leave this afternoon, as long as he rests for the next few days.'

'Where will he go?' Nick asked.

'He's told me that there's no family,' the Ward Sister said. 'Mum died a few years ago. He's going to have to go to a local authority children's home for the time being.'

Oh no. That's horrible.

Ruth's heart sank at the thought of it. Daniel had witnessed his father being murdered and now he was going to be placed in a home with a load of strangers. Although she knew that staff at the children's homes in Llancastell did an incredible job, the kids there were damaged and their behaviour challenging.

'Okay,' Ruth said sadly and gestured down the corridor. 'I've got a few things for him.'

Ruth and Nick turned and made their way towards Daniel's room.

Ruth gave a sigh. 'As far as our records show, he literally doesn't have anyone left in the world.'

For some reason, the news that Daniel would be placed into care had got to her more than other cases she had worked on. Maybe she was just getting soft in her old age?

Opening the door slowly, Ruth saw that Daniel was propped up in bed and sleeping. He blinked and opened his eyes as they came in.

'Hi Daniel,' Ruth said in a virtual whisper. 'How are you feeling?'

He nodded, thought for a second. 'Yeah, all right.'

Ruth held up the copy of *FourFourTwo* magazine and the bags of Haribo. 'I brought you a couple of things.' She went and placed them on the cabinet beside the bed. 'This is my friend Nick.'

'Is he a policeman?' Daniel asked.

'Yes, I'm a policeman.' Nick smiled. 'I hear you're a big Chelsea fan?'

Daniel nodded as he shuffled up in the bed and looked at them. 'Yeah. Who's your team?'

'Nick's not much of a football fan,' Ruth explained.

'I like rugby,' Nick stated. 'You ever played rugby?'

Daniel frowned and shook his head. 'My dad said that rugby was played by *meatheads*.'

Ruth and Nick laughed.

'Well, your dad was a very wise man,' Ruth said.

Nick grinned, pulled out his ear and squashed his nose with his forefinger. 'Yeah, you end up looking like this if you play too much rugby.'

Daniel smiled and gave a half laugh.

I just want to pick him up, take him home and keep him safe, Ruth thought.

Sitting slowly down on the chair next to the bed, Ruth looked at him for a moment. 'I know what happened last night was terrible and very scary. I wonder if there's anything else you can tell us about the man and woman who hurt your dad?'

She saw the colour drain from his face as he remembered all that had happened. He took a deep breath and shook his head.

'That's all right,' Ruth said gently. 'But if there is anything you can think of, can you tell me? It might help us catch whoever hurt him.'

Daniel nodded with a serious expression.

'How long have you been living in that van with your dad?' Nick enquired.

Daniel frowned as if he didn't understand the question. 'I wasn't.'

'You weren't living in the van?' Ruth asked, trying to clarify what he was saying.

'Not for a while,' he replied. 'We've been living in Llancastell for a few months. Then we packed up our stuff yesterday. Dad said we had to go and pick something up and then we were moving on.'

Nick looked over. 'Do you know where you were living in Llancastell?'

He shook his head and thought for a moment. 'Near a church. And there was a chippy on the corner.'

Okay, that does narrow it down a bit.

Ruth smiled at him. 'Do you think you would recognise it if we took you around Llancastell this afternoon?'

'In a police car?' Daniel asked.

'Yes, in my police car,' she replied.

He nodded brightly. 'Yeah, I think so.'

Chapter 10

Sipping her coffee, Ruth sat back in her temporary office and looked at the ridiculous amount of paperwork that had accumulated on her desk. Glancing outside into Incident Room 1, she could see that the CID team were busy chasing leads and intel on Vince Thompson. At this stage, they didn't have much to go on. Daniel had told them that they had packed up their stuff and they were leaving Llancastell. Vince was going to pick *something* up and he had £5,000 worth of marijuana in the van, plus £2,000 in cash. They stopped in a lay-by, there was some kind of altercation and Vince was shot dead. Her instinct was that his murder was drug related.

French approached and knocked on her open door. 'Boss?'

She smiled at the welcome distraction. 'What is it?'

'Vince Thompson hasn't paid any tax since 2003,' French explained, pointing to the document in his hand. 'Various claims for housing benefit and other benefits from all over the country. Everywhere from Essex to Norfolk, although he did seem to keep coming back to North Wales.'

'What about Llancastell?'

French shook his head. 'No, not here. From what I can see, he didn't stay in one place for more than six months before moving on.'

For a moment, she thought of Daniel. It must have been distressing to never put down roots anywhere. No real friends. No family. New school every six months.

'How did he think it was okay to drag his son around the country like that?' she snapped angrily.

'You know what it's like, boss,' French said. 'Some people just don't care. Or they think they're doing the best for their kids.'

'Okay, thanks,' she said. 'Let me know if you find out anything else.'

'Yes, boss.' French turned and left.

Ruth sat back in her chair and finished her coffee, which was now lukewarm. Getting up, she wandered out into Incident Room 1 and over to the scene boards.

Garrow came in through the door and looked at her. 'Think I've got something, boss.'

'What is it?'

Garrow pointed to a printout in his hand. 'A uniformed patrol stopped a car speeding on the outskirts of Llancastell last night at 11.30pm. When they checked the car, there was a shotgun in the boot. The driver claimed he had a licence for it. The officers issued him with a fixed penalty notice for speeding and told him to report to his local police station within 48 hours with the shotgun licence. It wasn't until they heard about what had happened in Chirk that they thought it might be linked.'

'Have we got a name for the driver?' Ruth asked, thinking that this was beginning to sound like a lead.

'Kevin Parks,' Garrow said with a knowing expression. 'So, I ran him through the PNC. Parks has a string of convictions for violence and drug dealing stretching back twenty years. He lives in Rhyl, so he was a long way from home last night.'

'Whereabouts in Llancastell did they stop him?'

'Out by St Mary's Park,' he replied.

Ruth raised an eyebrow. 'Which is on the way back from Chirk, isn't it?'

Garrow nodded. 'Yes. It's definitely the quickest way to Chirk.'

'I don't suppose he drives a Range Rover, does he?' Ruth asked hopefully.

'Grand Cherokee Jeep,' Garrow stated.

'That's a 4x4, right?'

'Yes, boss.'

'Could it be mistaken for a Range Rover?' she enquired.

'If you don't know much about cars then they definitely look similar,' he replied.

'And if you were a frightened ten-year-old boy looking into the darkness, you probably couldn't tell the difference either?'

'Probably not, boss.'

Kevin Parks was starting to sound very much like a viable suspect.

'We need to go and have a word,' Ruth said. 'Take Georgie with you. And get Rhyl police to send over a uniformed patrol to assist you. He sounds like a bit of a scumbag and I don't want him kicking off.'

'Yes, boss.' Garrow turned and went over to talk to Georgie.

Ruth looked over at French. 'Dan, is there any record of Vince Thompson ever living in Rhyl?'

French looked down at the paperwork. 'Yes, boss. From the looks of it, they were living over in Rhyl before they moved down to Llancastell.'

Ruth nodded. Was there a connection between the time Vince Thompson had spent in Rhyl and Kevin Parks? If they were both dealing drugs, did they know each other? Did they fall out over a deal or did Vince rip Parks off?

Chapter 11

Nick sat in his car on the Llancastell Business Park to the west of the town. He had told Ruth that he was going to talk to an informant to see if the name Vince Thompson rang any bells. However, he had taken a detour on the way.

He was parked outside the ACE Recruitment Agency where Fran worked. Even though he knew that *having a word* with her boss Paul Thurrock was not the right thing to do, he couldn't help it. What he should have done is rung his AA sponsor and talked it through with him. But Nick knew that his sponsor would have told him not to threaten Thurrock and he didn't want to hear that. In fact, Thurrock should count himself lucky that Nick hadn't dragged him into an alleyway and beaten him half to death after he'd attacked Fran.

Having searched ACE's website, Nick had a decent idea of what Thurrock looked like. In his profile photo as *Sales Director*, Thurrock was dressed in a cheap suit with a cocky grin.

He won't be fucking grinning in a minute, he thought.

Getting out of the car, Nick felt the wind against his face. It was still warm.

Right, let's do this.

Marching over to the building, he pushed open the glass door and spotted a reception area with a young woman sitting behind a desk and computer. She looked up and gave him her best cheesy smile.

'Can I help you?' she enquired in a slightly vacuous way.

Pulling out his warrant card, Nick smiled back but knew his expression was going to be tinged with sarcasm. He couldn't help it. 'Yes. DS Nick Evans, Llancastell CID. I'm looking for a Paul Thurrock?'

The woman nodded. 'Yes, I'll just see if he's available. Do you want to take a seat?'

'No,' Nick snapped. 'I'm fine just here.'

Her face fell. 'Okay. I'll just try his line for you.'

Nick turned and looked at a series of tasteful photographs of North Wales that were neatly arranged on the reception wall. He could hear the woman having a conversation but couldn't make out what she was saying.

'Sorry, do you have an appointment to see Paul?' she enquired. He could see that she was feeling uncomfortable at having to ask.

Are you bloody joking? What a cock!

Nick gave a sarcastic laugh. 'Erm, no. I don't have an appointment. But I am a police officer.'

The woman had her hand over the phone's mouthpiece. Thurrock was clearly still on the other end of the line.

'Paul is about to go into a directors' meeting,' she explained with embarrassment. 'If you could make an appointment, Paul said that he'd be more than happy to talk to you.'

Nick glared at her. 'Can you tell *Paul* that he has thirty seconds to get down here before I go up and find him.'

The woman went back on the line, explained what Nick had said and put down the phone. 'He said he'd be right down.'

I bet he did.

'Thank you,' Nick said through gritted teeth.

A minute later, Thurrock came trotting down the stairs wearing a surprised expression. Nick wasn't buying his bullshit. Thurrock knew what he had done to Fran last night and, underneath his innocent expression, he was shitting himself.

'Hi,' Thurrock chirped with a bemused expression. He held out his hand. 'Paul Thurrock. I understand that you want to talk to me?'

Nick didn't take his hand. He just fixed Thurrock with an icy stare. The receptionist noticed and made herself busy.

'Out here please,' Nick hissed under his breath, pointing to the double doors that led to the car park.

'Sorry?' Thurrock asked as if what Nick had requested was somehow amusing.

'You heard me,' Nick snapped. 'And I'm pretty sure you're not going to want anyone to hear what we're about to talk about. But we can do it here if you want an audience?'

Thurrock seemed rattled. He looked at the receptionist, gave a nervous laugh and shrugged. 'Okay. This all sounds very dramatic.'

Nick walked to the automatic doors which slid open and walked over to a flat piece of concrete, hopefully away from any prying eyes or ears.

Thurrock laughed as he approached. 'Is this really necessary?'

'Shut up, dickhead,' Nick thundered.

'Sorry?' Thurrock said, pulling a face to indicate that he was offended.

'You work with Fran, don't you?' Nick growled. 'In fact, you're her boss.'

Thurrock snorted and rolled his eyes. 'Oh, I know what this is all about.'

'She told me what happened last night, and the good news for you is that for some reason she isn't going to press charges. The bad news for you is that she told me.'

Thurrock smirked and shook his head. 'I don't know what she told you, but she was very drunk last night. She tried to make a move on me, made a bit of a fool of herself, fell over and I put her in a cab.'

Nick took an aggressive step towards Thurrock. 'Listen to me, you lying piece of shit. You sexually assaulted my eighteen-year-old step-daughter last night. And that means you're lucky I haven't waited for you after work and put you in a fucking coma …'

Thurrock visibly gulped. 'You can't threaten me like that,' he exclaimed, taking a couple of steps back. 'That's not what happened.'

Nick went closer so that there was only an inch or two between them. He could see Thurrock was panicking and his breathing was quick and shallow. 'Listen to me, you lowlife scumbag,' Nick whispered. 'This is what is going to happen. You are not going to talk to Fran, go anywhere near her or even make eye contact with her. And you are not going to tell anyone that we've had this conversation …'

'Who do you think you are?' Thurrock interrupted him. 'I could report you for police harassment.'

In a flash, Nick grabbed Thurrock's testicles hard. 'You could do. But I'm telling you now, go anywhere near Fran or reveal what we've talked about, and I'm going to be waiting for you. And I'm going to drive you out to Snowdonia and put you in a fucking hole where no one will find you. And that's a promise.'

Thurrock was now physically shaking.

Letting his grip go from Thurrock's testicles, Nick turned sharply on his heels and headed back to his car.

His heart was thumping and his body full of adrenaline. He knew he had crossed the line. As an alcoholic in recovery, he had also gone against everything he had been taught in the rooms of AA. He didn't care. Violence against women was his trigger. He had witnessed it at home when he was a kid. And he was happy to deal out his own brand of justice to the kind of men that got off by attacking women.

Chapter 12

Georgie and Garrow drew up outside an expensive-looking house on the outskirts of Rhyl. There was a black Cherokee Jeep parked on the large drive and a boat on a trailer. It was the address they had been given for Kevin Parks.

'Didn't know they had houses like this in Rhyl,' Georgie observed dryly as she took off her seatbelt.

'No,' Garrow said. 'Someone told me Rhyl was the most deprived part of Wales.'

Georgie opened the door, got out and gestured to the driveway. 'Well not this bit. He's got a bloody speedboat.'

At that moment, a local uniformed patrol car pulled up next to them. She wandered down, getting out her warrant card.

'Morning boys. Llancastell CID,' she explained, looking at the officer driving the car. He had coal black hair, mid 30s, handsome and looked like he worked out.

Hello, she thought.

'What's he done now?' the older officer in the

passenger seat enquired as he buzzed down the window and gestured to the house. She got a waft of stale coffee.

'Do I take it you know Mr Parks?' Georgie asked with a wry smile.

The officer snorted. 'I've been nicking him since he was bloody fourteen years old. Comes from a family of toerags.'

'One of our officers caught him speeding through Llancastell at 11.30pm last night with a shotgun in his boot,' Garrow explained.

'And it was the road that leads to Chirk,' Georgie said with a knowing look.

The officer raised his eyebrow as the penny dropped. 'You had a shooting out there, didn't you?'

Georgie nodded. 'We need to ask Parks what he was up to last night.'

The handsome officer got out of the car. He gave Georgie a twinkly smile. 'I'm coming with you guys. Parks put a mate of mine in hospital last year when we nicked him for possession.'

Georgie smiled. 'It's alright. I can handle myself.'

'I'm sure you can,' he said flirtily. 'But just to be on the safe side, eh?'

'Come on then,' Georgie gestured, feeling a little tingle of excitement. She wondered what Constable Handsome would be like in bed.

They wandered up to the front door and Garrow pressed the bell. He then gave Georgie a withering look as if to say *Please stop flirting your tits off.* She smirked back at him.

There was a sudden barking and snarling from inside the house. It sounded like there were two dogs – and they sounded big.

'Oh good,' Georgie remarked sarcastically. 'I really don't want to have to get the Canine Unit out.'

'Who is it?' shouted a man's gruff voice with a thick North Wales' accent.

'Police officers from Llancastell,' Garrow replied. 'We're looking for Kevin Parks.'

'Hang on a sec while I put the dogs away,' shouted the man.

A few seconds later, the door opened and a man in his 40s peered out at them. He was wearing a white vest and his muscular body was covered in tattoos. His face was angular and covered in black stubble.

'Mr Parks?' Georgie asked as she took out her warrant card. 'DC Wild and DC Garrow from Llancastell CID. Can we come in for a second?'

Parks gave her a sarcastic grin. 'You got a warrant?'

'No,' Georgie frowned. 'We just want to ask you a couple of routine questions.'

'Yeah, well you can ask them here,' Parks growled in an intimidating tone. 'I'm not having you lot contaminating my house.' He then looked her up and down and smirked. 'Although you can come in on your own if you like, darling?'

What a prick, Georgie thought.

'I understand that you were caught speeding in St Mary's Park at around 11.30pm last night?' Garrow enquired.

Parks shrugged. 'You've not come all this way to talk to me about a bloody speeding ticket.'

'And our officers found a shotgun in your boot,' Georgie said. 'Can you tell us why you were in possession of a shotgun?'

'I left it in there from the last time I went shooting,' he explained with a sneer. 'I forgot to lock it away. But, as you know, that's a recommendation not a requirement of the Firearms Act, so I'm not breaking the law.'

'You've got a licence for it, have you?' she asked.

Parks turned, reached over to a nearby table and handed her his shotgun licence. 'There you go, love. It's all in order. Why don't you scribble down your number on it?'

Georgie checked the name, address and date. It was fine. She gave him a forced smile. 'Thank you.'

'Can you tell us where you were coming from last night?' Garrow asked.

'I'd been to see my uncle,' Parks replied. 'He's got MS and he doesn't get out much.'

'And where does your uncle live?' Georgie asked in a dubious tone.

'Glyn Ceiriog. I'm happy to give you his name, address and number. And he'll tell you that I was with him until about eleven o'clock.'

'Okay,' Georgie said. An uncle providing an alibi didn't mean anything. 'We will need to talk to him.'

'I know why you're here,' Parks snorted. 'There was a fella shot dead in Chirk last night.'

'We can't discuss an ongoing investigation with you, I'm afraid,' Garrow said.

Parks looked at them. 'You think it had something to do with me?'

'When was the last time you fired your shotgun?' Garrow enquired.

Parks shrugged. 'Two days ago. Rabbit shoot out near the coast.'

Georgie looked at him. 'You do know that we can cross match any ammunition from the shooting last night.'

Parks shook his head and smiled. 'I suggest you take my gun and my ammunition and see what you find.'

Garrow looked at him. 'Don't worry. We will.'

75

'Does the name Vince Thompson mean anything to you?' Georgie asked.

'Nope.'

'You sure about that?'

Georgie watched him for a reaction but there wasn't a flicker. If he was involved in Vince Thompson's murder, he wasn't showing it.

Parks glanced at his watch. 'You know what, I'm a busy man, so unless you're going to arrest me, I've got things to do.'

'I'm going to need to take your shotgun and ammunition for forensic testing,' Garrow explained.

Parks reached into his pocket, took out some car keys and tossed them to Garrow. 'Knock yourself out, pal.' He then turned and slammed the door in his face.

Georgie gave Garrow a look and muttered, 'Cocky twat.'

Garrow smiled. 'Yeah, either he's got more front than Llandudno, or he's actually telling the truth.'

Chapter 13

Having spoken to the doctors and social services, Ruth and Nick had picked Daniel up from the hospital. There were no records of where Vince and Daniel had been living in Llancastell, but tracking down an address might give them some clues as to what Vince had been doing in recent weeks.

As they travelled through the centre of Llancastell, Ruth turned to look at Daniel in the back of the car.

'You okay?' she asked gently.

He nodded as he looked out of the window. 'Yeah.'

'Burger King or McDonald's?' she enquired.

He looked at her with a curious expression. 'Burger King.'

Ruth smiled over at Nick. 'Well that's lunch sorted.' She looked back at him again. 'What do you have from Burger King?'

'A Vegan Royale meal with a Sprite,' he said immediately.

Ruth laughed. 'A Vegan Royale, eh?'

Nick smiled over at her. 'He knows what he wants.'

'Me and my dad are vegetarians,' Daniel explained as he went back to looking out of the window. 'My dad always had the Plant Based Whopper meal with a Coke Zero.'

'Did he?' Ruth said and then looked directly at him. 'We've got a couple of places that we're going to take you that match the description you gave us. If you just have a look and tell us if you recognise it, that would be great.'

Daniel nodded but he was now lost in thought. It seemed that the mention of his father had got to him.

Five minutes later, they arrived at the area to the west of Llancastell which Ruth and Nick had identified as fitting his description.

A small church, St Luke's, sat on the left-hand side of the road. Opposite was a shabby white building with a bright red sign that read *Jack's Chippy*.

'Classy,' Ruth muttered under her breath as they slowed down and parked.

'I've lived here all my life and I've never been down here,' Nick remarked as they stopped.

'You've not missed much,' Ruth remarked.

Ruth looked back at Daniel who was gazing out of the window.

'Ring any bells?' she enquired.

He frowned. He didn't know what she was talking about.

She gave him a reassuring smile and then pointed. 'Do you recognise anything?'

Daniel nodded but didn't say anything. Maybe he was finding it upsetting to be back in the place where he had lived with his father.

'Shall we go and have a look?' Nick suggested.

'Yeah,' Daniel said.

'And you think this is the right place?' Ruth asked to clarify.

Daniel nodded.

'Would you be able to point out the house where you and your dad lived for us?' Ruth enquired.

Looking out for a few seconds, Daniel frowned. 'Can we get out?'

'Of course we can,' Ruth said as she reached down and unclipped her seatbelt. She got out and opened the rear door and Daniel stepped down onto the pavement tentatively.

'It was just down here,' he stated, pointing to a side street full of rundown houses.

Nick got out, beeped the automatic locking system and they all crossed the road and headed down Klea Avenue. The houses were small, squashed together and made from dark red brick. Front gardens were neglected, weed-strewn with an array of rubbish and discarded shopping trolleys, an old fridge and a mattress.

Ruth noticed Daniel slow down as he peered carefully at each house on the left-hand side of the road. 'It was one of these.'

'Do you know which number?' Nick enquired.

Daniel shook his head. 'No, sorry.'

Ruth gave him a sympathetic smile. 'You don't need to apologise. Just take your time.'

'Daniel?' called a cheery voice.

A blonde girl in her late teens waved at him from across the road. She was wearing grey trackies and a hoodie and was carrying a bag of shopping.

Without warning, Daniel jogged across the road to greet her. They embraced and she held him in her arms for a few seconds.

'Hello mate,' she chirped. 'I thought you guys were moving on?'

As Ruth and Nick crossed the road, Daniel looked very upset. He had tears in his eyes.

'My dad's dead,' he whispered as he sniffed.

'What?' the girl exclaimed and they hugged again.

'Hi there,' Ruth said as she took out her warrant card. 'We're police officers. We're trying to locate where Daniel and his father used to live.'

The girl pointed across the road at number 19. 'It was that one.' Then she looked at them and asked in a virtual whisper. 'Is that right? Is Vince dead?'

Ruth nodded with a serious expression. 'I'm afraid so.'

'Oh God, that's horrible.' She then crouched down to be level with Daniel. 'I'm so sorry, Daniel.'

Ruth looked at the girl. 'Sorry, I didn't catch your name.'

'Phoebe,' she said. She had a button nose with a sprinkle of freckles across the bridge. She wore more make-up than she needed, had false eyelashes and a pierced eyebrow.

Nick had grabbed his notepad and pen. 'And you live near here?'

'Number 17,' Phoebe explained. 'Next door, with my mum.'

'And you knew Daniel and his dad?' Ruth asked as they approached No. 19.

'She used to look after me when dad was out,' Daniel replied quickly.

Nick went to the front of the house, cupped his hands and peered through the window.

'There's no one in there,' Phoebe informed him. 'Not since Vince and Daniel left a few days ago.'

As Daniel watched Nick go and try the front door,

Ruth pulled Phoebe surreptitiously to one side for a quiet word. 'Do you know if Vince was renting the house from the council or privately?'

'I'm not sure. He never mentioned it,' Phoebe replied and then shook her head sadly. 'I can't believe he's dead. He was such a lovely bloke. And a brilliant dad to Daniel.'

'So, you knew them fairly well?' Ruth asked as she saw Nick crouch down and look through the letterbox.

'Yeah. I know it sounds weird,' Phoebe said, 'but me and Daniel were like friends, you know. And if Vince was late back, I'd go and cook him his tea and do some home-work, or watch the telly. That kind of thing.'

'How long did they live next door to you?'

Phoebe shrugged. 'I dunno. Six months. Might have been a bit longer.'

'And did they ever say where they were before?'

'I got the feeling they'd moved about a bit,' Phoebe explained quietly. 'Daniel said they'd been up in Rhyl, I do know that.'

'Did you see anyone else at the house? Did Vince have a girlfriend or any friends that you knew of?'

Phoebe seemed reluctant to say – she was hiding something.

'Cath,' Phoebe replied. 'Vince and Cath were having 'a thing'. Don't know how serious it was.'

'Cath?' Ruth asked.

'Yeah, Cath.'

Ruth looked at her. 'Don't suppose you know her surname?'

'No, sorry.' Phoebe shook her head and then pointed to the scruffy convenience store next to *Jack's Chippy*. 'She won't be hard to find though. She and her husband own that shop.'

'Her husband?' Ruth asked, realising that Vince and Cath might have been having an affair.

'Yeah, Stu,' Phoebe replied.

Nick hit the front door with his shoulder and it opened.

Ruth gave him a look. 'Front door was open was it, Sergeant?'

'Something like that,' he replied with a grin as he went inside.

Ruth went to follow him but then looked at Daniel. 'You okay to stay out here with Phoebe?'

Daniel seemed confused.

'Let's just check things in there first, eh?' Ruth said gently.

Phoebe put a reassuring hand on Daniel's shoulder. 'It's alright.' She pointed towards her house. 'He can come next door with me until you've finished.'

Ruth watched as Phoebe reached out her free hand, took Daniel's and they walked along the pavement before turning to her house to go inside.

It was then that Ruth realised why she felt such a connection and empathy to Daniel. He reminded her of her little brother Chris. He had the same colouring, the same quick, intelligent eyes. And the same vulnerability.

She and Chris had been brought up in a tiny council flat on the Winstanley Estate in South London, SW11. Even though there was no violence at home, her father was a petty criminal which was a source of considerable conflict with their mother. Ruth remembered the feeling of butterflies in her stomach every time there was an ominous knock at the door. Usually it was a local police officer wanting to speak to her father about something. Once in a while it was another local criminal looking to *fence* stolen jewellery or antiques. However, a couple of times her father had pissed off the wrong local villain and found himself on the end of a beating on their doorstep.

The chaotic nature of their upbringing seemed to affect Chris more than it did her. She was a few years older, so she found herself comforting or reassuring him. She remembered Chris's nervous blink when things got too much at home. It was identical to the blink that she had seen Daniel exhibit both in the hospital and since they picked him up.

Ruth took a step inside the house. It smelled damp and musty. Cloth hung at the downstairs windows as a substitute for curtains. Lightbulbs hung naked and exposed without shades. The floor was dirty and covered in junk mail and fast-food leaflets.

Nick looked at her and raised an eyebrow. 'Nice place,' he said sardonically.

'It looks like they were pretty much camping out here,' Ruth remarked as she wandered around. 'Let's get SOCOs in here. Let's see if we can find any fingerprints or DNA that don't match our elimination sample.'

'You think whoever killed Vince had been here at some point?' Nick asked.

'Possibly,' Ruth replied. 'Maybe we'll get a hit on the DNA database. I'm going to be interested in what Kevin Parks has to say for himself. And if he'd been here in the days leading up to Vince's death, then I want to know.'

Chapter 14

Walking into the local convenience store, Ruth and Nick looked around and spotted a young man stacking shelves which were stocked with Polish food and drinks – *Slaska sausages, pork loins, herby paprika sauces* and packs of *Tyskie Lager*. This part of Llancastell had a large Polish population that had roots that went back to the Second World War.

'We're looking for Cath?' Nick explained.

'Sorry, I …' The young man looked startled. 'I think she's out the back somewhere. I'll just go and give her a shout.'

'Thanks,' Ruth said as she looked around the shop, which was filled from floor to ceiling with tins and packets.

A moment later, a tall, spindly-looking woman in her 20s, with bright red hair, came out looking confused.

'I'm Cath,' she exclaimed. 'Is it me dad? Is he alright?'

Ruth gave her a kind smile. 'As far as I know, your father is fine. But we do need to talk to you. Is there somewhere we could go that's a bit more private?'

'There's a back office,' she stated, pointing to the back of the shop. She was clearly relieved that her father was okay.

Following her past the stockroom, they arrived at a small, dingy office where there was a ripped sofa and a couple of red plastic chairs.

'What's all this about?' Cath asked. She had a thick North Welsh accent, arms full of colourful tattoos and pierced eyebrows. She was attractive, Ruth thought.

'We understand that you know a Vince Thompson?' Nick said quietly.

The colour drained from her face. 'Vince? Yes. Why, what's happened?'

Ruth looked at her for a moment. 'I'm very sorry to tell you that Vince died last night.'

'What?' Cath's eyes widened with shock as she shook her head. 'No, no. That can't be right.'

'We're very sorry for your loss,' Ruth said gently.

'What happened?' Cath asked as her eyes roamed frantically around the room. 'Was it some kind of accident?'

'Vince was murdered,' Ruth explained.

'What?' Cath gasped as she wiped a tear from her eye. 'I don't understand … What happened?'

'I'm afraid we can't discuss the details of the case with you as it's an ongoing investigation,' Nick explained.

'You were close to Vince, were you?' Ruth enquired.

Cath frowned. 'We were … friends. He lived just across the street with his son.'

Ruth and Nick exchanged a look – Phoebe had led them to believe they were romantically involved.

Ruth looked at her. 'But your relationship wasn't anything more than that?'

Cath pulled a face as though this was a ridiculous question but she was definitely hiding something from them. 'No!' She pointed to the wedding ring on her finger. 'I'm married.'

That felt like an overreaction to me. Is that a sign of guilt? Ruth wondered.

Ruth nodded. 'Just routine questions, that's all.'

'We're just trying to build up a picture of Vince,' Nick explained as he scribbled in his notebook. 'What sort of bloke was he?'

The question obviously made Cath feel uncomfortable. She shrugged. 'I didn't really know him. He was a nice bloke. Friendly.'

Ruth looked at Nick. *That's weird because when we told you he'd died, you were totally shocked, upset and shed a tear.*

She was backtracking now. Maybe it was the suggestion that there was anything going on between them.

'When was the last time you saw Vince?' Ruth enquired.

Cath thought for a few seconds. 'A couple of days ago. He came in to tell us that he was moving on.'

'Did Vince mean he was leaving the area?' Nick asked to clarify.

'Yeah.' Cath nodded.

Nick stopped writing and looked up. 'Did he say where he and Daniel were going?'

'Somewhere up on the Llŷn Peninsular, I think he said. Close to Aberdaron.'

'Did he say why he was leaving? Ruth asked.

Cath shook her head. 'No. I got the feeling that he moved around a lot … It wasn't really any of my business, was it?'

'Can you tell us where you were last night at around 11pm?' Ruth enquired.

Cath shrugged. 'I was asleep in bed.'

'Can anyone confirm that?'

Cath pointed to the open door. 'Stu. He was asleep next to me.'

'And he was there all night, was he?' Ruth asked.

'Yeah, of course. Where else would he be?' Cath was now clearly rattled. She glanced down at her watch.

Ruth and Nick looked at each other and then got up to leave.

'That's all for the time being,' Ruth stated, 'but we might need to come back and talk to you again.'

They were distracted by the arrival of a man who was carrying a couple of cardboard boxes. He was short and stocky. His thick forearms were covered in Welsh tattoos and he wore a black baseball cap that looked a little faded by the sun.

'Where do you want these, love?' he asked, looking curiously at Ruth and Nick.

Is this the husband?

'Just in the storeroom,' Cath said. 'They need to go out later.'

The man gave her a look as if to ask who she was talking to.

'I'm just talking to these police officers, Stu,' Cath explained, almost as if talking to a child. 'You know that nice fella that used to come in here with his son? Vince?'

'Oh aye,' Stu stated, but it seemed that he didn't really remember.

'He's been shot and killed.'

'Oh, sorry to hear that like,' Stu said in a monotone voice that was devoid of any emotion. Then he turned and sauntered out.

Ruth looked at Nick for second and then asked, 'How do you know Vince Thompson was shot?'

Cath frowned. 'You told me just now.'

Ruth shook her head. 'No, we didn't. I told you he'd been murdered.'

Cath shrugged. 'I must have just guessed then.'

Chapter 15

Twenty minutes later, Ruth and Nick were sitting in a small living room at a dining table. Phoebe had made them a cup of tea and had just put a plate of biscuits in front of them. The room was decorated in various shades of brown and beige and smelled of polish and stale cigarettes. A small framed print of Constable's painting *The Hay Wain* had been hung on the wall beside a small Welsh dresser which was filled with Portmeirion china featuring dainty patterns of flowers. An old clock ticked on the wall above the doorway.

'Thanks,' Nick said as he reached out to take a custard cream.

Daniel was sitting on the sofa watching cartoons on the television, although Ruth could see that he was lost in his own thoughts. She didn't know how long it would be before he could see a child psychiatrist but he needed one now.

Ruth sipped her tea and smiled. 'Well, you make a great cup of tea, Phoebe.'

'Thanks,' Phoebe said with a satisfied smile. It was the

first time that Ruth had spotted just how young she actually was. Up until now, she had been conducting herself with a maturity way beyond her years.

Ruth looked at her. 'We've been across the road to talk to Cath. When we suggested that there had been something going on between her and Vince, she flatly denied it.'

'Of course she did,' Phoebe snorted as she turned her mug so the handle was in the right position. She then lifted the mug with her left hand. Ruth noticed a small tattoo on her forearm of two butterflies resting on dark green leaves.

'I see you're left-handed,' Nick remarked with a smile, gesturing to how she was holding the mug. 'Same as me. All the best people are left-handed.'

Ruth gave him a withering look. 'And it's a sign of modesty too.'

Nick gave her a sarcastic grin.

'It's really weird because I'm neither,' Phoebe explained. 'I iron with my left hand but I pour water from the kettle with my right. I throw darts with my left hand, but I play pool with my right.'

'It's called ambidextrous,' Ruth informed her.

'Ambi-what?' Phoebe asked with a frown.

'What about if you hit someone?' Nick enquired as though he was joking. Of course, the PM had revealed that Vince had been struck on the face by someone who was probably left-handed.

Phoebe shrugged with an innocent smile. 'I don't know. I don't go around hitting people.'

'Glad to hear it,' Nick said.

'Getting back to what we were talking about,' Ruth stated. 'You weren't surprised that Cath had lied to us?'

'She's married to Stu,' Phoebe replied.

'You don't like Stu?' Nick asked.

'No, he's a prick,' she replied. 'Especially when he's had a drink.'

'Is he violent?' Nick asked.

'Sometimes,' Phoebe said. 'I saw him fighting someone in The Red Lion a few months ago.'

'Any idea who it was?'

'Just some bloke who'd pinched Cath's arse at the bar. Stu decided to sort him out,' Phoebe explained. 'He gets jealous.'

'And you're convinced that Cath and Vince were having an affair?' Ruth enquired.

'That's what she told me in the pub a couple of weeks ago,' Phoebe replied. 'She was off her face. And she swore me to secrecy.'

'But you're telling us?' Ruth remarked, raising an eyebrow.

'You're police officers. And if someone killed Vince, it might help.' Phoebe shrugged. 'Cath seemed pretty scared when she told me.'

'Scared?' Nick asked. 'Why was that?'

Phoebe looked at him. 'She said that Stu would kill them both if he found out.'

Chapter 16

The sky was black by the time Ruth pulled up outside the *Clear View Children's Home* close to the centre of Llancastell. It had started to drizzle and the windscreen had steamed up. Taking a cloth from the glove compartment, Ruth gave the inside of the screen a quick wipe.

'That's better isn't it?' she said cheerily.

Daniel, who was sitting next to her in the passenger seat, didn't respond. She had tried to make conversation on the way over from Llancastell nick but it had been stilted and awkward. Daniel knew where he was going and he knew this was now going to be his home for the foreseeable future. She couldn't imagine how he must be feeling. If it hadn't been a sacking offence, she would have taken him back to Bangor-on-Dee to stay with her until something more suitable could be f0und.

'Here we go then,' she said quietly, looking out at the quiet residential street that was lined with large Victorian red brick houses.

The windscreen started to fill with tiny flecks of water that were getting heavier.

'How long will I be staying here?' Daniel whispered.

Ruth looked at him. 'I'm sorry but I'm not really sure.' She reached into her jacket and pulled out her card. She handed it to him and pointed to her mobile phone number. 'This is my card. And this is my number. And if you need anything or if you just want someone to talk to, please just ring me. Whenever you need to.'

Daniel shrugged sadly. 'I haven't got a phone.'

'Okay,' Ruth said. 'They'll have a landline in there that you can use. And let me see if I can't sort out a mobile phone for you.'

His face lit up. 'Really?'

'Yeah, why not.' Ruth then gestured to the house. 'Come on then.'

Getting out of the car, she felt the drizzle against her face as she jogged around the car to where Daniel was standing.

They made their way up the stone path to the large, dark red front door with a stained glass panel at its centre.

Ruth knocked and a few seconds later, a large, bearded man in his 40s wearing a dark Arran jumper answered the door and smiled.

'You must be Daniel?' he enquired brightly before Ruth had time to explain who they were. 'I'm Charlie.'

Crikey, he's very cheerful, she thought. I guess you need to have patience and a very positive outlook to work in a children's home.

'Come in, come in,' Charlie said and then gestured to a large living room where a couple of children were watching TV. 'Why don't you go and grab a pew while I have a word with Detective Inspector Hunter here.'

'Ruth,' she said. 'Please.'

'Everyone, this is Daniel,' Charlie announced loudly. 'He's going to be staying with us for a while.'

A teenage girl looked up and muttered 'Hi Daniel,' before going back to watching the TV.

Ruth watched Daniel wander uncertainly towards an armchair before stopping and looking at something on a small coffee table.

'What are the chances of Daniel being adopted?' Ruth enquired under her breath.

Charlie pulled a face. 'He's probably too old to be fully adopted if I'm honest. But we do have plenty of wonderful foster parents around.'

Ruth pulled out her card and handed it to him. 'Here are my details. If Daniel needs anything, and I mean *anything*, let me know.'

Charlie took the card and nodded. 'Thanks.'

Ruth gestured over to Daniel. 'I'm just going to say goodbye. I'll try and check in on him tomorrow.'

Wandering over to where Daniel was standing, she saw that he was holding something in his hand.

It was a leaflet for a local MP, Graham Wheeler, who was standing in the up-coming Llancastell by-election.

Ruth frowned. 'You okay?'

'My dad knew him,' Daniel said, gesturing to the flyer.

That doesn't sound likely.

'Are you sure?' she asked.

'Yeah,' Daniel nodded. 'We went out to his house a few weeks ago.'

Ruth wondered how Vince Thompson and Graham Wheeler's contrasting worlds could have collided.

'Do you know how your dad knew him?' Ruth enquired.

'No,' Daniel replied shaking his head. 'There was a girl there.'

'His daughter?'

Daniel nodded. 'Daisy. She was a bit younger than me. She showed me her pony that they had out in the field at the back. Its name was Harper.'

'What was your dad doing while you were out seeing Harper?' Ruth enquired.

'He was talking to this man,' Daniel said pointing to the photo of Graham Wheeler.

'And then you went home?' Ruth asked.

'Yeah, I think they'd had a row or something,' Daniel explained. 'He told my dad never to go there again.'

Ruth looked at the flyer again – *What on earth was that about?* she wondered.

Chapter 17

Nick opened his front door and got a lovely warm smell of cooking and bath time as he walked into the hallway. Taking off his coat and scarf, he took a moment to decompress. Knowing that he'd missed Megan's bedtime, he slipped off his shoes and padded very quietly up the stairs – as he always did when he'd missed seeing her.

Getting to the landing, he felt the soft carpet under his feet. For a moment, he wondered how Fran had got on at work. He hoped that his *little chat* with Thurrock would mean that she'd had nothing to do with him.

The door to Megan's room was slightly ajar. It had a little pink nameplate on it with two cartoon ponies smiling. He went in slowly and could see she was sleeping, bathed in the warm vanilla light of her night lamp. Her tiny blonde locks of hair were spread out on the pillow and her right hand was tucked under her head.

She looks perfect, he thought with a wave of gratitude.

He went over, kissed her on the forehead, turned and quietly left. Feeling the inner joy of having seen his daughter, he wandered down the stairs before heading to the living room where he assumed Amanda and Fran would be watching telly and chatting.

'Hiya,' he said as he pushed open the door. However, he was met with stern frowns. Something was up. Fran didn't make eye contact but instead took a sip from her glass of wine. 'Everything okay?'

'No.' Amanda shook her head and gave him a withering look. 'No, everything isn't *okay.*'

Nick went over and sat down in the armchair. This wasn't good. The atmosphere in the room was decidedly frosty.

'You couldn't do it, could you?' Amanda growled.

'Sorry, I'm lost,' Nick stated with a frown. He had no idea what she was talking about.

Amanda scowled at him. 'What did you say to Paul Thurrock?'

Oh shit.

'I haven't spoken to Paul Thurrock,' Nick lied. 'I don't know what you're talking about.'

He didn't know why he had bothered to lie. Amanda had an incredible bullshit detector.

'For fuck's sake, Nick, don't lie to us,' she snapped.

Fran was still avoiding looking at him.

'Okay, sorry,' Nick said. 'What's happened?'

Fran looked over and then asked in a virtual whisper, 'What did you say to him?'

'I told him that I knew what had happened and if he went anywhere near you, or even looked at you, there would be serious repercussions,' he explained.

'No one asked you to do that, Nick,' Amanda sighed. 'You've made things worse, you idiot!'

Nick looked at Fran. 'I'm really sorry. What's happened?'

'I've been moved off of my main accounts,' Fran explained looking very upset. 'They've also moved my desk so that I'm over by the factory section.'

Nick could feel his anger rising. 'Thurrock did this?'

'Not directly,' Fran said, 'but he told them to do it.'

Amanda sat forward and looked at him scornfully. 'Basically he's taken away all her good accounts, the stuff she loves working on, and moved her away from her friends in the office to punish her for telling you what happened.'

'What a prick!' Nick muttered. He looked over at Fran. 'Sorry. I was trying to protect you.'

Fran gave him a half-smile. 'I know you were. But I just wanted to forget about it. I love my job but …'

'But he's ruined it for you,' Nick stated. 'Maybe you should press charges?'

Amanda scowled at him. 'Fran's said she doesn't want to do that.'

Nick ran his hand over his beard. 'Look, I've met Thurrock. He's an arrogant dickhead who thinks he can get away with anything. He will have done this before and he'll do it again unless someone stops him.'

'It's not your decision to make, Nick!' Amanda thundered.

Fran had a tear in her eye. 'I'd been drinking. There were no witnesses. So it's my word against his, isn't it? I'm not stupid, Nick. I watch the news. I know how many cases like this don't get to court or the bloke just gets away with it.'

Nick knew she was right.

Fran looked at him. 'I'll press charges if you can guarantee that he'll be prosecuted for what he did.'

Nick didn't answer. There was no way he could guarantee that.

'Yeah, that's what I thought,' Fran sighed bitterly.

———

TAKING A LONG DRAG OF HER CIGGIE, RUTH BLEW A PLUME of smoke up into the night sky and watched it disappear. She was sitting out on the patio at the back of Sarah's house wrapped in a huge blanket. The sky was clear, black and speckled with stars. The moon was the colour of pale cream, gaining a hard-edged brilliance as it rose in the night sky.

A bright satellite, a man-made star, very slowly and somehow carefully crossed the sky in a great arc, from one side to the other. Ruth thought of it slowly going about its business round and round the globe. And then, much further away, stars were quietly disappearing. Silently being extinguished, lost in the utter silence.

'Thought I'd find you skulking out here,' said a voice.

It was Sarah.

'Skulking?'

'Yeah, it's a good word, don't you think?'

'It makes it sound like I'm up to no good,' Ruth protested.

'Are you?' Sarah laughed.

'Definitely not,' Ruth replied. 'I'm contemplating the meaning of life.'

'And smoking?'

'Yeah, and smoking, obviously. How could you look at the night sky and contemplate the mind-bending enormity of an eternal universe without smoking?' Ruth asked.

'Good point. Mind if I join you?'

'You don't smoke,' Ruth joked.

'Ha ha,' Sarah groaned as she approached with a tartan picnic rug wrapped around her shoulders.

'Did you ever smoke?' Ruth enquired. 'I can't remember if you ever told me.'

'I tried to smoke when I was a teenager,' Sarah replied, 'but it just made me feel sick every time. I smoked the odd spliff.'

Ruth looked at her. 'Well I know that. I've shared a spliff with you at Glastonbury.'

Sarah frowned. 'Was that the year we saw Amy Winehouse?'

'Yeah,' Ruth nodded. 'She wasn't very good was she?'

'No,' Sarah agreed. 'She looked detached. Like she wasn't really there.'

'I think she was off her head.'

'I remember thinking it was sad.' Sarah moved her chair closer and then gestured to an upstairs bedroom where her mother Doreen was resting. 'Mum's lost so much weight.'

Ruth nodded sadly. 'Is she sleeping okay?'

'She said she is but I know she's in quite of lot of pain.'

'Talking of spliffs,' Ruth said, 'there was an article in the paper the other day that said marijuana can really help with the side effects of cancer.'

'That's great but we don't have any marijuana,' Sarah pointed out.

Ruth gave her a look. 'I'm a police officer. I'm pretty sure I can get my hands on some. I was at a crime scene yesterday where we found five thousand pounds' worth of weed. I'll just *borrow* some.'

Sarah frowned. 'You can't do that. You'll get sacked.'

'No one will notice an ounce or two,' Ruth assured her. 'I'm not dealing, I'm using it to help an old woman who is in pain.'

'If you can get some, then thanks,' Sarah stated.

'How are you feeling about getting a trial date?'

'Nervous,' Sarah admitted, 'but at least there's an end to the whole thing, even if it's in five or six months' time.'

'They didn't give you the name of the judge did they?'

'Not yet,' Sarah replied. 'Shall I open a bottle of wine?'

'It's a school night, but yes,' Ruth said.

'I've only got white.'

'White is fine.'

Sarah disappeared back inside for a few seconds and Ruth stubbed out her cigarette. She thought of Daniel and wondered how he was getting on. She knew that on top of the grief he felt at losing his father, he would be feeling so incredibly lost and alone in the world.

'Here you go,' Sarah said, handing her a glass of wine.

'Thanks … Cheers.'

They clinked glasses and Sarah sat down.

'You said that you wanted to talk to me about something?' Sarah asked, and then took a gulp of wine.

'Yes,' Ruth replied. 'Do you remember a long time ago we talked about adoption?'

Sarah frowned. 'Jesus, Ruth, that was years ago. I mean before any of that stuff happened.'

'I know.' Ruth felt disappointed at Sarah's reaction. 'I know that.'

'Where are you going with this?'

'I don't know,' Ruth admitted. She didn't really know herself. 'I told you that there was a murder in Chirk the night before last.'

'Yes,' Sarah said as she put her glass down on the garden table. 'You didn't really tell me much more than that, except that a man had been shot at the roadside. And that his son had been taken to hospital.'

'Daniel,' Ruth said.

Sarah looked at her and frowned. 'Daniel, okay.'

'This boy is ten years old,' Ruth explained. 'His mother

died when he was young. Since then, he's travelled around the country with his weed-dealing father, stopping here, there and everywhere. He'd spend a few months at school before they moved on to the next place. He's got no friends.'

'Family?'

Ruth shook her head. 'None that we can find.'

'And now he's got no parents,' Sarah stated quietly. 'Where is he now?'

'*Clear View Children's Home* in the middle of Llancastell,' Ruth replied.

Sarah pulled a face. 'That's so incredibly sad, isn't it?'

'Yes, it is.'

Sarah furrowed her brow and looked over at Ruth. 'You want to adopt him?'

Ruth thought for a few seconds. 'I don't know. But when I dropped him off at *Clear View*, I know I just wanted to take him home with me and look after him.'

'Maybe someone will adopt him?' Sarah suggested. 'There are lots of parents who want to adopt.'

Ruth shook her head. 'He's too old. Adoption agencies are looking for babies or toddlers. It's virtually impossible to match anyone with a ten-year-old boy.'

'Have you thought this through?'

'No.' Ruth shook her head. 'I wanted to talk to you about it.'

Sarah looked up at the window. 'I've got Mum to look after.'

'I know,' Ruth said. 'I haven't thought it through.'

'Clearly,' Sarah said. 'You must have encountered kids like Daniel before?'

'Yeah, I have,' Ruth admitted, 'but there's something about him. I think it's because he reminds me of my brother Chris when he was that age.'

Sarah shrugged. 'It sounds like a nice idea. Maybe the timing just isn't right.'

'Maybe,' Ruth stated, 'but maybe the timing for that sort of thing is never right. You just have to take a deep breath and do it.'

Sarah looked at her pensively but didn't reply.

Chapter 18

Sipping at her flat white, Ruth took a look out of the window of her temporary office. They were on the opposite side of the building to where the CID offices were, so she was afforded a different aerial view of Llancastell and the surrounding area. Over to the north-west, the dark shapes of the Berwyn Mountains. If she could remember her geography correctly, they lay between Llangollen and Corwen, with Bala slightly to the west and Lake Vyrnwy to the south.

For a moment, she was transported back to one of the first nicks she ever worked at in South London. What an incredible contrast it was to where she worked now. A 19th century building – iron railings, red brick, with steep stone steps up to double doors. The single word *POLICE* was carved into a stone lintel above the doorway. She remembered thinking that it was a building that harked back to the days of blue police boxes and whistles.

Her DI, Terry Bulman, was a bear of a man but seemed to take her under his wing when she first arrived. He told her that being a decent copper was all about building a reputation. By that he meant a reputation both in the nick with the colleagues you worked with, as well as a reputation in the criminal fraternity in the local area. And reputation was built on the little things, he told her. How you handled yourself down at the custody suite while booking in a prisoner. Could you take the ribbing dished out by the male officers who were testing to see how tough you really were? And could you handle your drink in the local 'police' pub?

A noise from outside broke her train of thought. It was time for the morning briefing. She grabbed a folder, made her way out of her office and headed for the front of IR1. 'Morning everyone,' she chirped loudly. 'Let's get cracking shall we?'

Looking out, she saw the CID team move chairs around and settle themselves.

'Okay. Several developments in our investigation,' she explained, going over to the scene boards. She pointed to a photo of Kevin Parks that they had found on the North Wales' database. 'This is Kevin Parks. He has a string of convictions for violence and drug dealing stretching back twenty years. He currently lives in Rhyl. A uniformed patrol stopped Parks on the outskirts of Llancastell on Monday night at 11.30pm. He had a shotgun and ammunition in his boot.'

'Does he have an alibi, boss?' French asked.

Georgie looked over. 'He claims he had been to see his sick uncle over in Glyn Ceiriog.'

'Sick uncle?' French asked doubtfully.

'Have we managed to verify that?' Nick enquired.

Garrow shook his head. 'We're going down there to check his alibi this morning, Sarge.'

'Good,' Nick replied. 'To be honest, visiting his uncle is pretty lame as alibis go.'

'Anything on the forensics on the gun or the ammunition?' Ruth asked.

Garrow shook his head. 'No, boss. And given his eagerness to hand it over to us, my guess is that there's no match.'

'Or he's got some bloody front,' Georgie chipped in.

Ruth looked at the board again. 'We know from our records that Vince and Daniel were in Rhyl about nine months ago. And Parks lives in Rhyl. What if Vince was dealing on his patch or had some kind of dispute with Parks?'

Georgie frowned. 'Why wait eight or nine months to shoot him?'

Nick looked over. 'Maybe Vince got wind that Parks was after him and did a runner down to Llancastell to hide out. It's taken Parks this long to track him down.'

'That's a possibility … Parks was on his own when he was stopped, wasn't he?' Ruth asked, thinking out loud.

'Yes, boss,' French said.

'Daniel told us that there were two people in the 4x4 and one of them was a woman,' Ruth remarked.

Georgie shrugged. 'It was dark and he was terrified. He's only ten years old.'

'He might have been scared but he's sharp,' Ruth commented. 'If he says he saw a man and woman, then I think that's exactly what he saw.'

She noticed how defensive of Daniel she had become.

'That rules out Parks, doesn't it?' French asked rhetorically.

'Not if he dropped off the woman before he got back to Llancastell,' Nick pointed out.

'He's a drug dealer with a shotgun in the boot,' French stated, sounding a little irritated, 'and he's twenty minutes away from where another drug dealer was shot … with a shotgun.'

French clearly thought Parks was their man already.

Georgie smiled at French. 'I think we get the point, Dan.'

He gave her a sarcastic smile.

Ruth then pointed to another photo. 'We also have Cath and Stu Morton. According to the neighbour, Phoebe Evans, Cath Morton and Vince were having an affair. She denied it when we asked her.'

'But she would, wouldn't she?' Georgie pointed out.

'True,' Ruth replied. 'Phoebe also told us that she had seen Stu Morton beating up a man who had pinched Cath's bottom in the local pub. If Stu found out about the affair, then he's also a possible suspect.'

Garrow looked over. 'I've checked the shotgun register for the area. Stu Morton doesn't own a shotgun licence.'

A phone rang and French leaned over to answer it.

Ruth shrugged. 'Doesn't mean he doesn't own a shotgun though.'

Garrow looked at his computer. 'According to the DVLA, the Mortons only have one vehicle registered to that address. A 2016, black Citroën Berlingo van.'

'And we're looking for a dark coloured 4x4,' Ruth noted. 'Okay. Someone have a dig around Stu Morton. Has he got previous? Ask at the pub if they remember the fight and if they know him.' Ruth then pointed to a photo of Graham Wheeler. 'We also have this man, Graham Wheeler, who is the Conservative Party candidate for the up-coming by-election. Daniel pointed him out to me on a flyer that had come through the door.'

'What's the connection?' Nick asked.

'To be honest, I don't know,' Ruth admitted, 'but I can't see how someone like Graham Wheeler would come into contact with someone like Vince Thompson. Daniel told us that his dad and Wheeler argued about something. Nick and I will go and have a word but I'm not sure how relevant it is.'

French looked over and gestured to the phone. 'Boss, couple of things back from forensics. They've got a decent footprint from the murder scene. A male size 10. Not a trainer or a boot. More of a conventional shoe.'

'Good,' Ruth said. 'What else?'

French looked at her. 'The shotgun ammunition found in Parks' car is a match for the ammunition that killed Vince Thompson.'

It looked like Parks really was a suspect now.

Ruth gestured to the CID team. 'Jim and Georgie, go and check Parks' alibi for the time of the murder. If it doesn't check out, we bring him in for questioning.'

Garrow nodded and looked at Georgie. 'Yes, boss.'

Ruth tossed Nick the car keys. 'Come on, we can pay a visit to our next potential Member of Parliament.'

'I drive, you smoke?' Nick asked with a grin.

'Obviously,' Ruth smiled as she grabbed her jacket.

Chapter 19

Georgie and Garrow pulled up outside a small farmhouse to the south of Glyn Ceiriog. It was in the middle of a dark, wooded area. There was a pot-holed central yard with a couple of pieces of rusty farm machinery. On the far side was a series of old, dilapidated barns.

'It's all a bit *Texas Chainsaw Massacre* out here,' Georgie joked as they got out of the car. It's not somewhere she'd want to be on a dark night.

Garrow laughed.

The rain had stopped, but the ground was wet, the cold penetrating their shoes and chilling their toes. Georgie had pulled the hood of her waterproof jacket over her head while Garrow stood with his hands in his pockets, the collar of his overcoat pulled up. As they approached the house, two mangy-looking German Shepherds, who had been resting inside a huge metal cage, started to bark ferociously.

'Jesus!' Georgie exclaimed, feeling startled.

The dogs jumped up at the fencing, foaming fangs bared and snarling.

Christ, if they get out, we're dead.

The front door opened and a figure appeared on the wooden porch.

Garrow flashed his warrant card. 'DC Garrow and DC Wild, Llancastell CID. We're looking for an Alfred Parks?'

'Yeah?' said the giant of a man. He had grizzled features, long sideburns and a ripped, filthy camouflage jacket. His greying hair was long and greasy and swept off his face. 'What do you want?'

Charmer.

It was hard to hear anything over the commotion of the dogs barking.

Alfred walked down the wooden steps and aimed an almighty kick against the cage where the dogs were barking. 'SHUT UP!' he thundered.

Georgie was feeling decidedly uneasy. She was glad that Garrow was with her.

'Alfred Parks?' Garrow asked.

'Aye,' Alfred stated with a deep frown. His thick eyebrows formed a V as he peered at them. 'What do you want?' he growled.

'We wanted to ask you a couple of routine questions as part of our investigation,' Georgie explained.

'Oh yeah?' Alfred said before he noticed the two dogs heading back to the side of the cage. He kicked the cage again. 'Go on, scram!' The dogs turned and wandered away again. 'What do you want to know?' he asked.

'Can you confirm that Kevin Parks is your nephew?' Garrow asked as he took out a notebook and pen.

'Kevin?' Alfred asked. 'Aye, he's my sister Julie's eldest.'

'We spoke to Kevin yesterday,' Georgie explained. 'He

claims that on Monday night and early on Tuesday morning he was here with you. Can you confirm that?'

Alfred rubbed the stubble on his chin. 'Yeah, he was here with me on Monday night.'

Garrow looked up from his notebook. 'Can you tell us what time he left here?'

Alfred thought for a few seconds. 'What time did he say he left here?'

Nice try but that's not how we work.

'If you could just tell us what time Kevin left here on Monday night, that would be really helpful,' Georgie asked with a forced smile.

'Suppose it must have been about nine, ten at the latest,' Alfred stated, scratching his face.

It was about a ten-minute drive to Chirk from where they were. If they believed that Vince Thompson was shot between 10pm and 11pm, then Kevin Parks didn't have an alibi for the time of the shooting.

'You can't be more specific than that?' Garrow asked.

Alfred pulled a face and frowned. 'Eh?'

'We're wondering if you can tell us exactly what time Kevin left here on Monday night?' Georgie asked, trying to clarify.

Alfred shook his head and gave them a withering look. 'I just said, didn't I? Nine, maybe ten.'

Georgie looked at Garrow – they weren't going to get a more specific time than that.

'Can you tell us why Kevin was visiting you on Monday night?' Garrow asked.

Alfred shrugged. 'He's my nephew. Came down for a brew and a catch up.'

Georgie nodded. 'Do you know where he was going when he left here?'

'Home,' Alfred snorted as if this was a stupid question.

'He told you that?'

'Aye. Where else would he be going?'

'Has Kevin ever mentioned the name Vince Thompson to you?' Georgie asked.

Alfred bristled for a second as if he recognised the name. Then shook his head adamantly. 'No, never heard of him.'

You're lying, Georgie thought to herself.

'Are you sure about that?' Georgie asked, probing. 'Vince Thompson?'

'I just told you, didn't I?' Alfred snapped aggressively.

Georgie and Garrow looked at each other – time to go.

'Thank you for your help,' Garrow said with a polite smile as they turned and headed back towards the car.

Georgie looked at him. 'I'd better let the boss know that Kevin Parks doesn't have an alibi for the time of the murder.'

R uth and Nick pulled up on the large, circular gravel drive in front of an enormous Georgian house. A sign read *Theakstone Hill Hall.* It had been built in the 1850s and boasted over 50 rooms. It was the address they'd been given for Graham Wheeler.

'Nice pad,' Ruth observed. It was an impressive home.

'Made his money in online shopping apparently,' Nick stated. 'Although I heard he married into money too.'

Getting out of the car, Ruth felt the cool breeze against her face. The sky was a uniform metallic grey but there were blue skies over to the west. A falcon hovered over a nearby field, using the wind currents to float silently above whatever prey it was targeting below.

'Morning!' boomed a confident, male voice.

Graham Wheeler was 40s, slim, with a balding head and glasses. He was wearing a rugby shirt and jeans.

'Can I help?' he asked with an enquiring expression as he approached.

Ruth gave him a half-smile, took out her warrant card and showed it to him. 'Mr Wheeler?'

'Yes?' He now looked confused and concerned.

'DI Hunter and DS Evans, Llancastell CID,' she explained. 'We've got a couple of routine questions we'd like to ask you about an ongoing investigation.'

'Of course,' Wheeler said with a serious nod. 'Anything I can do to help.' He then gestured to the house. 'Would you like to come inside?'

'Thank you.' Ruth gave him a polite smile. People weren't always this well-mannered and polite when the police wanted to talk to them.

The inside of his home was tastefully decorated in keeping with the style of the house, with antiques, dark carpets and oil paintings on the walls.

'We'll go into the drawing room,' Wheeler suggested, opening a door. 'We won't be disturbed in here.'

Drawing room? Now that is posh, Ruth thought.

The drawing room was also well-furnished, although Ruth thought it was a little old-fashioned looking. There was a grand piano on the far side and the walls were lined with bookshelves that reached from floor to ceiling. It smelled of furniture polish and coffee.

'Please.' Wheeler gestured for them to sit down on a mustard-coloured sofa.

Ruth settled and then looked over at him. He seemed very calm, controlled and not at all anxious that they wanted to talk to him.

'We understand that you know a Vince Thompson?' she asked.

Wheeler nodded. 'Yes, that's right.'

'Can you tell us how you know him?' she asked.

'Erm ...' Wheeler hesitated.

The door opened and a girl wandered in holding an iPad. Ruth guessed that she was about seven or eight years old.

'Daddy, can I show you this?' she asked, without taking her eyes from the screen.

'Darling, I'm just talking to these people,' Wheeler explained gently. 'I won't be long.'

The girl looked up from the screen and gave Ruth and Nick a curious look. 'Okay.' She then wandered out of the room, closing the door behind her.

Ruth smiled. 'She seems very sweet.'

'Daisy.' Wheeler smiled. 'Yes, she is.'

'Only child?' Ruth asked.

'Yes,' Wheeler replied with a smile. 'We weren't lucky enough to have any more … Sorry, where were we?'

Nick had his pen poised over his notebook. 'Vince Thompson.'

'Yes, of course,' Wheeler said, nodding. 'Vince rents one of my houses in Llancastell.'

Nick flicked through his notebook. '19 Klea Avenue?'

'Yes, that's right,' Wheeler stated.

'And how long has he rented the house from you?' Ruth asked.

Wheeler frowned. 'Has something happened to him? Is that why you're here?'

Ruth looked at him for a moment. 'I'm afraid that Vince was murdered on Monday night.'

Wheeler narrowed his eyes. 'Good God, that's awful.'

'So, Vince lived with his son Daniel in one of your properties, is that right?' Ruth asked.

'Yes,' Wheeler said. 'It's a bit delicate actually, especially now I know that he's …'

Ruth looked at him. 'Sorry? What's delicate?'

'I'm afraid Vince wasn't very good at paying his rent on time,' Wheeler stated with a sigh. 'In fact, he wasn't very good at paying his rent at all.'

'His son Daniel said that he and Vince drove up here a few weeks ago?' Ruth asked.

'Yes, that's right,' Wheeler replied.

Nick looked up from his notebook and asked, 'Can you tell us what that was about?'

'He was trying to negotiate an extension on paying his rent,' Wheeler explained.

'What did you say?' Ruth asked.

Wheeler shrugged. 'His rent was six weeks late already. I'd asked him several times when he would be able to pay it. I knew that he had his son living with him, so I wasn't about to throw them out onto the street. But he was making it very difficult for me.'

'So, you had an argument?' Nick asked.

Wheeler thought for a few seconds. 'I guess there was a heated conversation, yes. I told him that I couldn't extend the time he had to pay me. I'd been more than accommodating. And then he became very abusive, stormed off and drove away.'

'And that's the last time you saw him?'

'Yes,' Wheeler said. 'Is Daniel okay? He wasn't hurt or anything?'

Ruth shook her head. 'No. He's fine. Very shaken up but he's not hurt.'

'Was he with Vince when he was murdered then?' Wheeler asked. 'That's terrible.'

'We can't really discuss the details of the case with you, I'm afraid,' Ruth informed him.

'Of course, of course. I completely understand,' Wheeler said getting up from his armchair. He was clearly signalling that he wanted them to go. 'I'm sorry that I couldn't be of any more help. I'll show you out.'

Ruth and Nick followed him outside and then headed for the car. Wheeler's explanation seemed to be genuine enough but Ruth's instinct was that he was hiding some-thing from them. Maybe it was just her innate dislike or distrust of all politicians, whatever their political allegiance.

Before she could discuss it with Nick, her phone rang.

It was Georgie.

'Hi Georgie. How did it go with Alfred Parks?' she asked.

'He confirmed that his nephew was here on Monday evening,' Georgie explained. '*But* he told us that he left between nine or ten o'clock.'

Okay, that's very interesting.

'It's about ten minutes to drive from Glyn Ceiriog to Chirk, isn't it?' Ruth asked. She might have been in North Wales for several years, but she still wasn't always certain of such details.

Nick looked over and gave Ruth the thumbs up to confirm that her estimate was about right.

'About that, boss,' Georgie agreed.

'And that means that not only does Parks not have an alibi for 11pm on Monday night,' Ruth stated thinking out loud, 'he also lied to us about where he was at that time.'

'Exactly,' Georgie agreed.

'Right, meet me back at the nick,' Ruth said. 'We need to get a search warrant executed.'

Chapter 21

'Kevin Parks?' Ruth asked as she stood on the doorstep of Parks' home in Rhyl waving her warrant card. The sound of the dogs barking somewhere inside of the house was jarring.

Parks shrugged and gave her a withering look. 'What do you want?'

Ruth pulled out the Section 18 Search Warrant that she had requested DCI Drake execute an hour earlier. Parks had provided a false alibi, his shotgun ammunition matched that found in the victim and he was a known drug dealer. They now had reasonable grounds to search his home.

'Are you fucking kiddin' me?' Parks thundered.

Nick smiled at him. 'Do we look like we're kidding, Kevin?'

Parks took an aggressive step towards Nick. 'And who the fuck are you, dickhead?'

Nick continued to smile. 'Your worst nightmare, if you don't step aside. And make sure those dogs remain safely out of the way. If we think any of our officers are in danger, we'll have them put down.'

Ruth was surprised at Nick's underlying aggression. It wasn't like him. 'If you don't mind stepping out of the way, please.'

Parks knew it was no use protesting and stepped to one side as Ruth and Nick entered, along with four uniformed officers who were there to help with the search.

'I'm going to talk to my brief about this,' Parks growled.

Ruth ignored him and directed two of the uniformed officers to go upstairs. She then looked at Parks who seemed to be gritting his teeth. 'Anyone else in the house, Kevin?'

'No,' he snarled. 'My wife is at the gym and the kids are at school. You're not going to find anything.'

Walking through the ground floor of the house, Ruth noted the tacky, studio photos of Parks, his wife and his children, who looked like they were in their early teens.

She reached the open-plan kitchen which was enormous and expensive-looking. There were more black and white photos and a row of framed Liverpool football shirts. Parks clearly had a lot of disposable income.

Parks followed her in a few seconds later.

'Nice kitchen,' Ruth observed. 'Wife, kids, house. You've got the lot, haven't you Kevin?'

Parks grinned at her. 'I've got a lot more than you'll ever have, that's for certain.'

'I'm assuming you can account for where the money for all this came from?' Ruth enquired. 'HMRC can be right bastards if they think you're diddling them on paying your taxes.'

Parks gave her a smirk. 'It's all legit. Ask my accoun-

SIMON MCCLEAVE

tant. As I said, you'll find nothing here. I run my own import/export business.'

At that moment, Nick walked in holding an evidence bag. Inside were a pair of smart-looking brown brogue shoes.

'What the hell are you doing with those?' Parks snapped.

Nick ignored him and looked over at Ruth. 'Size ten brogues, boss. Flat, smooth sole. Seems to be some dirt and gravel which could match our crime scene.'

Ruth looked at Parks. 'I'm sure our forensics can see if it's a match.'

Parks shook his head. 'I don't know what the fuck you're talking about.'

'Kevin Parks, I'm arresting you on suspicion of murder. You do not have to say anything, but it may harm your defence if you do not mention when questioned something which you later rely on in court. Anything you do say may be used as evidence in a court of law,' Ruth said. 'Do you understand your rights?'

Parks looked rattled for the first time. 'This is ridiculous!'

Chapter 22

It was an hour since Parks had been brought into custody. Ruth marched out of her office and across to the scene boards. Most of the CID team were in IR1, working at computers or on the telephone.

She looked out at them for a second and then pointed to the photo of Parks. 'Right, guys. We have 24 hours to find something that will allow us to charge Parks with Vince Thompson's murder. How are we getting on with matching the tyre tracks at the scene of crime to Parks' Jeep?'

French looked over. 'Forensics are still working on it, boss. I told them to fast-track it.'

'Good.' Ruth was feeling fired up. Parks was the kind of scumbag that got a thrill from flaunting his criminal wealth and never seemed to get caught for the major offences that he actually committed. 'If we can put his car at the scene of crime, we might reach the threshold for the CPS. Anything else?'

Georgie looked over. 'We've taken his clothes and

swabbed him. If there's any gunshot residue, forensics should be able to find it.'

'I want us to look again at the money and drugs that we found in Vince's campervan,' Ruth stated. 'If Vince had stolen from Parks, that's our motive for his murder. Let's sweep them both for fingerprints and DNA.'

Nick frowned. 'If Vince had stolen the money and drugs from Parks, why didn't Parks take them with him once he'd shot Vince?'

'Maybe he saw Daniel running off into the woods?' Ruth suggested with a shrug.

French looked over from where he had answered the phone. 'Boss, there's been a call from the *Clear View Children's Home.* They've had a prowler at the back. Uniformed patrol are there now.'

Ruth nodded. 'Right, I'll get over there.'

Chapter 23

R uth pulled up outside the *Clear View Children's Home*. It had occurred to her that if Kevin Parks had murdered Vince Thompson, then the only eyewitness to the killing was Daniel. It was likely that Parks had some very nefarious *associates*. Did that mean that Daniel was now in danger? Did the person that had been spotted lurking around the premises have something to do with Parks?

Grabbing her Tetra radio, she clicked the grey *Talk* button. 'Control from three six, over.'

'Three six receiving, go ahead, over,' came the voice of the Computer Aided Dispatch officer.

'I'm going to need a uniformed patrol stationed outside the *Clear View Children's Home* on Holmes Road. We have an eyewitness who is in potential danger,' she explained.

'Three six from Control, received,' the CAD operator stated. 'I will advise immediately, out.'

Ruth ended the call. She knew that DCI Drake would okay the use of a permanent patrol car once she explained that Daniel was witness to a murder and Kevin Parks was a well-connected drug dealer with a record of violence.

Getting out of the car, Ruth saw that the patrol car that had responded to the call was parked further up the road. She walked up the garden path and knocked on the door. A second later, Charlie answered the door.

'Come in,' he said quietly.

'Everything okay?' Ruth asked.

Charlie nodded and gestured. 'The officers are just out the back.'

'What happened?' Ruth asked in a virtual whisper as they stood in the hallway.

'A couple of the girls saw a man in the back garden,' Charlie explained. 'They screamed their heads off.'

'Did you see him?'

Charlie shook his head. 'No. I think they might have scared him off.'

'Could they describe him?' Ruth asked.

'They said he was wearing black and had a balaclava over his head,' Charlie explained.

Ruth didn't like the sound of that. Whoever had been out the back was taking no chances.

'Listen, I have no idea whether this has anything to do with what happened to Daniel or his father,' Ruth said, 'but I've stationed a patrol car outside permanently.'

She could see Charlie's eyes widen in fear. 'You think someone was here because Daniel saw his father being killed?'

'Possibly,' Ruth said. 'It might be that we take Daniel elsewhere while all this is going on. I don't want everyone else's safety in here to be jeopardised … How is he?'

Charlie gave her a look. 'Not great.' He gestured for her to follow him down the hall and they came to the door into the living area. Daniel was sat on the far side on an armchair. 'He's been in there nearly all day and not said a word. He hasn't really eaten very much either.'

Ruth nodded. 'I'll go and have a word, shall I?'

Daniel's face was motionless as he gazed at the television. As Ruth approached, he looked up at her and his whole face lit up.

'Hi Daniel,' Ruth said with a smile.

'Hi,' he replied with a toothy grin.

'What are you watching?' she asked.

Daniel shrugged. 'Just some silly cartoons.'

'Charlie says that you haven't eaten much today?'

He looked a little embarrassed. 'I dunno. Not really.'

'What was it again? A Vegan Royale meal with a Sprite?' Ruth asked and gave him a wink.

Daniel nodded, his eyes bright and beaming.

'Come on then sunshine,' Ruth said gesturing to the door. She looked at Charlie. 'I'm just gonna take Daniel out for a while and then I'll drop him back.'

＝

Pulling up at the speaker at Burger King in Llancastell, Ruth looked over at Daniel who was sitting in the passenger seat.

'What do you think I should have then?' she asked him.

'My dad always had a Plant Based Whopper Meal with a Coke Zero,' he explained.

Ruth nodded. 'Well that sounds good to me.'

She gave her order, pulled around to the window, paid and then drove forward to the next window to collect the food and drinks.

'Here you go,' Ruth said, handing him the bag and drinks.

Daniel pointed to a parking bay in the far corner of the

retail park car park. 'Me and dad used to go and sit over there and eat our food,' he explained. 'There's a nice view.'

'Okay. Let's do that then.'

She pulled the car over and stopped.

For a few seconds, they sat in a comfortable silence as they ate and looked out across Llancastell's skyline.

'How are you settling in?' Ruth asked as he fished out the fries from the bag.

Daniel shrugged. 'They all keep fighting.'

'Yeah,' Ruth said with an empathetic look. 'It's going to take some getting used to after it's been just you and your dad.'

'Yeah,' Daniel murmured with a mouthful of burger.

'Your mum not around?' Ruth asked gently.

Daniel shook his head and then looked at her. 'She died.'

'Oh, I'm really sorry to hear that,' she stated.

'She died giving birth to my sister, Jodie.'

Ruth looked at him for a moment. The vanilla light from the car park highlighted his face. He looked so incredibly young and vulnerable.

'You've had a hard time of it, haven't you?' Ruth remarked. 'And you've been incredibly brave, you know that?'

Daniel didn't respond. Instead, he took his drink and slurped on the straw.

'I'm going to find out who hurt your dad,' Ruth said, looking at him. 'I promise you that.'

Daniel nodded but continued to gaze out of the car.

Reaching into her pocket, Ruth pulled out her phone. She clicked onto a photo of Kevin Parks.

'Can you do me a favour, Daniel?' she asked quietly.

He looked up at her, the straw still in his mouth, and nodded.

'Have you ever seen this man?' Ruth asked.

Daniel looked at the phone, frowned and then shook his head. 'No.'

'You're sure?' Ruth asked. 'When you were living up in Rhyl?'

'No,' he said. 'I don't know who he is. Did he shoot my dad then?'

'We're not sure yet,' she replied.

Daniel reached over to the radio that had been playing music almost imperceptibly.

As the volume increased, Ruth recognised the song as *The Long and Winding Road* by *The Beatles*.

'You like this?' she asked.

He gave her a look as if that was a ridiculous question. '*The Beatles*? Of course. They were the best band in the history of music.'

'Were they?'

'Everyone knows that. My favourite album is *Rubber Soul*. Everyone goes on about *Sgt Pepper's*, but I think *Rubber Soul* is the best *Beatles'* album.'

'Right,' Ruth nodded with a bemused smile. 'Good to know. I think I've got that on CD at home.'

'CD?' Daniel asked with a frown.

Christ! He doesn't know what a CD is. That makes me feel very old.

'If you're an old fuddy duddy like me, you have your music on CDs.'

'You're not old,' Daniel protested.

Ruth smiled at him. 'Thank you … I feel old.'

The song finished and noisy adverts started to play on the radio station. Ruth turned down the volume and looked over at Daniel.

'I guess we should be getting back soon,' she said. 'I need one more favour from you, if that's okay?'

Daniel shrugged. 'Okay.'

'The other night, your dad told you he was going to pick something up before you moved on to wherever you were going. Do you know what he was talking about?'

Daniel frowned. 'No. He said we were going to pick *someone* up.'

'Someone?'

'Yeah.' Daniel nodded.

'Do you know who you were going to pick up?' Ruth asked.

'No, sorry,' he replied. 'Dad said not to worry. There was plenty of room for her in the back with me.'

'Her?' Ruth asked, seizing on this.

'Yeah.'

'He definitely said *her*?'

'Yeah.'

'But you don't know who that was?'

'No.'

Ruth looked at him again. 'I know this is really difficult for you to think about, Daniel, but is there anything you can remember about the two people who got out of the car when you stopped the other night?'

He thought for a second. 'I know that one of them was a woman. She had long hair.'

'How long?'

Daniel touched his shoulder. 'Down to here.'

'What about the man?'

Daniel shrugged. 'I don't know. I couldn't really see his face.'

'Why not?'

'He had a black baseball cap pulled down over his face,' Daniel explained.

128

Ruth paused for a second – the last person she had seen wearing a black baseball cap was Stu Morton.

Chapter 24

It was 8am the following morning by the time Ruth and Nick went to interview Kevin Parks. His solicitor, Jack Harding, had arrived and had been briefed on his arrest. Parks was now dressed in a regulation grey tracksuit as his clothes had been taken for forensics. He had also been swabbed for traces of DNA and gunshot residue. Nick leant across the table to start the recording machine. A long electronic beep sounded as Ruth opened her files and gave Nick a quick look of acknowledgement.

'Interview conducted with Kevin Parks, Llancastell Police Station. Present are Detective Sergeant Nick Evans, Solicitor Jack Harding and myself, Detective Inspector Ruth Hunter.' Ruth then glanced over at Parks. 'Kevin, do you understand you are still under caution?'

Kevin was staring down at the table as if he hadn't heard her.

'Kevin?' Ruth said.

Kevin slowly looked up and met her eyes. 'No comment.'

Ruth knew that Parks had been advised to reply 'No comment' to all their questions. She had come across the solicitor Jack Harding before. He was an experienced defence lawyer.

Reaching into her folder, Ruth pulled out a photograph of Vince Thompson. 'For the purposes of the tape, I am showing the suspect a photograph, Item Reference 7WT. Kevin, can you look at this photograph and tell me if you recognise this man?'

Parks let out a sigh, looked at the photo for a second. 'No comment.'

'This man's name is Vince Thompson and he was murdered at around 11pm on Monday night in Chirk,' she stated. 'Is there anything you can tell us about that?'

'No comment.'

'Can you tell us where you were at 11pm on Monday night?' Nick asked.

Parks sat back, let out a loud yawn and grinned. 'No comment.'

'You told our officers that you were with your uncle, Alfred Parks, at that time,' Ruth remarked. 'However, Alfred told us that you left his home between nine and ten pm on Monday night. Can you tell us why you lied about your whereabouts at the time of Vince Thompson's murder?'

'No comment.'

'When you were stopped on the outskirts of Llan-castell,' Ruth said, 'our officers found a shotgun and ammunition in the boot of your car. Can you tell us why it was there?'

'No comment.'

Nick glared over at him. 'Would it surprise you to know that the ammunition we found in the back of your car matches the ammunition that was used to murder Vince Thompson?'

'No comment.'

By the time Ruth had sat down to conduct the morning North Wales Police press conference, she was already aware that someone had leaked to the press the story of Daniel being present at Vince's murder. She was furious. It now put Daniel in more danger as he was effectively the only eyewitness to his father's killing. Her phone buzzed and she took it out of her jacket pocket. There was a tweet in Twitter:

BBC Wales@BBC Wales Breaking News
Sources claim that the ten-year-old son of Vince Thompson was present and witnessed his father's murder. Thompson, who had been living in Llancastell, was brutally gunned down in Chirk on Monday night. North Wales Police are appealing for witnesses who might have been in the area at the time.

Looking out at the assembled reporters, Ruth took a moment. She had never liked holding press conferences. Even though she had held about half a dozen since arriving in North Wales, it was her least favourite part of the job. She wondered if she would ever get used to it.

Sitting next to her was Kerry Mahoney, the Chief Corporate Communications Officer for North Wales Police, who had come up from the main press office in Colwyn Bay. Ruth had met her before and there was little love lost between them.

On the table in front of Ruth was a row of microphones. She cleared her throat. 'Good afternoon, I'm Detective Inspector Ruth Hunter of North Wales Police, and I am the Senior Investigating Officer in the murder of Vince Thompson. Beside me is Kerry Mahoney, our Chief Corporate Communications Officer. This press conference is to update you on the case and to appeal to the public for any information regarding Mr Thompson's murder on Monday evening between approximately 9pm and 12pm. Mr Thompson was killed close to his distinctive orange VW campervan on a road close to Chirk Castle. If you were in or around the Chirk Castle area on Monday evening, we would like you to get in touch with us. If you saw anything out of the ordinary, however insignificant you think it might be, please contact us so we can come and talk to you. I have a few minutes to take some questions.'

'Can you confirm that Vince Thompson's ten-year-old son was present at his father's murder?' asked a reporter from the front row.

Bloody great! Ruth thought.

'Yes. I can confirm that Mr Thompson's son was present. However, he wasn't harmed and he is helping us with our enquiries.'

'Can you tell us if his son saw his father's killer?' asked another journalist.

I'm not getting into this bloody discussion. Let's wrap this up, Ruth thought.

'I can only reiterate what I've already told you. We are keen to talk to anyone who was in the Chirk Castle area on Monday evening,' Ruth said, but she knew she sounded a little irritated. 'Right, thank you, everyone. No more questions.'

As Ruth stood and gathered up her files, she noticed Mahoney giving her a slightly conceited look. She had spotted that Ruth was a bit rattled and she was judging her.

Right, I need a ciggie and a coffee, Ruth thought.

Chapter 25

'Right everyone,' Ruth said as she strode into the middle of IR1, coffee and folders in hand. 'A few things to go through. We now have eight hours to find something that we can take to CPS, or we're going to have to release Kevin Parks. What have we got?'

French looked over and pulled a face. 'Bad news, boss. Forensics came back on the footprint and the shoes we took from Parks' house. Results are inconclusive on both the shoe and the soil sample on the sole.'

'What does that mean?' Ruth asked, feeling frustrated.

'The shoe *might* be the one that created the footprint at the crime scene. And the soil sample wasn't specific or distinctive enough for a decent match.'

'Right,' Ruth stated. 'Tyre prints?'

French shook his head. 'We're still waiting on those, boss.'

'Bank records, phone, anything?' she asked starting to sound frustrated and hoping that something had turned up.

Garrow pointed to the printout he was holding.

'There's nothing on his bank records or the phone records. He's probably got a 'burner' but we didn't find any evidence of that.'

'So, all we have is the shotgun ammunition and no alibi,' Ruth groaned, thinking out loud. 'Any forensics that put Parks at the crime scene?'

The CID team looked blankly back at her. It looked like Parks was going to walk out of Llancastell nick unless a significant piece of evidence turned up very soon.

At that moment, Georgie walked through the door.

'Nice of you to join us, Georgie,' Nick quipped.

She gave him the finger and everyone smiled.

Holding a printout, Georgie looked over at Ruth. 'Boss, I've tracked down the address that Vince and Daniel used to live at in Rhyl.'

'Good work,' Ruth said. 'Go and have a word with the neighbours. See if they remember anything and see if they ever saw Parks hanging around.'

Georgie nodded and then frowned as she pointed to another sheet. 'I just picked up some more results from forensics, boss. They found a match to the sets of finger-prints that they found on the money and the bags of weed in Vince's campervan.'

'Go on,' Ruth prompted her.

Georgie raised an eyebrow. 'They belong to Phoebe Evans, the girl that lived next door to Vince and Daniel in Klea Avenue. She was arrested for shoplifting a couple of years ago.'

Ruth frowned and looked over at Nick.

I wasn't expecting that.

Chapter 26

It was an hour later by the time Georgie and Garrow got to the outskirts of Rhyl, one of the most deprived towns in the UK. The centre looked like a ghost town as shops were boarded up or derelict. A couple of teenagers in black hoodies glared at them as they vaped on a bench.

'Welcome to Rhyl,' Georgie quipped sardonically.

'Don't think I've ever been,' Garrow admitted.

Georgie rolled her eyes. 'And why doesn't that surprise me?'

Garrow gave an expression of mock offence. 'That's not very nice.'

'Nice university-educated boy like you wouldn't survive five minutes in a place like this,' Georgie remarked.

'Yeah, well neither would the SAS,' Garrow joked.

That's what she liked about Garrow. Unlike most male coppers she had worked with, he never felt the need to demonstrate his masculinity. And despite her teasing, she liked his quiet assuredness. In her experience, the male coppers who puffed out their chests and went toe to toe with every criminal they met were overcompensating for something.

'True,' Georgie laughed. 'There used to be a sign as you came in to the town. It said *Welcome to Rhyl*. Some joker had graffitied under it *Twinned with Kandahar.'*

'Good one.' Garrow rolled his eyes. 'You've spent a lot of time in Rhyl then?'

'My Taid used to live up here,' she explained quietly. It made her sad to think of him.

'Spoilt you rotten, did he?' Garrow asked brightly.

'Not really. He was a junkie,' Georgie replied. 'He died from a smack overdose when I was nine.'

'God. Sorry,' Garrow said pulling a face.

'You weren't to know. It's just a bit weird when I come back here, that's all.'

Garrow nodded. 'Yeah, I can imagine. Sounds horrible.'

For the next few minutes, they didn't speak. Georgie could feel the emotion of being back weighing on her. By the end, her taid had been a skeletal seven stone. He had been ravaged and eventually killed by his addiction.

They drove along the seafront, with the dark, black, choppy Irish Sea stretching away to their left as far as the eye could see. To the right, a long terrace of cream-coloured Victorian houses that housed B&Bs. Paintwork was old, damp and covered in mould. Guttering was broken and pathways strewn with weeds. Next came a string of gaudy amusement arcades in lurid colours – *Play-zone, Casino Lounge* and *Geronimo's*.

Turning left, they soon found the address where Vince and Daniel had lived before they moved to Llancastell. What they were hoping for was some kind of link to Kevin Parks or anything that might shed light on Vince's life.

Getting out of the car, Georgie looked at the house. It

138

was pebble-dashed with a bright blue front door. The house to the left had been boarded up.

'Let's try the neighbours to start with,' Garrow suggested as they walked up to the adjacent house.

Knocking at the door, they got out their warrant cards.

A few minutes later, a middle-aged woman in a grey tracksuit peered out at them. 'Hello?' It sounded like she had some kind of accent. Maybe Eastern European.

'DC Wild and DC Garrow, Llancastell CID,' Georgie said. 'We'd like to ask you a couple of questions about former neighbours of yours. Vince and Daniel Thompson?'

The woman nodded. 'Yes.'

'You remember them?' Garrow asked.

'Yes, of course,' the woman said cheerily. There had clearly been no bad feeling between them as neighbours. She gestured to her flat. 'My daughter is asleep so it's okay to talk out here?'

Georgie smiled and nodded understandingly. 'Of course. Did you know Vince and Daniel well?'

'Oh, yes.' The woman smiled. 'Sometimes Daniel come and sit with me when Vince is out. We watch TV. Football. He likes Chelsea. He is a lovely boy.'

'Yes.' Garrow pulled out his phone, found the photo of Kevin Parks and showed her. 'Did you ever see this man around here or at their home?'

'Yes, maybe,' the woman replied uncertainly. 'I think they were friends, no?'

'His name is Kevin Parks,' Georgie explained. 'Does that ring any bells?'

'Yes, Kev.' The woman nodded.

'Did you ever see Vince and Kev argue or was there any trouble when he was around?' Garrow asked.

'No, no,' the woman said with a shrug. 'They play their

music too loud sometime. I go and complain because my daughter is only one years old. But they turn it down and say sorry.'

'So, they were friends?' Georgie asked.

'I think so,' the woman replied and then she mimed smoking. 'I think they smoke too much weed. I can smell it in my house sometimes.'

'Did you ever see Vince arguing or having any trouble with anyone while he was living here?'

'Yes,' the woman nodded readily and pointed to the phone. 'But not with this man.'

Georgie looked at her. 'What exactly did you see?'

'A man in a very nice car. He was rich, you could tell. He had nice clothes,' the woman explained. 'It was late and he was banging on their door. He was shouting for Vince to come and open the door. He was very angry.'

Georgie and Garrow exchanged a look.

'When was this?' Garrow asked.

'Oh, maybe one or two days before Vince and Daniel move away, so last year,' the woman explained. 'My husband had to go and see what was going on.'

'Was Vince in?'

The woman shrugged. 'I don't know. But this man kept banging the door. My husband told him to be quiet.'

'And you saw this man?' Garrow asked.

The woman pointed to a downstairs window. 'Yes, I saw him from my window. Then he jumped in his car and he drove off.'

'Can you describe the man for us?'

'He is maybe forty years old,' she explained. 'Grey hair. Handsome man.'

That sounds a bit like Graham Wheeler, Georgie thought to herself.

Garrow looked at her. 'What about the car?'

'A sports car. Red,' she remembered. 'My husband said it is Lotus … A Lotus Elise I think he said.'

Georgie took out her phone, clicked on a photo of Graham Wheeler and showed the woman. 'Is this the man who you saw?'

The woman peered and shrugged. 'I think so. He definitely looks like him.'

Chapter 27

The front door to No. 17 Klea Avenue opened and Phoebe looked out at Ruth and Nick, who were standing on her doorstep. Her hair was pulled back tight and then secured in a top knot.

'Hi?' Phoebe said with a quizzical expression.

'Can we have a quick word, Phoebe?' Ruth asked. She gestured to show that they wanted to come inside. 'It won't take long.'

'Erm, okay.' Phoebe looked anxious and ushered them inside. 'Is everything all right? Is Daniel okay?'

Ruth smiled at her and gave her a reassuring nod. 'Yes, he's fine.'

They followed her down to a small, dark kitchen. It was tidy, clean and very basic. There were photos and an array of colourful magnets on the fridge. The photographs mainly showed Phoebe as a child or with her mother. One photo showed Phoebe, aged about five, sitting on the lap of a blond-haired man with her mother standing behind. Ruth assumed that was Phoebe's father.

'Do you want tea or coffee or something?' Phoebe asked as they all sat down, but she was clearly nervous.

'We're fine thanks, Phoebe,' Ruth replied gently. 'There's just a couple of things that we'd like to talk to you about.'

Phoebe nodded and folded her arms defensively. 'Okay.'

Ruth looked at her and leaned forward so her arms were resting on the table. 'What was your relationship to Vince Thompson?'

Phoebe frowned and replied too quickly, 'I don't know what you mean.'

Ruth shrugged. 'Were you close? Were you friends … or was there more to it?'

'No.' Phoebe pulled a face. 'There was nothing like that. He was old enough to be my dad.'

Nick had pulled out his notebook and pen. 'But you'd describe Vince as a friend?'

'Yeah,' Phoebe agreed. 'I suppose so.'

'Did you know what Vince did for a living?' Ruth asked.

Phoebe frowned, visibly took a breath and then thought for a few seconds.

She's not hiding the fact that she knows he dealt drugs very well, Ruth thought.

Phoebe still had her arms crossed as she gave a little shrug. 'No, not really.'

'Would you be surprised if we told you that we suspect that Vince was dealing drugs?' Nick asked.

'I … don't know … I,' Phoebe stammered and shook her head. 'It wasn't really my business.'

Ruth gave her a half-smile. 'It sounds like you did know that Vince was dealing drugs, Phoebe?'

Phoebe nodded but didn't say anything. She looked embarrassed.

Ruth was trying to read her. Phoebe's fingerprints were on the money and bags of marijuana they had found in the campervan. She clearly knew that Vince dealt drugs but was there any more to it? Was her nervous innocence an act? It didn't seem like that but it was hard to tell.

'When we searched Vince's campervan, we found some cash and five bags of marijuana,' Nick explained. 'Is there anything you can tell us about that?'

Phoebe frowned and shook her head. 'No.'

'Are you sure about that?'

'No,' she replied in a virtual whisper. 'I don't know why you're asking me about that?'

Phoebe was clearly hiding something. Ruth waited for a few seconds so that the tension in the room could increase. 'When you were sixteen, Phoebe, you were arrested for shoplifting.'

'That was a big mistake,' Phoebe snapped as she unfolded her arms and glared across the table. The façade of the timid, harmless girl had dropped suddenly.

Ruth ignored her. 'It means that we have your fingerprints on a database. And your fingerprints were found on the cash and the bags of marijuana that we found in Vince's campervan. Can you tell us why that is?'

Phoebe looked rattled as she thought for a few seconds. 'When they were leaving, I helped Vince and Daniel put all their stuff in the van. I opened a small cupboard to put something inside it, and I saw the cash and weed. I picked them up to ask Vince what the hell he was doing. I was worried about Daniel.'

'And you expect us to believe that?' Nick asked.

'It's the truth!' Phoebe growled. 'I don't care if you believe me or not. You can't arrest me for touching some money and someone else's weed. I was worried and I didn't want Daniel getting mixed up in anything dangerous.'

'So you confronted Vince?' Ruth asked.

'Yeah.'

'What did he say?'

'Not a lot. He said it was just a bit of weed, nothing serious,' Phoebe explained.

Ruth looked over at Nick – it sounded plausible.

'Were you working for Vince?' Ruth asked.

Phoebe pulled a face. 'No, of course not.'

Nick stopped writing, narrowed his eyes and looked at her for a second. 'You really expect us to believe you happened to find the money and drugs in the campervan, and that's the only reason why your fingerprints are present?'

Phoebe shrugged as she bit her fingernail. 'That's what happened.'

'Come on, Phoebe,' Ruth sighed. 'We're not interested in a bit of petty dealing. We want to know who murdered Vince.'

'I don't know,' Phoebe insisted. 'I'd tell you if I knew.'

'Had he pissed off a local dealer who caught up with him?' Nick asked.

'Why are you asking me all this?' Phoebe huffed. 'I don't know anything.'

Ruth got out her phone, found the image of Kevin Parks and showed it to Phoebe across the table. 'Do you recognise this man?'

'No,' she replied as she peered at the photo. 'I've never seen him before.'

'And you're sure about that?' Nick asked.

'Yes.'

There were a few seconds of uncomfortable silence.

'You told us that Cath and Vince were in some kind of relationship,' Nick said.

'Yeah, so what?' Phoebe enquired with a frown.

'Did you ever see Stu and Vince talking?' he asked.

Phoebe shifted in her chair. 'Only in the shop.'

She thought of what Daniel had told her about seeing a man with a black baseball cap the night Vince had been murdered.

'You never saw Stu at Vince's home?' Ruth asked.

'No,' Phoebe said adamantly. 'They weren't mates or anything.'

'Okay. Have you got any idea who might have killed Vince?' Ruth asked. 'Any disputes, any arguments that you heard?'

Phoebe's eyes roamed around the room as she took a deep breath. She had thought of something.

'What is it?' Ruth asked, sensing that Phoebe wasn't telling them everything.

'Nothing.'

Ruth leaned forward again. 'Listen, Phoebe. I get the feeling that you, Vince and Daniel were close. Someone shot and killed Vince and we want to find out who that was. And I think Daniel deserves to know what happened to his dad, especially as he grows up, don't you? And I think you know something that you're not telling us.'

Phoebe bit the skin around her nails again but it looked as if Ruth's words about Daniel had struck a chord. 'Vince asked me not to tell anyone.'

'What is it?'

'One night, I heard Vince arguing with someone out the back. It woke me up,' Phoebe explained. 'I looked out of my window and saw Vince struggling with another man in the garden. I opened the window and shouted down to ask Vince what the hell was going on.'

'Go on.' Ruth sensed that Phoebe wasn't comfortable recounting what she had seen.

'By the time I went out onto the street …' she said 'they were shoving each other. This other man punched Vince and knocked him to the ground. He told him that if he didn't leave his family alone, he would kill Vince. Then he drove off.'

'Why didn't you tell us this before?' Nick asked.

'Vince told me to swear not to tell anyone what I'd seen or heard. He said it was complicated and he didn't want Daniel to get hurt or taken away,' Phoebe explained. 'So, I just kept it to myself.'

'Can you describe the man?' Ruth asked.

'That's the weird thing,' she stated. 'He definitely wasn't from around here.'

'How do you know that?'

'He was dead posh,' Phoebe said. 'You know, the way he spoke, his clothes. And he had a sports car.'

Ruth had a thought as she took out her phone and got a photo up onto the screen.

'Is this the man you saw?' Ruth asked.

Phoebe nodded.

Ruth looked at Nick. 'It's Graham Wheeler.'

Chapter 28

Georgie and Garrow approached the bar in The Red Lion pub. It was a five-minute walk from Klea Avenue and was where Phoebe claimed she had seen Stu Morton fighting with someone who had pinched his wife Cath's bottom. If Stu Morton had been violent over this incident, maybe he lost control when he found out that Cath and Vince were having an affair.

The Red Lion was dark, dingy and looked like it hadn't had a lick of paint or any kind of renovation since the 1980s. Dark red stools were scattered around stained wooden tables. There was a couple of old men sitting at the bar, nursing pints and watching horse racing on the silent television above the bar. *Don't Play* by *Anne-Marie* and *KSI* was playing somewhere in the background and sounded completely out of place in these surroundings.

'Thanks Jim. You take me to all the nicest places,' Georgie joked under her breath.

'It's very … retro, isn't it?' Garrow smiled taking out his warrant card as a middle-aged woman approached. She had short blonde hair that was ruffled and spiked on top.

148

'DC Garrow and DC Wild, Llancastell CID. I wonder if we could ask you a couple of questions?' Garrow asked her.

The woman smiled. She had crooked teeth. 'Yeah, go for it,' she said with a thick North Wales accent.

'What can you tell us about a customer who drinks in here called Stu Morton?' Georgie asked.

'Big Stu?' the woman asked with a broad smile. 'Bloody hell. He's not in trouble is he?'

'We understand he got into a fight a few weeks ago?' Garrow asked.

'That?' The woman rolled her eyes. 'Christ, I wouldn't have described it as a fight. Just a bit of bloody handbags, that's all.'

Garrow fished out his notebook and pen. 'Can you tell us what happened?'

'Some little tosser was celebrating his eighteenth birthday with a couple of his mates,' the woman explained. 'They'd had too much to drink. In fact, I'd told him I wasn't going to serve him anymore. He pinched Cath's arse at the bar and waved over to his mates. Stu told him to pack it in. The nobhead tried to start on Stu but he was bloody shit-faced. He came at Stu, so Stu gave him a push and he fell back over a table. It was his own bloody fault.'

'And that was it?' Georgie asked.

'Sort of,' the woman said. 'One of his mates threw a glass at Stu but it missed. Stu went over and they all ran out.'

'But it was nothing more than that?' Garrow enquired.

'No. Like I said, it was just kids not handling their drink properly, if you know what I mean? Stu thought it was funny, if I'm honest.'

'You know Stu and Cath Morton well, do you?' Georgie enquired.

'Should do,' the woman snorted. 'I went to bloody school with the pair of them. They've been together since Year 9.'

Garrow looked up from his notepad. 'Would you describe Stu as the jealous type?'

'Stu?' the woman scoffed. 'God no. He's a big, bloody softie. I'm surprised it wasn't Cath giving that little twat a thump.'

Georgie frowned. 'Why do you say that?'

'Cath's got a hell of a temper,' the woman laughed as she raised an eyebrow. 'I wouldn't want to mess with her, especially when she's had a couple of drinks.'

Georgie reached for her phone and clicked on a photo of Vince Thompson. 'Do you recognise this man?'

The woman peered at the image and shook her head. 'No, sorry.'

'He never drank in here?' Garrow asked.

'Not as far as I know,' she replied. 'Are Stu and Cath in some kind of trouble?'

Georgie ignored her as she remembered that it had been Phoebe Evans who said she witnessed Stu Morton fighting in the pub.

Georgie clicked onto a photo of Phoebe. 'What about this girl? Have you ever seen her before?'

The woman rolled her eyes and sneered. 'Phoebe bloody Evans? Yeah, that little bitch is banned from here.'

'Why's that?' Garrow enquired.

'Caught her dealing in the toilets. Twice,' the woman growled. 'Looks like butter wouldn't melt but she's not right in the head. Her mum, Mel, is a lovely woman. I've known Mel for years.'

Georgie and Garrow exchanged a look. Was there a link between Phoebe dealing drugs, the marijuana they found in the campervan and Vince's murder?

'Phoebe was dealing drugs in here?' Georgie asked to clarify.

'Yeah. Bit of weed and some coke,' the woman replied. 'Someone told me she works for some headcase who lives up on the coast.'

Kevin Parks lives in Rhyl. Is that the connection? Georgie thought to herself.

Garrow frowned. 'Do you know his name?'

The woman shook her head. 'No. But he came in here a couple of times looking for her. Nasty piece of work. All tattoos and jewellery. Full of himself, if you know what I mean?'

Georgie went to her phone yet again and found a photo of Kevin Parks. 'Was this him?'

The woman nodded. 'Oh yeah. That's him. Flash git.'

'Did he say why he was looking for Phoebe?' Garrow asked.

'No,' she replied. 'But he knew she drank in here. He didn't look very happy when I told him she was banned.'

'Did he say anything else?' Georgie enquired.

'Yeah, as a matter of fact,' the woman stated. 'As he went to the door he muttered that she was a thieving little skank and he was gonna sort her out.'

A s Ruth and Nick drove through the countryside, Ruth took out a ciggie and buzzed down the window. She hadn't slept well. But then again, she hadn't slept well in years. She supposed she had seen and experienced too much violence, horror and despair to sleep well. She remembered that she had dreamed that Sarah was a ballet dancer. Ruth had sat in the circle of a huge theatre watching Sarah circling the stage in a black tutu and a headdress of sparkling diamonds and black feathers. And she leapt into the air and seemed to levitate before crashing to the stage. Ruth had frantically tried to make her way down to help her but had been confronted by a series of locked doors and dark corridors. She just couldn't get to Sarah. Ruth assumed when she woke with a start, it had been yet another anxiety dream.

Taking a drag on her cigarette, Ruth blew the smoke out of the window and let the wind grab it away. Graham Wheeler's house loomed into view as Ruth and Nick pulled up onto the sweeping gravel drive. Ruth spotted that there was a tennis court to the rear of the house. She hadn't played tennis since she was a kid and she and her brother Chris had sneaked onto a court at Battersea Park. It had been the summer of 1982 and they had just watched Jimmy Connors beat John McEnroe in an epic five-set battle in the Wimbledon final. Ruth and Chris both had old wooden rackets that had seen better days, and a single ragged tennis ball. After about twenty minutes, someone had come to collect money for the court and they'd scarpered.

Parked to one side of the Wheelers' driveway was a navy-coloured Volvo XC90. Above, the sky was a perfect blend of white clouds and blue background as though from a film. As Ruth and Nick got out of the car, the air was starting to fill with the smells of spring.

Nick pointed to the Volvo. 'Dark-coloured 4x4, boss.'

Ruth nodded. 'Yeah, I saw that. Unfortunately, dark-coloured 4x4s seem to be two a penny around here.' Her phone buzzed and she answered it. 'Georgie?'

'Boss,' she said. 'The neighbour in Rhyl confirmed she had seen Kevin Parks at Vince's flat. She said they were friends and never saw anything suspicious between them.'

'Shame,' Ruth remarked. It wasn't enough, so it looked like they'd have to release Parks from custody in a couple of hours.

'But she did witness a man banging on Vince's door for quite some time. Apparently this man was angry and shouting. She didn't know if Vince was out or if he was just hiding?'

'Any description?'

'Description matches Graham Wheeler,' Georgie stated.

'That doesn't make any sense,' Ruth said with a deep frown. 'According to Wheeler, he only knew Vince because he rented that house from him. How did he know Vince back then?'

'Doesn't add up, does it?'

'No. Did the neighbour say anything else?'

'The man she saw was driving a red Lotus Elise sports car. Shouldn't be difficult to check with the DVLA,' Georgie explained.

'We've just had something similar from Phoebe Evans. She saw a man fitting Wheeler's description fighting with Vince at his home in Llancastell,' Ruth said.

'Okay. Well we've got something interesting on Phoebe,' Georgie stated. 'The landlady at The Red Lion banned her for dealing drugs a few weeks ago. She'd heard a rumour that Phoebe worked for Kevin Parks. And then Parks turned up at the pub looking for her. Parks said something that implied that Phoebe had stolen from him.'

That is very interesting.

'Right. Well that changes a few things. Thanks Georgie. Good work,' Ruth said. 'I think we'll get a search warrant and pull Phoebe in for questioning tomorrow morning.'

'Yes, boss.'

'We're at Graham Wheeler's home now,' Ruth explained. 'I'll see you back at the nick.'

Ruth ended the call.

'Something interesting?' Nick asked.

'Yeah. Looks like Phoebe Evans has been lying to us. She's possibly involved with Parks,' Ruth explained as they walked up to the front door, their shoes crunching noisily on the gravel.

'What?' Nick asked with a frown.

'She's told us a pack of lies, so we'll bring her in first thing tomorrow morning.'

Nick nodded and then knocked forcefully on the door.

A moment later, it opened and a rather snooty woman with blonde hair and a ruddy face peered out at them. 'Can I help you?' she enquired in an upper-class accent.

Ruth flashed her warrant card. 'DI Hunter and DS Evans, Llancastell CID. Is your husband around?'

'Graham?' she enquired. 'No, I'm afraid he's down in London on business.'

'And you're his wife?' Nick asked.

The woman gave him a slightly bemused look. 'Yes, I'm Liv Wheeler - his wife.'

'We've got a couple of routine questions we'd like to ask,' Ruth explained. 'Is it okay if we come in?'

Liv thought for a few seconds, gave an audible sigh and gestured for them to come inside. 'I suppose so.'

As they followed her down to the kitchen, Ruth gave Nick a look as if to say *She's rather snooty.*

Liv pointed to the kitchen table. 'You can sit down there if you like?'

Ruth gave her a forced smile. The heavy smell of roses and coffee filled the room. Ruth had always thought there was something terribly sad about the smell of roses. They lacked the light, carefree smell of other flowers.

'Thank you.' Ruth moved a chair from under the table.

'I would offer you coffee or tea but we appear to be out of milk,' Liv muttered as she looked in the fridge.

'We're fine, thank you.' Ruth and Nick sat down at the long, oak table with an empty cafetiere at its centre. There were copies of all the day's broadsheet newspapers – *The Times, The Telegraph, The Guardian* etc …

Nick took out his notebook and pen.

'Does the name Vince Thompson mean anything to you?' Ruth enquired.

'It didn't until yesterday,' Liv replied.

Ruth gave her a quizzical look.

SIMON MCCLEAVE

'Graham told me you spoke to him yesterday,' Liv said as a way of explanation. 'He said that Vince Thompson had been killed.'

'That's right,' Nick stated. 'Did you know him?'

Liv shook her head as if that was a ridiculous question. 'God no. I don't have anything to do with our tenants. Graham sorts out all that kind of thing.'

'So, Vince Thompson was a tenant of yours?' Ruth asked.

'That's right,' Liv replied. 'I'm pretty sure my husband told you all this when he spoke to you yesterday.'

'Yes, he did,' Ruth said. 'I take it that you and your husband own a number of properties that you rent out? Is that right?'

Liv nodded as she leant back against the expensive-looking granite work surface. 'Yes, that's right. We've got about nine or ten.'

God, she really is horribly full of herself.

Nick looked up from writing. 'And they're all in Llancastell are they?'

'Mainly,' Liv replied. 'That sort of area. As I said, Graham deals with our lettings so I couldn't tell you exactly where they are.'

Ruth nodded and looked at her. 'I don't suppose you own properties up as far as Rhyl though, do you?'

'Rhyl?' Liv snorted and pulled a face. 'God no. Why would you ask that?'

Let's see how she explains this.

'We have an eyewitness that saw your husband banging at the door of a property in Rhyl. The witness said he seemed very angry,' Ruth explained.

'Rhyl? I don't think so,' Liv stated with a deep frown.

'The strange thing is, the property was being rented by Vince Thompson,' Ruth said, 'And your husband was

156

shouting for Vince to come outside. Do you know anything about that?'

'When was this?'

'Last year. Probably around six months ago,' Ruth stated.

'No.' Liv gave her a look of disbelief. 'Sorry, but that's not possible. Vince Thompson was one of our tenants in Llancastell not Rhyl. I can't remember Graham ever even going to Rhyl. I think your eyewitness must be mistaken.'

'Possibly,' Ruth shrugged. 'The witness said that the man was driving a sports car.'

Liv laughed. 'Graham doesn't own a sports car.'

'A red Lotus Elise?' Ruth stated.

Liv glared at her. 'I just told you, we don't own a sports car.'

Ruth didn't believe her. She was hiding something.

'Just for our records, can you tell me where your husband was on Monday night?' Nick asked.

'What time?'

'Between ten and midnight?'

'Sleeping next to me,' Liv explained.

'Thank you,' Nick said.

Daisy, Graham and Liv's daughter, wandered in and looked at them.

'Hi there,' she said confidently.

'Hi.' Ruth smiled. 'It's Daisy, isn't it?'

'Yes.'

'That's a lovely name,' Ruth remarked as she got up from the table and looked over at Liv who had the expression of someone who had chewed a wasp. 'Thanks for your help, Mrs Wheeler. If you can tell your husband we'd like to speak to him, that would be much appreciated.'

'Yes, of course,' Liv said in a way that suggested she had no intention of doing that.

As they went down the stone steps to the driveway, the front door slammed behind them.

'She was charming,' Ruth joked sardonically. She spotted Nick looking at something – a newly-built garage on the far side of the driveway.

'Might just take a look, boss,' he explained as he strolled casually over. He then cupped his hands as he peered in through a door on the side.

'Anything?' she asked.

Nick gave her a meaningful look. 'Yeah. There's a red Lotus Elise sitting in there.'

Chapter 30

Strolling to the centre of IR1, Ruth looked out at the CID team. It was late afternoon and the investigation was developing fast, with various lines of enquiry. She walked over to the scene boards and pointed to a photograph.

'As most of you know, we've had to release Kevin Parks pending further investigation,' she explained. There were a few disgruntled noises from a couple of detectives. Parks was a drug-dealing scumbag who had avoided prosecution for nearly a decade. 'However, I'm still convinced that Parks is involved in Vince's murder somewhere along the line. I want us to focus on our trace, investigate and eliminate strategy.' She pointed to two photos. 'Jim, what did you dig up on Stu and Cath Morton?'

Garrow looked over from where he was sitting. 'According to the landlady in The Red Lion pub, Stu Morton is a big softie. The incident that Phoebe reported seeing sounds like nothing more than a couple of teenagers drinking too much, getting lairy and Stu telling them to get lost.'

Georgie nodded. 'She told us that Stu wasn't the jealous type. I'm not even sure there's any truth to Phoebe Evans' story about Cath Morton and Vince having an affair.'

Ruth raised an eyebrow. 'Yeah, well the more I learn about Phoebe Evans, the more I think she's smack bang in the middle of all this.'

Garrow looked down at his notepad. 'Just to bring us all up to speed, boss, Phoebe Evans had been banned from The Red Lion pub for dealing in their toilets. The landlady knew Kevin Parks and thought Phoebe worked for him. Parks recently came into the pub looking for Phoebe and made a comment that she had stolen from him.'

Nick looked over. 'The money and bags of weed we found in the campervan?'

Ruth frowned and thought for a moment. 'Phoebe is dealing for Parks in Llancastell. She steals the money and drugs from him, hands them to Vince who decides to disappear. Maybe she tells Parks that Vince stole them from her.'

'Maybe Vince did steal them from her?' French suggested.

Georgie frowned. 'But if we think that Parks tracked down Vince, ran him off the road and shot him, why didn't he take the stolen money and drugs from the van?'

'Daniel ran from the van,' Garrow stated. 'Maybe that spooked Parks?'

'What time did that farmer Charles Winner call it in?' Ruth asked.

'11.30pm,' Garrow replied. 'But he said he didn't see anyone else around.'

'Didn't Daniel say he saw a woman in the car that stopped that night?' Georgie enquired.

'Phoebe Evans?' Ruth suggested.

'Could have been,' Nick said with a shrug.

Ruth perched herself on a table. 'Listen, my instinct is that Phoebe is the key to this. I'm getting a search warrant tonight which I want to execute bright and early tomorrow morning. And we bring her in here for questioning.' She then pointed over to the board again. 'Phoebe Evans also told us that she had seen a man fitting Graham Wheeler's description arguing and fighting with Vince at his home.'

Georgie looked over. 'Yeah, that fits in with what the neighbour up in Rhyl told us. She saw the same.'

Ruth raised an eyebrow. 'Up until now, we thought the only connection between Vince and Wheeler was that he rented the property in Klea Avenue from him. However, we now have a positive sighting of Wheeler banging and shouting at a property being rented by Vince, long before he ever moved to Llancastell. So, the question is, how did Wheeler and Vince know each other?'

Nick looked over. 'Wheeler told us that Vince owed rent. But Wheeler couldn't have been demanding rent from Vince for a house he didn't own. He's lying to us.'

French nodded. 'I've done some digging on Wheeler. He's worth several million. And he's running for Parliament. He's not likely to get into a fight with a tenant over some missing rent.'

'No,' Ruth agreed. 'Whatever it was, it was very heated and emotive. Liv Wheeler also lied about the car that her husband drives. The neighbour from Rhyl claimed the man she saw left in a red Lotus Elise. When we asked Liv Wheeler about it, she stated that her husband didn't own a car like that. Nick spotted one sitting in the garage. Someone check with the DVLA on that.'

Georgie narrowed her eyes. 'So, they're covering up something.'

'Yeah,' Nick agreed. 'And it's not a bit of late back-rent.'

Chapter 31

The kettle boiled and Nick took it over to a pan that was full of pasta and a pinch of salt. He was preparing his *famous* pasta Arrabiata for Amanda and Fran, who were in the living room watching telly. He poured the boiling water into the pan and cranked up the heat.

Twelve minutes should do it, he thought.

For a moment, his mind turned to the investigation into Vince Thompson's murder. He wondered what the connection between Graham Wheeler and Vince could be. In terms of lifestyle, they couldn't be more different. And Wheeler didn't strike him as someone who would be involved in drugs. So what were the Wheelers trying to hide from them?

Little Bit of Love by *Tom Grennan* started to play on the radio. Nick turned it up and began to sing along – *A little bit of love, I need a little love.* He had just bought Tom Grennan's new album *Evening Road*. Even Ruth admitted that she liked it.

Taking a small pot of dried chillies, Nick continued to sing as he went over to the pan of sauce.

'Careful with the chillies, buster,' warned a voice.

It was Amanda.

Nick gave her a defensive frown. 'I'm making Arrabiata. It has chillies in it.'

'Yeah, but it's meant to be a subtle heat, not volcanic,' she teased him.

Amanda smiled at him as she joined in with the song for a moment and took him in her arms.

'Oh, back in your good books, am I?' Nick teased, raising an eyebrow.

'Maybe,' she replied. 'I know you meant well but going to *chat* to Thurrock wasn't really working a twelve-step programme was it?'

'No. Sorry.' Nick smiled. 'Has Fran mentioned if everything is okay at work?'

'Apparently Thurrock has given her a wide berth and hasn't even looked at her,' Amanda replied.

'See?' Nick said with a self-satisfied grin. 'Maybe it wasn't the worst thing to have done.'

Amanda gave a growl. 'You do know you're a total nobhead?'

Nick gave her a wink. 'But I'm your total nobhead, you lucky lady.'

There was a loud knock at the door.

Amanda frowned, looked at Nick and said, 'I'll get it.'

As she disappeared, Nick went over and stirred a pinch of chillies into the sauce.

Amanda came back into the kitchen and looked perplexed. 'There's a couple of police officers that want to talk to you.'

'Uniform?' Nick enquired, wondering why they were on his doorstep.

'Yeah,' she replied.

'I'll be back in a sec,' Nick told her as he walked out of the kitchen, headed down the hallway to the front door where two uniformed officers stood.

'DS Evans?' the older officer asked. He was short with a chubby face and small eyes.

'Yes?' Nick had no idea why two uniformed officers were standing on his doorstep. It wasn't likely to be anything to do with work.

'Sorry to trouble you, sir,' the officer said. 'We were called to an assault earlier in Llancastell. The victim had cuts to his face and a suspected fractured jaw. He's been taken to the University Hospital.'

'Okay.' Nick was still none the wiser.

Amanda joined him by the door. 'Everything all right?'

'I'm not sure,' Nick replied.

'The thing is, sir,' the officer said. 'The victim is claiming that you assaulted him.'

Nick narrowed his eyes and frowned. 'What?'

'Can you tell us where you were at 7.30pm this evening, sir?' the officer asked.

Nick shrugged. 'I was driving home from work.'

'Were you on your own?'

'Yeah.' Nick was starting to feel very uneasy. 'Who is the victim?'

The officer looked down at his notepad. 'Victim's name is Paul Thurrock.'

Chapter 32

Ruth sat on the end of Doreen's bed with her legs crossed looking at one of the women's magazines that Sarah had bought for her mother.

'These magazines are hilarious, Doreen,' Ruth laughed, turning the front cover to show her. 'In this one we've got *Devil Doll Keeps Setting My House On Fire.*'

Doreen giggled. 'Maybe you should bring it in for questioning.'

'I think I should.' Ruth pointed to another magazine. '*I Had Eyebrows Made Out Of Socks On Our Wedding Day.*'

They both burst out laughing.

A figure appeared at the doorway and looked in. It was Sarah.

'You two are making a right racket,' she stated with a grin. 'And Mum, you're meant to be getting some rest.'

Doreen rolled her eyes, put out her own hand and gave it a smack. Then she looked at Ruth and whispered, 'It's like living with Hitler.'

Sarah raised an eyebrow. 'I can hear you. I *am* actually standing here.'

As Ruth got off the bed, she looked over at Doreen. She did look tired so it was probably best to leave her to rest. 'I was hoping that you'd remembered another 60s musician that you slept with.'

Doreen laughed. 'I wish I'd slept with Elvis.'

'Mum!' Sarah exclaimed.

'Yeah, I don't think you were the only one,' Ruth commented with a wry smile.

'I met that Billy Fury once,' Doreen explained. 'He told me he was Liverpool's answer to Elvis. And I looked at him and said, 'Well you're not really are you dear?' I remember he had terrible breath.

Ruth chortled. 'But you didn't sleep with him though?'

'Ruth!' Sarah said.

'No dear,' Doreen sighed. 'I think he batted for the other side.'

Sarah rolled her eyes. 'Mum, you're not meant to say stuff like that these days.'

'Sorry.' Doreen winked at Ruth.

'See you later, Doreen,' Ruth said as she left, pulled the door to and walked along the landing with Sarah. 'Your mum is officially hilarious.'

'Yeah,' Sarah sighed. 'And I think you bring the worst out in her. But I know she loves chatting to you.'

They began to walk down the stairs.

'How's that Daniel doing?' Sarah asked as they reached the bottom of the stairs.

'I haven't seen him today,' Ruth replied. 'I checked in with the children's home and I think he's struggling to settle in. I took him to Burger King last night.'

'Did you?' Sarah asked with a smile as they went into the living room and sat down.

'Yeah, he's ten years old and he's a vegetarian,' Ruth

explained. 'He told me his mum had died giving birth to his sister.'

Sarah sighed. 'Poor little thing.'

'To make matters worse,' Ruth said, '… the press have got hold of the story, so now everyone knows that Daniel witnessed his dad's murder.'

'You think he's in danger?'

Ruth shrugged. 'The kids at the home saw a man prowling around at the back so I've put a uniformed patrol outside the house. But I'm not happy that he's the only eyewitness. Our prime suspect is a drug-dealing scumbag.'

Sarah looked at her. 'You really do care about him, don't you?'

'Yeah,' Ruth admitted. 'Of course. He's been through so much in his short life.'

'Can't he come and live with you temporarily?'

'I wish he could,' Ruth sighed. 'I'd have to get a temporary foster care order from social services and I don't think they sort those out in just a few days.'

'I thought about what we talked about the other night.'

'You mean adoption in general?' Ruth asked.

'I think I was a bit of a cow about it,' Sarah admitted. 'Maybe we should think it through. Or at least have a proper conversation about it.'

'Yeah, I'd really like that.' Ruth smiled at her.

Chapter 33

I
t was nearly 9am when Ruth sat back in her chair as
Nick looked at her. He'd just told her that Paul Thurrock was in hospital, claiming that Nick had assaulted
him.

'Have you even met this Thurrock?' Ruth asked.

Nick gave her a look that made her feel uneasy.

'Okay,' she said. 'Your silence isn't filling me with confidence, Nick. What happened?'

Nick pulled a face. 'I had *a little chat* with Thurrock in
the car park at his work.'

'Anyone see you?' Ruth enquired.

Nick nodded. 'Yeah. I asked for him at reception. Then
we went outside.'

'Jesus. And what exactly did you say to him?'

'I told him not to talk to Fran, or even make eye
contact with her,' Nick explained.

'Did you threaten him?'

'Yeah,' Nick sighed. 'I told him that if he did, I'd take
him out to Snowdonia and put him in a hole.'

'Bloody hell, Nick,' Ruth growled. She knew that Nick could be a bit hot-headed but this wasn't good.

'Could anyone hear you?'

He shook his head. 'No. We were in the middle of a car park.'

'Anyone see you?' Ruth enquired.

Nick shrugged. 'I guess so. If anyone had looked out of one of the office windows, they could have seen me and Thurrock talking.'

'At least you didn't touch him.'

Nick winced as he looked at her.

Ruth narrowed her eyes. 'What the bloody hell did you do?'

'I might have accidently grabbed him by the balls,' Nick admitted.

'In full view of a building full of office workers!' she thundered.

'Yeah, I don't know what I was thinking,' he mumbled.

'It's pretty clear you weren't thinking,' Ruth stated shaking her head. 'Jesus, Nick.'

'But I have no idea why he would say that I assaulted him last night.'

Ruth looked at him for a second. He looked worried. 'Okay, I'm going to ask you this once. Did you go looking for Thurrock on the way home from work last night?'

'No,' Nick exclaimed. 'Bloody hell. Of course not.'

'You grabbed him by the balls and threatened to kill him, Nick,' she pointed out. 'It's not beyond the realms of possibility that you went to have another *little chat* and things got out of hand.'

'No. I swear to you, I went straight home from here last night. I didn't go anywhere near Thurrock,' Nick explained anxiously.

'Well someone did,' Ruth said. 'And he says it was you. What the hell is that all about?'

'I wish I knew.'

'Any idea if he's going to press charges?'

Nick shrugged. 'I'm waiting to hear.'

French appeared at the door and looked in. 'Boss, we've had a call from a uniformed patrol.'

'What is it?'

'They attended an emergency call to a house on Klea Avenue,' French explained. 'They found a young woman dead and they think it's Phoebe Evans. They think she was murdered.'

Chapter 34

Ruth and Nick pulled up outside Phoebe Evans' home. Uniformed officers had already cordoned off the area with blue evidence tape and several neighbours were out on the pavement trying to find out what had happened. Directly outside the house was the SOCO van. Its back doors were open and a SOCO, in full nitrile forensic suit, hat and mask, was putting evidence away inside.

Walking towards a young officer who was manning the cordon and keeping the neighbours away, Ruth got out her warrant card. She didn't recognise the young officer.

'DI Hunter and DS Evans, Llancastell CID,' she explained. 'What have we got Constable?'

'Mother, Mel Evans, works nights in a local factory. She came home this morning and found her daughter in the living room,' the constable explained. 'She called us.'

'Where exactly did you find the victim?' Nick asked.

'Lying in the middle of the carpet,' he replied. 'She had serious blows to the back of her head and there was a substantial amount of blood.'

172

'Any sign of forced entry?' Ruth enquired.

'No, ma'am.'

Ruth looked at him. 'Start running a scene log, please. No one comes onto the crime scene without my say so.'

'Yes, ma'am.'

The constable pulled up the police tape and Ruth and Nick headed for the house.

As they arrived, they showed their warrant cards and a SOCO handed them a full forensic suit. It smelled of chemicals and rustled noisily. Ruth could still remember when CID officers just popped on some gloves and trod all over crime scenes.

Snapping on her blue latex gloves, Ruth looked at Nick and gestured for them to go inside. There were already steel stepping plates across the carpets going into the house. Several SOCOs were dusting surfaces and examining the carpet for forensic evidence.

Ruth made her way through to the living room and saw Phoebe's body lying on the floor. A SOCO was taking photographs.

She immediately recognised the Chief Pathologist as Professor Tony Amis.

'We really must stop meeting like this,' Amis joked as he used a torch and tweezers while examining the body.

'What have we got, Tony?' she asked.

'Blunt force trauma to the back of the head,' Amis explained, pointing to where the hair was matted, sticky and black. 'I'm pretty sure her skull's been fractured.'

'Time of death?' Nick asked.

'She's been here for quite a while given the lividity. At least ten hours, maybe longer.'

That took the time of death back to twelve o'clock the previous evening or earlier.

Amis pointed to the palms. 'Some defensive wounds here and here. A couple of broken bones in the hand.'

'Any idea about a weapon?' Nick asked.

'Something big and heavy,' he replied. 'Baseball bat. Maybe even a mallet.'

Ruth looked around the room. A table had been turned over and the armchair wasn't straight. 'Looks like there was a struggle.'

'No sign of forced entry though,' Amis remarked.

Nick looked at Ruth. 'You think Phoebe knew her attacker?'

'Looks like it,' she replied as she moved away from the body and gave Nick a dark look. 'And we released Kevin Parks at 5pm yesterday.'

Nick nodded. 'And a few hours later, Phoebe was killed.'

Chapter 35

Twenty minutes later, Ruth and Nick had found Mel Evans, Phoebe's mother, who was sitting in the kitchen of the neighbours across the road. No longer dressed in their forensic suits, they settled themselves at the kitchen table.

Mel's face was streaked with tears – she was in utter shock.

'I'm so sorry for your loss,' Ruth said quietly.

'I can't believe it,' Mel whispered, staring into space. 'How can she be gone? She was my little girl.' She began to sob and the neighbour, a woman in her 40s, came over and rested a comforting arm on her shoulder.

'I know this is an incredibly difficult time for you, Mrs Evans,' Ruth stated gently, 'but I wonder if we could ask you a couple of questions?'

Mel nodded as she wiped her face with a tissue. 'It's Mel.'

'Can I get anyone any tea?' the neighbour asked.

Nick smiled at her as he got out his notebook and pen. 'We're fine thanks.'

Ruth looked at her. 'Can you tell us exactly what happened this morning?'

Mel took a deep breath. 'I finished work at about six. I'm on nights, see.'

'Where do you work, Mel?' Nick enquired gently.

'The Canto factory on the Industrial Estate,' she replied. 'Plastic mouldings, stuff like that. I got the bus home. And then I walked up from the bottom to our house. And then …'

Ruth nodded sympathetically. 'What time did you leave your house last night?'

'I leave at ten on the dot,' Mel replied.

Nick looked over. 'And Phoebe was home?'

'Oh yeah,' Mel said sadly. 'Watching telly. I still can't believe what's happened.' She then bit her lip and blinked as a tear rolled down her face.

'On your way out, did you see anyone around, or any cars parked nearby?'

Mel thought for a second. 'I don't think so. It was late so there's not normally anyone around.'

'Are you sure?'

'I saw Stu Morton driving up the road, but no one else,' Mel stated.

'Stu Morton?'

'Well, I saw his van drive past, so I assumed it was him,' Mel replied.

Ruth looked over at Nick – *I wonder how significant that is?*

She then gave Mel a reassuring look. 'And what happened when you got home?'

'I got to the house, opened the door and came in.' Mel started to shake. 'And that's when I saw Phoebe.' She blinked as tears rolled down her face. 'I … don't know what I'm going to do without her, you know.' She wiped her face and then looked directly at Ruth. 'Why would anyone do that to her? I don't understand.'

'I promise you, we're going to find out,' Ruth replied. 'And when you came in, you didn't see or hear anything?'

Mel shook her head sadly. 'No. Nothing.'

'Can you tell us what you did next?' Nick asked.

'I went over to see if I could do anything but Phoebe wasn't moving.' Mel's voice broke a little with emotion. 'There was blood everywhere. Then I rang 999.'

Nick looked over at her. 'Okay. Did you then stay in the house until the paramedics arrived?'

'No,' Mel said, shaking her head. 'I ran out of the house and started to shout for help.'

'Did you see anyone when you went outside?'

'No.'

'Just to check,' Ruth said. 'The only thing you saw when leaving or coming home was Stu Morton's van?'

'Yeah,' Mel replied and then she frowned. 'You don't think Stu had anything to do with what happened to Phoebe do you?'

'We can't really discuss that with you, I'm afraid,' Ruth explained gently.

'Yeah, but Stu is lovely. Heart of gold,' Mel remarked. 'I don't know how he can be married to that woman though.'

'You don't think much of Cath Morton then?' Ruth asked.

Mel snorted. 'She's a psycho bitch, that one. Especially when she's had a drink.'

Ruth and Nick exchanged a look. They needed to speak to Stu and Cath Morton.

Chapter 36

Ruth and Nick sped north towards Rhyl. As they cut along the coastline, Ruth buzzed down the window an inch and caught the last of the fresh sea breeze before the downpour began from the hooded grey clouds overhead. To their right, the Irish Sea – a vast, black and green mass that stretched for as far as the eye could see. In fact, the Isle of Man was just over a hundred miles to the north. Another hundred miles on from that was the coast of Northern Ireland.

'Anything from the children's home?' Nick asked after a while.

Ruth shook her head. 'I'm hoping that no news is good news though.' She looked over at him. 'Any more on this Thurrock thing?'

Nick shrugged. 'No, nothing.'

'And no idea why he would implicate you in his assault?' she asked.

'No, no idea,' Nick said. 'I've got to speak to my Federation Rep later just in case it goes any further.'

Ten minutes later, they arrived at Parks' house. They marched up to the front door, knocked aggressively and stood back. The dogs began to bark as the door opened. Parks peered out. His eyes were bloodshot and he was unshaven.

'Are you fucking joking me?' he thundered. 'What the hell do you want now?'

'We need to know where you were last night,' Nick sneered.

'Why?' he hissed.

Ruth could smell the booze on his breath.

'Did you go and see Phoebe Evans after you were released yesterday?' she enquired.

'What? No,' Parks mumbled. He looked seriously hungover. 'Who the fuck is Phoebe Evans?' he asked.

'Don't mess us about, Kevin,' Nick snapped. 'We know that Phoebe worked for you. You were in The Red Lion a few weeks ago looking for her.'

'So what?' Parks shrugged. 'And no, I didn't go and see Phoebe.'

'Where did you go?' Ruth enquired.

'I came straight back here. Had a shower and went out,' Parks explained.

'And you can prove that, can you?'

'Yeah, I can actually,' Parks scoffed as he reached into his pocket and pulled out his phone. He clicked and showed them the screen. 'These are photos of me and my mates out last night on the piss. And these are the times that they were posted.'

'That doesn't prove anything,' Ruth said. 'Those photos could have been taken ages ago.'

'Jesus! I'll give you their names and you can go and ask them if you like?' Parks shook his head. 'What the hell's happened? Why are you asking me about Phoebe?'

SIMON MCCLEAVE

Ruth looked at him. 'Phoebe was murdered at her home last night.'

Parks' eyes widened. 'What? You're joking aren't you?'

He seems genuinely shocked. Or he's a very good actor.

'We are going to need the names and addresses of everyone you were with last night,' Nick explained.

'Fine.' Parks shrugged but he did now look rattled. 'I didn't have nothing to do with Phoebe being killed though.'

Nick raised an eyebrow and pointed over to Parks' Cherokee Jeep. 'Nice car.'

Parks gave him a withering look. 'What?'

'You do know that there's a GPS tracker in there,' Nick informed him. 'So, there will be a record of everywhere you drove yesterday. And if you went anywhere near Klea Avenue in Llancastell, we can find that out.'

Parks smirked. 'Well I didn't, so knock yourself out, sunshine. You can have my car keys if you want to have a look.'

Ruth looked at Nick – either Parks had nerves of steel or he wasn't responsible for killing Phoebe.'

180

Chapter 37

'*Flanaghan's Irish Bar*' was on the seafront in Rhyl. It was where Parks claimed he had spent the previous evening and was the location mentioned on his social media posts. It was dark and overcast. The flat, sandy beach was deserted except for a couple of dog walkers. It might have been just the weather, but Ruth thought there was something sinister and desolate about the abandoned Welsh seafront.

Ruth squinted as she and Nick entered the bar. It was dark with old fashioned wooden booths along the walls. Traditional Irish instruments - such as a bouzouki, fiddle and a bodhran drum – hung on the wall. Old adverts for Guinness adorned the bar along with bright green images of shamrocks and photos of Dublin.

Ruth approached the bar and flashed her warrant card to a young barman with a dark ponytail. 'DI Hunter and DS Evans from Llancastell CID. I wonder if I could speak to anyone who was working here last night?'

The barman shrugged with a touch of arrogance. 'You can talk to me if you like?' He had a thick Irish accent.

'Do you know a man called Kevin Parks?' she enquired.

The barman thought for a moment. 'I've heard the name, aye.'

Ruth fished out her mobile phone, clicked on a photo of Parks and showed him. The barman peered at it for a moment and then gave a wry smile. 'Oh yeah. That fella was in here last night. Really going for it, him and his pals.'

Nick looked over. 'Any idea what time he came in?'

'I started at six,' the barman informed them. 'I guess they came in around seven.'

'And they were here all night?'

'Pretty much. I think they were on *the sniff*, if you know what I mean?' the barman said, and then something occurred to him. 'Tell a lie. They actually left an hour or two before we closed.' He pointed to Ruth's phone. 'Your wee man there paid for all the drinks on a credit card.'

'What time do you close?' Ruth asked.

'Midnight.'

'So you think they left between ten and eleven?' Nick enquired.

'At a guess, although I couldn't swear to it.' The barman shrugged. 'I'm pretty sure they said they were going on somewhere else.'

'We're going to need to see what time Kevin Parks paid for the drinks,' Ruth explained. 'I assume it's on your till roll or somewhere.'

The barman nodded and pointed. 'It'll be on that computer over there if you want me to check for you?'

'Please.'

The barman left them and Ruth turned to look at Nick.

'If Parks left here at ten last night, that still gives him two hours to get over to Llancastell to murder Phoebe

Evans, if we're using Amis' estimated time of death,' she said.

'Maybe coming here last night with his mates was a deliberate attempt to give himself an alibi for the evening,' Nick suggested.

'If you're hammering it, how fast do you think you can get from here to Klea Avenue in Llancastell?' Ruth asked.

Nick shrugged. 'Forty-five minutes, give or take.'

'So, even if he left here at eleven, he could have got to Phoebe's house at the time of her murder,' Ruth stated, thinking out loud.

The barman returned. 'Yeah, I've had a look. Kevin Parks signed for those drinks at 10.17pm last night.'

Ruth gave Nick a meaningful look – Parks didn't have a viable alibi.

'Thanks,' Nick said as they headed for the door.

As they came out, Ruth took a cigarette out, popped it in her mouth and lit it. She took a deep drag.

That's better.

'I don't know what it is but being in places like that makes me want to smoke.'

'We just need to hope that forensics find something that links Parks to the murder scene,' Nick stated.

Ruth's phone buzzed. It was Garrow.

'Jim.'

'Boss,' Garrow said. 'I've just had that *Clear View Children's Home* on the phone. Someone called Charlie. He says that Daniel has gone missing.'

'What?' Ruth exclaimed, feeling a sudden panic. 'Is he sure?'

'Yes, boss. He's checked everywhere inside and out,' Garrow explained. 'There's no sign of him anywhere.'

Chapter 38

Half an hour later, Ruth and Nick had cut down from Rhyl to the A55 and had hammered cross country towards Llancastell. They pulled up sharply outside *Clear View Children's Home.*

Ruth spoke to the officers in the patrol car that had been stationed permanently outside the house ever since one of the children had seen a man in the back garden. They hadn't seen anyone enter or leave the house in the past two hours. Ruth's head was now whirring with all the different scenarios of what might have happened to Daniel, where he might have gone – or who might have taken him.

Ruth and Nick hurried along the pavement.

'Our best possibility is that Daniel has run away,' Ruth said, thinking out loud.

'If he ran away, where do you think he might go?' Nick asked.

Ruth looked at him. 'My guess is that he would have headed to where he used to live and gone to Phoebe's house on Klea Avenue.'

'Makes sense,' Nick agreed. 'It looked like they were very close the other day. The only problem is that the house is now a major crime scene and cordoned off.'

'And that will make him panic. And of course the other possibility is that someone has taken him.'

Nick nodded with a concerned expression. 'Yeah. He's the only eyewitness to his father's murder.'

'And at the moment, we're no closer to finding out who the two people were in that car,' Ruth sighed frustratedly as she rang the doorbell.

A few seconds later, Charlie answered the door. He looked frightened. 'Hi. I don't understand how this has happened.'

He ushered Ruth and Nick inside.

'Anyone see anything?' Nick asked.

'No.' Charlie shook his head. 'Most of them were playing out in the garden when someone asked where Daniel was.'

'When was the last time anyone saw him?' Ruth enquired.

Charlie glanced at his watch. 'About an hour ago. Daniel was playing outside and then he just seemed to vanish.'

Ruth looked at Nick and gestured to the garden. 'Let's go and have a look.'

Charlie pointed. 'We can go out that door there.'

They followed Charlie through a door that led from the living area onto a large patio where there were wooden tables and chairs. Beyond that, the garden stretched away to a long brick wall. There were two goals, a couple of footballs and some coloured plastic cones dotted around the grass.

Ruth immediately marched across the garden towards the back wall. 'Daniel didn't go out the front otherwise our officers would have spotted him. But if he came this way and over the back wall …'

Charlie stopped to talk to two boys who had come over to talk to him about something.

Nick frowned. 'If he'd gone over the wall, someone would have seen him, wouldn't they?'

Ruth shrugged. 'I'm not sure yet.'

The wall was about eight foot high and covered with moss and thick ivy. Where they were standing, it was in full view of the house and the garden. Scanning her eyes down to the left, Ruth saw where trees, an overgrown hedge and scrubs encroached over the lawn and untidy footpath.

'Down here,' Ruth pointed as she strode away.

Reaching the trees, Ruth moved around the wall and looked at Nick. The house and garden were no longer visible.

'It's a blind spot,' she said, gesturing to the far-left edge of the wall. 'If Daniel went over the wall there, no one would have seen him.'

Before they had time to continue their discussion, Charlie approached looking concerned. He had a boy of about thirteen in tow.

'Callum has just told me that he saw a van parked up at the back of this wall this afternoon,' Charlie explained.

Callum, who had a shock of blond hair that was shaved around the back and sides nodded. 'Yeah, it was there for ages. Lara threw a frisbee over the wall so I climbed up to see if I could see where it went.'

'Can you show us where?' Nick asked.

'Yeah,' Callum replied as he turned and led them towards the middle of the wall. 'Just here.' He then used the small cracks and ledges to scale the wall to the top in a couple of seconds. He pointed. 'It was just down here. But now it's gone.'

'And it was there before Daniel went missing?' Charlie enquired.

Callum jumped down and nodded. 'Yeah. I climbed up to the top to see if I could see Daniel anywhere. That's when I saw the van had gone.'

Ruth gave Nick a look – she didn't like the sound of what Callum had seen.

'Can you tell us what kind of van it was, Callum?' Nick enquired.

Callum shrugged. 'I dunno. Not one of those big ones.'

Ruth looked at him. 'Can you remember what colour it was?'

'Black, I think,' Callum said with a frown. 'It might have been dark blue. Sorry.'

Ruth gave him a smile. 'Don't worry. You're being very helpful, Callum.'

Remembering that the only van that they had come across in their investigation was Stu's black Citroën Berlingo, Ruth fished out her phone and used Google to bring up a photo of that make and model. She then showed it to Callum. 'Did it look like this?'

Callum peered at the image. 'Yeah, I think so.'

Ruth looked at Nick. 'It might have been a Citroën Berlingo van. And there's only one person we know who drives one of those.'

Chapter 39

R uth and Nick screeched to a halt outside the corner shop that Cath and Stu Morton owned. A quick check had revealed that they lived in a flat above the shop. Ruth had spent the journey across Llancastell making sure all police officers in the town and the surrounding area knew that Daniel was missing. At the moment, they still had no idea if he'd been taken or if he'd walked off on his own accord. CAD operators were sending out an APB as well as sending all units a photo of Daniel so they knew who they were looking for.

As they arrived at the door to the side of the shop, Nick pointed to the blue Berlingo van which was parked on the road outside. He went over to the back, cupped his hands and looked inside. 'I can't see anything. Just a few old cardboard boxes.'

Already Ruth was beginning to have doubts that if Daniel had been taken, Stu Morton was involved. You don't kidnap a child and then park the vehicle you used directly outside where you lived and worked.

Entering the shop, Ruth scoured the aisles and saw a figure crouched down, stacking packets of breakfast cereal on the shelves. He was wearing a black baseball cap which sat too high on his head as though it hadn't been pulled on properly.

It was Stu Morton.

'Mr Morton?' Ruth enquired as she approached.

He looked up from where he was kneeling and immediately looked scared. 'Yes? It's Stu.'

'We're police officers,' Ruth explained as Nick joined her. 'We spoke to your wife the other day?'

'Yes, that's right,' Stu nodded as though it had taken him a few seconds to put two and two together. He then frowned. She might have been mistaken but she got the distinct impression that Stu had some kind of learning difficulty.

'We'd like to ask you a couple of questions,' Ruth stated. The anxiety of Daniel's whereabouts was weighing heavily on her.

'Erm, okay,' Stu mumbled. 'But I'm on my own in the shop.'

'That's fine,' Nick said. 'We need to check your whereabouts in the past few hours.'

Stu furrowed his eyebrows. He didn't understand the question.

Ruth looked at him. 'We need to know where you've been in the past few hours.'

Stu gestured to the interior of the shop looking baffled. 'I've been in here all day.'

Nick pointed to the CCTV cameras up on the walls. 'Do your cameras work?'

Stu gave him a defensive nod. 'Yeah.'

'So, if we had a look at the CCTV from today,' Nick continued, 'we would see you here all day?'

SIMON MCCLEAVE

'Yeah.' Stu gave them a bemused look. 'But I don't understand why you'd want to do that.'

Ruth had a thought. 'Where's your wife Cath at the moment, Stu?'

Stu pointed to the ceiling. 'She's got one of her migraines. She's having a lie down.'

'What time did she go for a lie down?' Nick asked.

Stu shrugged. 'Quite a while ago.'

Ruth wondered if they needed to speak to Cath about her whereabouts.

'Your van is outside the shop, isn't it?' Nick enquired.

Stu nodded. 'Yeah, that's right.'

'Has it been there all day?' Ruth asked.

Stu shrugged. 'I suppose so. I haven't driven it.'

'What about Cath?' Ruth asked. 'Did she take the van out?'

Stu shook his head adamantly. 'No. She can't drive when she has a migraine.'

Nick looked over at him. 'Does anyone else use the van?'

'Phil,' Stu said as if they should know who Phil is.

'Phil?'

'Yeah, Phil. He's the young lad that works part-time for us,' Stu explained.

'Could he have taken the van out today?' Ruth enquired, wondering if they were now going down a dead end.

'He's away on holiday,' Stu explained. 'Stag do, I think.'

Ruth looked at Nick. If Stu had killed Vince Thompson because he'd had an affair with Cath, he might have taken Daniel as he was an eyewitness. Stu had an alibi for the whole day. Plus, her instinct was that Stu didn't have a clue about what they were talking about and certainly didn't seem to have the mental capacity to hide anything from them.

Nick got out his phone and showed him a photo of Daniel. 'Do you know this boy?'

Stu nodded. 'Yeah. It's Vince's lad. I think his name is Darren, isn't it?'

'Daniel,' Nick corrected him. 'Have you seen him today?'

Stu shook his head. 'No, I haven't seen him for a while now.'

'Okay, thanks for your help.' Ruth was feeling frustrated and now eager to get on with the search for Daniel.

Ruth and Nick walked out of the shop and stopped on the pavement.

'It's not him, is it?' Nick asked.

Ruth shook her head. 'No. As my dad would say, Stu's *not the full shilling*.'

Nick nodded and then gestured to the front door. 'Maybe we should have a quick word with Cath Morton.'

Before Ruth could agree, her phone buzzed. It was French.

'Boss,' French stated with an urgent tone. 'Officers have had a report of a boy walking alone up by Chirk Castle. I haven't got much of a description, but it sounds like he's about the same age. I wondered if Daniel had gone back there?'

'Okay, thanks,' Ruth said. 'We're on our way.'

As she ended the call, Nick looked at her. 'What's going on?'

'We need to get to Chirk Castle.'

Chapter 40

While the rest of CID were chasing leads in the search for Daniel, Georgie and Garrow had been sent to see Graham Wheeler and find out why he and his wife had been lying to them. There was clearly a link between Wheeler and Vince which had nothing to do with unpaid rent.

Georgie glanced out of the window for a moment. As they turned off the main road towards Wheeler's home, they passed rough, patchy land to their left. A dozen or so rabbits scattered away towards their burrows in response to the noise of the car. She could hear the faint sound of music playing.

'Is that classical music you're trying to sneak into this car, Jim?' she asked with a bemused smile.

'You don't like classical music?' Garrow asked sardonically. 'Now there's a surprise.'

'I don't. But to be honest, I don't know anything about it,' Georgie admitted.

Turning up the music, Garrow gave her a look. '*The Lark Ascending* by *Vaughan Williams.*'

'The Lark did what?' Georgie asked, half-teasing him.

'The composer came from Welsh heritage,' he informed her.

She listened to the rising violins and had to admit that it sounded beautiful. 'Yeah, fair play, Jim. It is nice.'

'Nice?' Garrow rolled his eyes.

'Don't be such a snob,' Georgie groaned. Looking down at her phone, she saw that a message had arrived from the DVLA. She looked over at Garrow. 'DVLA has confirmed that Graham Wheeler owns a 2016 red Lotus Elise.'

Garrow shook his head. 'Why lie to us? They must have known we can run a check?'

Georgie shrugged. 'I guess his wife panicked and didn't think it through. Luckily, not everyone we deal with is an arch-criminal who's used to covering their tracks.'

Garrow gave a wry smile. 'That's true. A couple of weeks ago, I worked a burglary. I did a quick scoot round the surrounding roads and spotted the burglar walking down the road carrying a huge plasma TV.'

Georgie laughed. 'Jesus. What a dickhead.'

'Yeah.' Garrow rolled his eyes. 'Sad thing is, he'd only been out of prison for twenty-four hours.'

'I think some of them can't wait to get back,' Georgie said scornfully.

As they turned a corner, Wheeler's large house loomed into view. As Georgie glanced out of the car window, she could see that they were high up. The beautiful Welsh countryside swept down and away as far as the eye could see.

They pulled up on the driveway and got out.

Georgie gestured to the garage where Nick said Wheeler's Lotus Elise had been sitting.

'Let's go and have a look, shall we?' she asked with a playful grin.

They walked over, their shoes crunching on the gravel drive. Georgie went to the door, cupped her hands and peered inside.

The garage was empty.

'What a surprise,' she snorted.

'Don't tell me,' Garrow said. 'There's nothing in there anymore.'

'Nope, empty.'

'Can I help you?' boomed a very posh male voice.

It was Graham Wheeler. He was dressed in a red Welsh rugby jersey, shorts and trainers. His face was red and sweaty and it looked like he'd been for a run. A black labrador trotted around his feet.

Georgie reached into her jacket and pulled out her warrant card. 'DC Wild and DC Garrow, Llancastell CID.'

Wheeler rolled his eyes as he wiped his forehead with the cuff of his jersey. 'Again? I think me and my wife have told you everything we know.'

Garrow pointed to the garage. 'Where's your car gone?'

Wheeler gave them a look as if to say he had no idea what they were talking about. 'What car?'

Georgie looked at him. He seemed suddenly nervous. The question had clearly caught him off guard. 'The Lotus?'

He shook his head. 'I don't know what you're talking about. I don't own a Lotus.'

Georgie frowned. 'That's very strange because the DVLA have a red 2016 Lotus Elise registered to you at this address.'

Wheeler seemed lost for words.

Garrow pointed to the house. 'Maybe we could go

inside, Mr Wheeler? There are a few questions we'd like to ask you.'

Wheeler nodded sheepishly. 'Yes, of course. That's probably a good idea.'

Following him through the front door, they crossed the hallway and down to the huge open-plan kitchen.

'Please, come and sit down,' Wheeler stated as he gestured to a large oak table. He seemed to have composed himself again. 'Would you like tea or coffee?'

Garrow shook his head. 'No. We're fine thanks.'

'Okay.' Wheeler grabbed a glass of iced water. He came and sat down at the far end of the table and stroked the labrador's head.

'She's beautiful,' Georgie said of the labrador. 'What's her name?'

'Bess,' Wheeler replied looking lost in thought. He then turned and gave them a meaningful look. 'Listen, I think I know why you're here. And I'm happy to admit that my wife and I haven't been entirely honest with you about how we knew Vince Thompson.'

Georgie raised an eyebrow and glanced over at Garrow. They weren't expecting that. She was used to people lying until every avenue had been exhausted and then continue to lie anyway.

'Okay.' Garrow fished his notebook and pen from his pocket. 'Can you tell us how you did know Vince Thompson.'

'Vince was my tenant at that house in Llancastell,' Wheeler explained. 'But that's not really the full story. But what I do need to clarify is that what I'm about to tell you won't go any further than this kitchen?'

Georgie narrowed her eyes. 'I'm afraid we can't promise that. Not if what you're telling us is pertinent to the case.'

Wheeler nodded. 'It's not. I can assure you.'

Garrow looked over at him. 'I think you need to let us decide that, Mr Wheeler.'

'Graham,' he stated. 'It's Graham.'

'Okay,' Georgie said. 'Let's start with how you know Vince Thompson.'

Wheeler moved his chair around and sat forward at the table. 'Vince and I were in sixth form together over in a school in Cheshire. We were friends and we both ended up at Cardiff University.'

'Can you tell us when this was?' Garrow asked.

'Late 90s,' Wheeler said. '1998. I could check the exact dates ... Anyway, Vince didn't even make it through to the end of the first year. He got involved in drugs, missed all his lectures and then dropped out. And that was the last I heard of him.'

'You lost contact?' Georgie stated to clarify.

'Exactly.' Wheeler nodded. 'I started to get involved in local politics. And then I started to explore the idea of standing as a candidate for Parliament for this constituency when the next general election was called.'

'When did all this happen?' Garrow enquired.

'It was two years ago, I guess,' he explained. 'Somehow Vince got wind of my political ambitions and turned up on our doorstep one night.'

'What did he want?' Garrow asked.

Wheeler looked uncomfortable. 'Unfortunately, Vince had a couple of photographs of me that he said could ruin my career as a politician.'

'Did he show you those photographs?' Georgie enquired.

'Yes, he did.'

'What were they of?'

'I'd rather not say.'

Georgie gave him a stern look. 'This is a murder investigation. You need to tell us what those photographs contained.'

Wheeler took a few seconds. 'I was taking drugs – cocaine, during a party in my first year at Cardiff. It was nothing more than youthful experimentation. And I assure you that I've never taken drugs since then. But Vince said that he wanted money or the photos would end up in the press.'

'So, he blackmailed you?' Georgie stated.

'Exactly,' Wheeler said. 'I paid him £2,000, he gave me the photographs and I hoped that would be the end of it.'

Garrow looked up from his notepad. 'But it wasn't?'

'No,' Wheeler sighed. 'He called again a few months later. He said he still had the negatives and he wanted me to give him money and a place to live in Llancastell. I managed to track him down to where he was living in Rhyl and I went up there to reason with him.'

Georgie nodded. 'We spoke to Vince's neighbour who remembers you banging on his door one night.'

'Yes. Either he was out or he wasn't answering,' Wheeler said. 'Eventually I agreed that he and his son could live in a house I owned in Llancastell.'

'Klea Avenue?' Garrow asked to clarify.

'Yes. They moved in. But months went past and Vince still wouldn't give me the negatives to destroy. I went round there a couple of times to have it out with him but he dug his heels in. And then about two weeks ago, Vince told me that he and Daniel were going to move on. He said that if I gave him £2,000 he would give me the negatives and I'd never see him again.'

Georgie looked at Garrow. 'I'm assuming that was the £2,000 in cash that we found in his campervan.'

Wheeler shrugged. 'I guess so.'

'And you gave him the money?' Garrow enquired.

'Yes.'

Georgie raised an eyebrow. 'Did you get the negatives?'

'Yes. It was a huge relief, as you can imagine,' Wheeler admitted.

'Do you have them now?'

Wheeler shook his head. 'God no. I burned them as soon as I got home.'

Georgie glanced at Garrow – it would have been useful to have them to validate what Wheeler was telling them.

'Vince gave you these negatives in return for £2,000 and he and Daniel left your property in Llancastell?'

'Yes,' Wheeler replied. 'I assumed that was the last I'd see of him. And then I discovered that he'd been murdered. Obviously I panicked. And I didn't want anyone to know why Vince and I had been in contact or that I'd paid him off.'

'Obviously without the negatives …' Garrow said, 'you can't prove that what you've told us is true.'

Wheeler's face fell. 'I know it doesn't look good. But I promise you, I had nothing to do with Vince Thompson's murder. I swear on my family's life.'

Chapter 41

Ruth had commandeered several uniformed officers to scour the area surrounding Chirk Castle. Having walked up the wide, sweeping pathway to the castle, Ruth and Nick looked out down to the car park and the fields beyond. Even though it was a weekday, the castle was relatively busy with visitors. However, it was term time so there were virtually no children around which certainly made Ruth think the sighting of Daniel was real.

'Why would he come back here?' Nick asked as they scoured the area.

Ruth shrugged. 'Maybe he wanted to see where he last saw his father? I don't know.'

'I thought he'd never want to come back here after what happened,' Nick stated.

Out of the corner of her eye, Ruth spotted a young boy walking down the steep pathway and away from the castle towards the car park. He was definitely Daniel's age and build, but he was wearing a white baseball cap so it was impossible to see his hair colour or his face.

'Down there,' Ruth pointed.

They broke into a jog as they weaved in and out of the bemused-looking tourists coming the opposite way.

The pathway was steep. Ruth could feel the pressure of running downhill in her legs. She wished she'd kept up the running that she had started when she first moved to North Wales.

Halfway down, the pathway took a sharp right. Due to the high stone walls either side, the next section of path wasn't visible.

They hurtled around the bend and then stopped.

Where the hell has he gone?

Looking down, Ruth could see that the boy they were chasing had disappeared from view.

Shit!

Nick shrugged. 'He's got to be down there somewhere. Come on.'

As her jog became a run, Ruth feared she was going to lose her footing and fall. Nick was now about twenty yards ahead.

She spotted the boy further down on the right-hand side. Breaking into a full sprint, she only just avoided knocking into an elderly couple as she hurtled down the hill.

'Daniel?' she called as she approached.

He didn't respond.

'Daniel?' she said as she finally reached him, gasping for breath.

The boy turned and looked startled. He had black hair and olive skin.

Shit! You're not Daniel.

The boy said something angrily in a language that she didn't understand – possibly Italian.

'Sorry, I thought you were someone else,' she panted.

From out of nowhere, a man and woman arrived looking worried. From the way they spoke and looked, Ruth could see they were his parents and they were probably wondering why their son was being accosted by a strange middle-aged woman.

They frowned and babbled at her angrily.

Ruth gave them a forced smile as Nick arrived. 'Mi scusi,' she said, which she vaguely remembered was Italian for 'sorry'. She got out her warrant card to show them as a way of an explanation.

'Bollocks,' Nick muttered under his breath as the Italian boy scurried away under the protective arms of his parents. 'Where the bloody hell is he?'

Ruth's phone rang. It was a Llancastell landline number that she didn't recognise.

'DI Hunter?' asked a voice that she recognised but couldn't place. 'It's Charlie from *Clear View Children's Home.*'

'Oh hi, Charlie.' Ruth tried to get her breath. 'I'm really sorry, but we still don't have any news on Daniel.' She assumed that's why he'd called her.

'Oh right,' Charlie replied, sounding despondent. 'I don't know if this helps but I logged onto our computer downstairs using Daniel's login. I saw him on it early this morning. Then I checked his search history.'

'Okay.' Ruth wondered what Daniel had been looking at.

'Daniel had been looking up St Mary's Church which is over in Eaton,' Charlie explained.

Eaton was an affluent suburb of Llancastell and Ruth knew roughly where St Mary's Church was.

'Any idea why he was looking at that?' Ruth enquired.

'No, sorry,' Charlie replied.

'Thanks, Charlie. We'll check it out.' Ruth ended the call.

'Where are we going?' Nick asked.

'St Mary's Church in Eaton.' Ruth pulled a cigarette and looked at him. 'You drive, I'll smoke.'

Nick raised an eyebrow. 'Smoke. You can hardly get your breath.'

Ruth held the cigarette. 'For some reason, this is exactly what I need right now.'

Nick shook his head as they turned and headed for the car.

Chapter 42

Thirty minutes later, Ruth and Nick pulled up outside St Mary's Church in Eaton. It had been built as a parish church in the 1850s in a 14th century Decorated Gothic style. Its imposing tower had a broach spire. To the left of that were four naves with a row of intricate coloured stained-glass windows.

Getting out of the car, they quickly scanned the churchyard before going through the wrought iron gates. Up above them, starlings flew in a perfect formation, banking left and then right, as if they'd rehearsed the manoeuvre a thousand times. Their incredible patterns across the sky signalled that the day was drawing to a close.

The tranquility was broken by the chimes of the church bell to signal that it was 4pm.

Ruth had no idea why Daniel had looked at the church online. However, she soon had her answer.

A figure sat on a bench on the far side of the graveyard.

It was Daniel.

Thank God! she thought and then registered the irony.

SIMON MCCLEAVE

'He's over there,' Ruth exclaimed to Nick with a huge sense of relief.

They approached slowly. The last thing they wanted to do was startle him or cause him to run away.

'Why don't you go over there on your own?' Nick suggested under his breath as they got closer. 'Two of us might freak him out.'

Ruth nodded and whispered, 'Good idea.'

Taking a few steps along the path, Ruth saw that Daniel was deep in thought as he sat on the bench slowly swinging his legs to and fro. He became aware of her presence and looked up. He didn't move. Ruth was relieved that he didn't seem to want to run.

The late afternoon clouds moved past the sun so that its rays lay across the churchyard, bringing a modicum of warmth.

'Hi, Daniel,' Ruth said gently as she went over.

He glanced up at her and blinked at the sunshine. 'Hi.' He clearly wasn't startled – nor was he upset at having been found.

'Mind if I sit down?' she asked.

He gave a shrug and shifted over a few inches.

Ruth sat down and gave a little sigh. 'It's beautiful here, isn't it?'

'Yeah.'

'We've been looking for you,' Ruth explained after a few more seconds.

'Have you?'

'In fact, we've been worrying about where you were.'

'Sorry,' he said.

There was silence as they sat together – still and connected.

'Do you like it here?' Ruth asked.

204

Daniel pointed to a grave opposite them. 'I came to see my mum.'

Ruth peered over at the black, granite gravestone with gold writing – *Charlotte Emma Taylor 1990 – 2013. Loving daughter and mother*

'Have you been here before?' she enquired.

'No,' he shook his head. 'But my dad told me this is where she is. The only thing is I can't find my sister anywhere.'

Ruth frowned. 'Your sister?'

'Yeah.' Daniel nodded. 'Dad said that mum and my sister Jodie were buried up here.'

Ruth gave him a benign smile. 'Oh, I didn't know you had a sister.'

'Yeah,' he said with a slow nod of his head. 'She died with my mum when she was born.'

Ruth put a comforting hand on the top of his arm. 'I'm sorry to hear that.'

'I wish I'd met her.'

'Of course you do. And your dad said that Jodie was here?'

'Yeah. But I've looked everywhere and I can't find her,' Daniel explained.

They sat in silence for a while.

'How did you get up here?' Ruth enquired. Eaton was about three or four miles from the centre of Llancastell.'

'I walked.'

'It must have taken ages.'

'I don't mind.' Daniel shrugged.

'Tell you what,' Ruth said. 'When you're ready, we can take you back in the car. Okay?'

'Can we sit here for a bit longer?' he asked.

'Of course we can.'

'I was talking to my mum before you came,' Daniel explained.

'Were you?'

'It's a bit weird, because I don't really remember her,' Daniel said with a slight frown. 'I can sort of. And I've seen her in some photos that my dad had.'

Ruth nodded. He was such a sweet, lovely-natured boy.

Daniel reached into his pocket and pulled out a small canvas wallet that had a Velcro fastener. 'I've got some in here.'

Ruth smiled. 'Oh right.'

He pulled out a couple of creased Polaroid photos. The first featured a pregnant woman with a small boy.

'This is me and my mum.' Daniel handed Ruth the photo to look at.

'She's very pretty isn't she?' Ruth remarked quietly.

'Yes.' Daniel nodded. He handed her another photo of the same woman standing on the driveway of a house.

Ruth did a double take as she looked again at the photograph. She recognised the house in the photo. It was Theakstone Hill Hall, Graham Wheeler's home.

'Do you know this house, Daniel?' Ruth asked.

'Yes,' Daniel nodded. 'My dad said I used to live there. But I can't remember.'

That doesn't make any sense, Ruth thought to herself.

'You used to live there?' Ruth asked, trying to work out what on earth was going on.

'That's what he said when we went up there,' Daniel replied as he looked at some of the other photos. 'Dad said that I had a Spiderman poster on my wall.'

Chapter 43

It was dark by the time Ruth pulled up outside *Clear View Children's Home* with Daniel. They sat in the car quietly for a while, listening to the radio. Ruth was still trying to get her head around the photo of Daniel's mother Charlotte outside Graham Wheeler's house, and Daniel's claim that he had once lived there. It was something they needed to go and quiz Wheeler about. They also needed to look up Charlotte Taylor's death certificate and check that she did actually die in childbirth.

'How's your Vegan Royale?' Ruth asked with a smile as Daniel tucked into yet another Burger King.

'Great,' he said stuffing food into his mouth.

'How long have you been a vegetarian then, Daniel?' she enquired.

'I dunno … Are you a vegetarian?'

'No,' she replied. 'I've thought about it. I think I like bacon too much.'

He frowned at her. 'Isn't bacon bad for you though?'

'Yes, very,' Ruth laughed. 'I'm afraid I've got a few bad habits.'

'Have you got children?' he enquired as he picked up his drink.

'Yes. A daughter called Ella,' Ruth replied.

'Does she live with you?'

'Not anymore,' she replied with a smile. 'She's twenty-three so she's got her own life.'

Daniel looked puzzled. 'Don't you miss her then?'

Ruth thought for a second. 'Yes, I do miss her. I miss her a lot. But she doesn't live very far away so I get to see her lots.'

'Oh, okay,' he nodded, now deep in thought.

Ruth pointed to the children's home. 'I should probably get you back now.'

Daniel nodded. 'Can I take my drink with me?'

'Of course you can,' Ruth replied as she unclipped her seatbelt and got out of the car.

Spotting the uniformed patrol car that was parked outside the house, Ruth gave the officers a little wave. They had been there all day in case Daniel had decided to return. They waved back. She didn't envy them the job of sitting there all night, trying to stay alert.

Ruth and Daniel walked together along the pavement and up the path to the front door. As Ruth rang the doorbell, she could already hear the noise of raised voices coming from inside.

Charlie opened the door. He looked flustered. 'Sorry, just give me a second.' Leaving the door open, Charlie hurried away.

What the hell is going on? Ruth wondered.

She looked down at Daniel – he was clearly apprehensive. As they walked down the hallway, Ruth could see two teenage boys beating the crap out of each other on the floor. Some of the other children were cheering them on or filming the fight on their phones.

Jesus Christ!

Charlie was trying to pull them apart but it looked like he needed help.

Ruth marched over, grabbed the older, larger boy, pushed him to the floor and pinned him down. 'Right, stay there and don't move.'

'Who the fuck are you, bitch?' the boy yelled.

Ruth put her knee on the small of his back. 'I'm a police officer. And if you don't calm down right now, I'm going to handcuff you, put you in my car and put you in a cell for the night.'

'You can't do that!' the boy yelled as he stopped wriggling and tried to throw her off.

'Try me,' Ruth snapped.

'All right, all right,' the boy said. 'Just let me go, okay.'

Moving slowly up from the floor, Ruth could see that Charlie had taken the other boy away.

'Right, if I have to come back here …' Ruth said, fixing the boy with a stare. His nose was bleeding from where he had been punched. '… I promise you, I'm putting you in a cell.'

The boy shrugged and walked over to the sofa where he slumped down with an irritated huff.

Charlie came back and rolled his eyes at her. 'Thanks.'

'No problem,' Ruth stated.

'Good to see you back, Daniel,' Charlie said. 'You had us worried there for a bit, mate.'

Ruth nodded. 'Yeah, I've explained to Daniel that he can't go wandering off without talking to you first.'

Daniel still looked frightened from witnessing the fight. He looked up at her.

'Can I come and stay with you?' he asked.

Ruth leant down and took his hand. 'I really wish you

could. But it wouldn't be allowed. But I promise I'll come and see you tomorrow, okay?

Daniel nodded - he looked terrified.

Ruth's heart hurt at the sight of him looking back at her as she left.

Chapter 44

Nick drummed his fingers on the steering wheel. He was parked outside the ACE Recruitment Agency waiting for Paul Thurrock. He still had no idea who had beaten up Thurrock or why he had decided to claim that Nick had been responsible. Although he knew it probably wasn't a good idea, he had decided to follow Thurrock to get an idea of what he was up to and to see where he lived. He had told Amanda that he was working late which made him feel guilty, especially as he was missing Megan's bedtime. But he needed to know why Thurrock had made the allegation – and it wasn't as if he could just walk up to him and ask.

A few minutes later, the doors to ACE Recruitment opened and Thurrock strolled out with a self-satisfied grin and a laptop bag slung over his shoulder. He still had the remnants of a black eye.

Dickhead.

Watching Thurrock as he got into his BMW, Nick started the ignition and pulled out of the parking space.

Thurrock headed out of the car park and turned left. Nick followed.

For the next five minutes, Nick tailed Thurrock as he made his way through the centre of Llancastell, heading west. When he turned left towards the multi-storey car park, Nick wondered if Thurrock was planning on doing some shopping.

Trying to keep his distance, he entered the ground floor of the multi-storey which was starting to empty out at the end of the day.

They worked their way up to the first and then the second floor. As they got to the third floor, Nick could see there were virtually no cars left. He wondered why Thurrock wasn't parking.

As Thurrock turned right up the ramp, Nick realised he was heading to the top floor of the multi-storey. It was essentially the roof of the building, open to the elements and, even though it had parking bays and a ticket machine, it was usually empty.

What the hell is he doing?

Realising that if he drove up to the roof parking he might well arouse Thurrock's suspicion, Nick parked in a nearby bay.

He got out and closed the car door quietly. The car park smelled of oil and urine.

Making his way to the ramp up to the rooftop, Nick's shoes echoed around the low concrete ceilings of the car park. Hugging the left-hand wall, he moved slowly up the ramp so he could see across the roof.

He glanced behind to make sure no one was watching him.

It had started to rain heavily. The raindrops battered noisily onto the concrete in front of him.

Nick peered over to see that Thurrock had parked

beside a black Range Rover with darkened windows. Both cars had their headlights on and their beams lit the rain as it fell.

Thurrock is definitely up to something very dodgy Nick thought to himself.

The driver's door to Thurrock's car opened and he got out. Pulling up the collar on his coat, he moved to the back of the Range Rover where a window had just lowered. Thurrock shook hands with whoever was sitting in the back seat. He then reached into his pocket, pulled out a package and handed it over. He was handed a smaller package back which he tucked into his coat.

Right, that's got to be drugs or money.

Getting back into his own car, Thurrock pulled away, which allowed Nick to see the licence plate of the Range Rover. Fishing out his phone, Nick took a photograph and hurried back to his car before he could be spotted.

He looked at the photograph and grabbed his Tetra radio.

'Three six to Control, over,' he said.

'Three six from Control, receiving, go ahead,' said a female voice.

'Requesting a DVLA check on a black Range Rover, licence plate TD19 FDF, over,' Nick stated.

'Received three six, stand by,' said the voice.

A few seconds later, the Tetra radio crackled again. 'Three six from Control. Car is registered to a Curtis Blake in Croxteth, Liverpool, over.'

Opening the door to Sarah's house, Ruth took off her coat and popped it on the coat rack in the hallway.

'Hello?' she called.

'I'm in here,' Sarah called from the direction of the living room.

'Have we got wine?'

'In the fridge,' Sarah replied.

Thank God for that, Ruth thought. She had forgotten to pick up a bottle.

Strolling across the hallway, she smiled at the thought of a ciggie, a glass of wine and a cuddle on the sofa with Sarah.

She stuck her head around the living room door only to see Sarah watching the television intently.

Sarah gave her a dark look and pointed. 'I think you should come and watch this.'

Ruth frowned. There was some kind of news programme on. Aerial footage showed the back garden of a house that was now covered in police tents. A SOCO, dressed in a full white forensic suit, appeared from one of the tents and walked across the garden carrying a plastic box in their hands.

'What's going on?' Ruth asked, still none the wiser as she sat down next to Sarah.

'Shh.' Sarah put her finger to her lips.

A news reporter's voice started over the footage. *'Does the answer to an eight-year-old mystery lie here? In the back garden of a house in Semley, Wiltshire, they are looking for Gabriella Cardoso. The current owner of the house, who has no connection to the case, says that he hopes the search will bring an end to the investigation.*

Gabriella Cardoso went missing in London in November 2013. Gabriella was an eighteen-year-old Portuguese au pair working for a family in Holland Park. She left on the evening of the 1ˢᵗ November, saying she was meeting friends in nearby Notting Hill. She never arrived.

Her parents never gave up hope that their daughter would be found alive somewhere. However, there have been significant developments in the case in the past six months that led the Metropolitan Police to issue a statement saying that they believed Gabriella had been murdered that night.

Officers from Scotland Yard arrived at the property in Semley early this morning and have been working closely with Wiltshire Police. A garage to the rear of the property has been identified as a specific area of interest. Forensic officers will be using ground-penetrating radar to aid their search.'

'Bloody hell.' Ruth turned to Sarah and raised an eyebrow. 'I'll get us both a very big glass of wine shall I?'

Chapter 46

Walking over to the scene boards in IR1, Ruth looked out at the CID team who had assembled for the 9am briefing. She knew they were frustrated that they still didn't have a prime suspect – and now they were dealing with a double murder.

'Right guys, listen up.' Ruth put her coffee down and then pointed to the scene boards. 'I know this investigation is proving to be very complicated, but I promise you that we are moving closer and closer to finding out who killed Vince Thompson and Phoebe Evans.'

Nick looked over. 'I'm assuming that our theory is that the same person, or persons, murdered them both?'

'At the moment, yes.' Ruth nodded. 'There are way too many coincidences for us to think that the two murders aren't connected.' She pointed to the board. 'Right, Kevin Parks. He doesn't have a watertight alibi for the night that Vince was shot. And we know that he knew Vince while he and Daniel were living in Rhyl. And both Parks and Vince were dealing drugs.'

'Maybe Vince ripped Parks off?' French suggested. 'If

we think that Phoebe worked for Parks, maybe she was carrying the drugs and cash in her house? That explains why her fingerprints are on both. Vince decides to steal them and do a runner. Parks and Phoebe chase Vince, run him off the road and shoot him dead. However, Parks begins to panic that Phoebe is an eyewitness to the murder. Maybe she tries to blackmail him and he kills her to keep her quiet?'

Ruth nodded. 'Yeah, I think that really works as a hypothesis but at the moment we have nothing to link Parks to either crime scene. No fingerprints, no DNA and no forensics. He definitely has the motive, means and opportunity. But the CPS are never going to allow us to charge him until we have solid evidence against him.'

Garrow frowned. 'His shotgun ammunition matches the ammunition used to kill Vince.'

Nick raised an eyebrow. 'Apparently it's the most popular shotgun ammunition in Wales. In fact, you'd be struggling to find anyone who didn't use it.'

'And we've got nothing on his phone or bank records?' Ruth enquired.

Garrow shook his head. 'Nothing, boss. Clean as a whistle.'

Ruth looked at the boards again. 'Okay, we've got Stu and Cath Morton. Phoebe alleged that Cath was having an affair with Vince. That gives Stu motive.'

Georgie looked over. 'Does he have an alibi?'

Ruth shook her head. 'Both Stu and Cath claim to have been at home on the evening of the murder. At the time of Phoebe's murder, Stu told us that he was in their shop all day and has given us CCTV to corroborate that.'

'What's his motive for killing Phoebe Evans?' French asked.

'Phoebe had been telling everyone she met about

217

Cath's affair with Vince,' Ruth said. 'Maybe he went down there to tell her to keep her mouth shut and things got out of hand.'

'I haven't managed to look at the shop CCTV footage yet, boss,' Nick admitted. 'But I'd be surprised if he'd give it to us if he wasn't there. He's not exactly the sharpest tool in the toolbox.'

Georgie frowned. 'What if Cath wasn't having an affair with Vince? What if it was just Phoebe spreading rumours?'

Ruth looked over and nodded. 'Go on.'

'Stu gets the wrong end of the stick and shoots Vince,' Georgie said. 'Cath kills Phoebe for bad mouthing her.'

Ruth frowned. She wasn't sure that sounded plausible. 'Maybe. Daniel remembers that the man who shot his father was wearing a black baseball cap. And that fits with Stu Morton. But Daniel also says he saw a woman in the car too. And if that was Cath, it doesn't make any sense.'

'Plus they have a small van not a 4x4,' Nick pointed out.

'But we do have Phoebe's mother, Mel Evans, claiming she saw the Mortons' van driving past as she got home,' Garrow stated.

'Okay, I think the Mortons have to go on the back-burner for now,' Ruth said. 'And I do believe Kevin Parks is our prime suspect. He's just been clever enough to cover his tracks effectively.' Ruth went back to the boards. 'And then we have Graham and Liv Wheeler. Georgie, can you bring everyone up to speed on your interview with Graham Wheeler?'

Georgie looked up from where she was sitting. 'So, Wheeler and Vince went to sixth form and university together. Vince dropped out but he had photographs of

Graham Wheeler taking cocaine at a university party. Twenty years later, when Wheeler announces that he's going into politics, Vince turns up on his doorstep looking for a handout or he'll release the photos to the press. Wheeler is eventually forced to allow Vince and Daniel to live rent-free in Llancastell in return for the negatives to those photos. However, Vince stalled, asking for a final £2,000 in return for the negs. Wheeler finally agreed and he claims that he handed Vince the £2,000 which we found in the campervan.'

'Where are the negatives?' Nick enquired.

'Wheeler claimed he burned them,' Garrow said, 'which isn't that surprising.'

'That all makes sense,' Ruth said, trying to process what Georgie had fed back.

Nick shifted forward in his chair. 'How do we know that Vince didn't just drive off with the negatives?'

Ruth shrugged. 'We don't. We only have Wheeler's word that Vince handed them over and he burned them.'

'If Vince took the money without handing over the negs and then did a runner, that would give Wheeler motive for killing Vince,' French suggested.

Ruth frowned. 'But it doesn't tally with what Daniel told us. Vince went to the car with a baseball bat and was then shot. Wheeler wanted the negatives to those photos. If he, and whoever he was with, looked through the campervan for them, they would have ripped the place apart trying to find them. Me and Nick saw the campervan and it was tidy.'

'Unless Vince had the negs about his person?' Nick suggested. 'If they shot him, then searched the body and found them, they would have just left.'

Ruth wasn't convinced and it was frustrating that they

hadn't got the break they needed. 'Okay everyone. Let's keep working at this. Nick, after the photos that Daniel showed me, I think we need to go and have another chat with Graham Wheeler.'

As Ruth and Nick pulled round the corner and onto Graham Wheeler's driveway, they saw that an ambulance was parked outside.

Ruth glanced at Nick as if to say *I wonder what's going on?*

Getting out of the car, Ruth saw a paramedic helping Wheeler's daughter Daisy from the house and helping her up to the ambulance. She had a clear mask over her mouth and nose that was attached to small, green oxygen tank.

Wheeler came down the steps, looking concerned. When he spotted Ruth and Nick's arrival, his face twisted in anger.

'As you can see, this isn't a good time,' he snapped.

Liv Wheeler came out and rolled her eyes when she saw them. 'Haven't you got better things to do than harass us?'

Ruth looked at Wheeler. 'Sorry, but I do have a few questions that I need to ask you. And it is urgent. But we could wait or talk to you at the hospital?'

'Stay here and sort this out, darling,' Liv said to Wheeler. She pointed. 'I'll go with the ambulance, okay?

I'll give you a call when we get there and I've spoken to the doctors.'

Wheeler nodded. 'Okay, thanks.'

As the paramedics closed the rear doors and Liv made her way over to her car, Ruth gave Wheeler a sympathetic look. 'Is she going to be okay?'

Wheeler nodded. He seemed to have calmed down a little. 'Daisy has a condition that flares up every now and then. She'll be in good hands once she's at the hospital.'

Ruth gave him an empathetic nod. 'Good. And I apologise for our bad timing.'

'You'd better come in,' Wheeler said reluctantly. 'But I'm pretty sure I explained everything to the other officers who were here yesterday.'

Ruth and Nick followed Wheeler down the hallway and into the huge open-plan kitchen. He gestured for them to sit at the table and then sat down himself.

Wheeler sighed. 'I'm not sure what else I can tell you.'

'Actually, we wanted to ask you about something else.' Ruth fished out the polaroid photo of Charlotte Taylor standing in front of Wheeler's house and pushed it across the table for him to look at. 'Do you recognise this woman?'

Wheeler peered closely at the image and then shook his head. 'No.' Then he looked at Ruth. 'Should I?'

'It's Charlotte Taylor,' Nick stated. 'Does that name mean anything to you?'

Wheeler shrugged. 'No. I've never heard of her.'

'Charlotte and Vince Thompson had a child, Daniel,' Ruth explained. 'And I take it you've met Daniel at some point?'

'I saw him once when I went to visit Vince in Llancastell,' Wheeler replied. He then pointed to the photo. 'I don't understand what this has to do with me?'

'I'm surprised you haven't recognised the house that's behind Charlotte,' Nick said with a tinge of sarcasm. 'Why don't you have another look?'

Wheeler clearly didn't like Nick's tone but looked anyway. 'Yeah, okay, it's this house.'

'How long have you and your wife lived here?' Ruth enquired.

'Twenty years, give or take.'

'Polaroids have a date stamp on the back,' Ruth explained. 'That photograph was taken in June 2010.'

'Okay,' Wheeler said with a nonchalant shrug. 'We used to rent this house out for weddings and functions in the summer. We also have a series of summer garden parties here. This … Charlotte, is it?'

'Yes. Charlotte Taylor.'

'She could have attended any one of those functions,' Wheeler stated very calmly. He certainly didn't look like he'd been rattled by the photo. 'Can't you ask her when the photo was taken and why she was here?'

Ruth shook her head. 'She's dead, I'm afraid.'

'Oh, right,' Wheeler mumbled. 'Well I'm sorry to hear that.'

'There is something else that we need to talk to you about. Daniel, Vince Thompson's son. When he showed me this photo, he also told me that he had lived in this house when he was very young.'

Wheeler looked perplexed. 'What? No. I don't know what he's talking about.'

'Yeah, he seemed very certain,' Ruth explained. 'He said there was a picture of Spiderman on the wall.'

Wheeler gestured to the hallway. 'If you want a quick guided tour, I'm more than happy to show you around. But I don't know where he got that from.'

'Okay.' Ruth nodded and then looked at Wheeler as

they got up. He had a curious expression as if he was deep in thought. 'It's strange that Daniel would say that, don't you think?'

Wheeler shrugged. 'If he was very young, maybe he just got confused.' He gave her a sarcastic look. 'I think I would have noticed if a small boy was living here.'

Ruth gave him a forced smile as they headed for the huge staircase that swept in an arc to the first floor. The wall flanking the stairs had a series of oil paintings – some portraits, some landscapes.

'How many bedrooms do you have here?' Ruth asked as they climbed the carpeted steps.

'Seventeen, if you include the two small rooms at the top,' Wheeler replied.

Nick glanced at some framed photos of a private aeroplane. One showed it flying, the other two had Wheeler standing beside it.

'You've noticed my pride and joy,' Wheeler commented.

'That's your plane?' Nick asked.

'Yes,' he replied. 'I keep her down at Rednal Airfield.'

Ruth ignored him and pointed to the stairs. 'Okay if we have a look around?'

'Be my guest,' Wheeler stated.

For the next ten minutes, Ruth and Nick wandered through Theakstone Hill Hall but found nothing remotely suspicious – or anything that could help their investigation.

Chapter 48

As Ruth entered IR1, she could feel her frustration growing. As she headed over to her office, she could hear that members of the team were talking in hushed voices.

Something's going on, she thought.

'Everything all right?' she asked as she turned to look at them. 'I could really do with some good news.'

Georgie gave her a smile and nodded. 'Stu Morton.'

'Stu Morton? What do you mean?' Ruth asked.

'Forensics found a follicle of his hair in some carpet fibres beside Phoebe's body,' Georgie explained. 'They matched it to his DNA.'

Ruth felt a little buzz of excitement. 'That's brilliant.'

French looked over. 'Gets better, boss. I've checked the CCTV from the night Phoebe was murdered. Morton told you he was in the shop all night. Except he was lying because he turned off the CCTV recording at 9.30pm, which is 90 minutes before the shop closes.'

'Jesus,' Ruth sighed.

'Plus, the tyres that Morton has on his van match the

tyre tracks at the crime scene the night that Vince was shot,' Garrow said. 'I know Daniel told us that he saw a 4x4, but he might have been mistaken. Maybe he just saw Morton's van?'

Ruth nodded. 'Yes, that's possible. Right, I want Stu Morton arrested and brought in right away.

Chapter 49

'Interview conducted with Stuart Morton, Friday 19th March, 11.32am, Llancastell Police Station. Present are Stuart Morton, Detective Sergeant Evans, Duty Solicitor Cliff Patrick and myself, Detective Inspector Ruth Hunter.' Ruth then glanced over at Stu who looked lost. 'Stu, do you understand that you are still under caution?'

Stu was staring down at the table as if he hadn't heard her.

'Stu?' Ruth asked.

Stu slowly looked up and met her eyes with an icy glare that was more than unsettling.

'Stu, do you understand you are still under caution?' Ruth asked again slowly.

The duty solicitor leant in and whispered something in his ear.

'Yes,' Stu nodded. 'This is bloody stupid. I haven't done nothing.'

'Okay.' Ruth moved the files so that they were in front of her. 'I'd like to ask you about your whereabouts last Monday evening.'

Stu shrugged. 'I was at home, I think.'

'You think?' Nick asked.

Ruth sighed. 'Monday evening and night. Monday of this week, Stu.'

'Yeah, well I must have been in,' Stu said.

'Why's that?' Ruth enquired.

'I never go out on a Monday night,' he replied as if it was a silly question. 'Cath doesn't let me do anything. And I definitely can't go down The Red Lion.'

Ruth fished out an image from a folder and turned it to show Stu. 'For the purposes of the tape, I am showing the suspect item reference 361T. As you can see, this is a photograph of the tyres on your van. And here is a mould made from tyre tracks of a vehicle that we found at the place where Vince Thompson was murdered.'

Stu looked utterly baffled. 'What does that mean?'

'Would it surprise you to know that the tyres on the mould are a match for the tyres on your van?' Ruth asked.

Stu shook his head. 'They can't be 'cos I wasn't there.'

Nick frowned. 'But this mould shows us you have the same tyres.'

Stu pulled a face. 'Why would you think I'd kill a bloke like that Vince?'

Ruth took a few seconds and then looked over at him. 'We believe that your wife Cath and Vince were having an affair.'

Stu snorted. 'Don't be bloody daft. Cath?'

'And we think that you found out that Cath was having an affair and you decided to follow Vince and shoot him,' Nick said. 'Is that right, Stu?'

'No, that's not bloody right,' Stu snapped. 'You've got all this wrong.'

'We have an eyewitness who saw a man wearing a black baseball cap, standing beside a car which looks almost identical to yours, when Vince was murdered,' Ruth said. 'Was that you?'

Stu was starting to look upset. 'No, it wasn't me. I don't know why you're saying all this.'

Nick looked over and gave him a half-smile. 'I get it, Stu. If I found out that my wife was having an affair, I'd want to go and kill the bloke. It's only natural isn't it? I mean, this man was having it away with Cath so no one is going to blame you for wanting to kill him, are they?'

Stu's breathing was shallow. 'But he wasn't doing that. I know Cath. She wouldn't do that kind of thing.'

'But we know your van was there, Stu,' Ruth stated. 'And we have an eyewitness who saw someone who looked just like you. How do you explain that?'

Stu looked nervously at the duty solicitor. 'I can't explain that. It doesn't make any sense.'

'Okay.' Ruth took another folder from the table and pulled out a photo. 'For the purposes of the tape, I'm showing the suspect item reference 473E. Stu, can you look at this photo for me and tell me if you recognise the person in it?'

Stu took a deep breath, leaned forward and peered at the image. 'Yeah, that's that Phoebe girl from down the road.'

Ruth nodded. 'That's right. Phoebe Evans.'

Stu shrugged. 'If you say so.'

'How well did you know Phoebe?' Nick enquired.

'I dunno. She came in the shop,' Stu mumbled. He now looked shaky.

'You weren't friends then?'

'No, 'course not.' Stu's hands were shaking as he ran his hand over his shaved scalp.

Something about this is really getting to him.

Ruth fixed him with a stare. 'Had you ever been to Phoebe's house?'

'No,' Stu snapped as if he was offended by the suggestion.

'And you're sure about that?'

'Yeah,' Stu mumbled and then looked at the duty solicitor. 'Can we stop this for a bit? I don't feel well.'

The duty solicitor shook his head and then whispered something into his ear.

'Just answer the question, Stu,' Nick said loudly.

Stu looked startled. 'No, no. I told you.'

Ruth reached into the folder. 'For the purposes of the tape, I'm showing the suspect item reference 383T.' She turned the image for Stu to look at. 'What I'm showing you Stu is a tiny hair fragment we found in carpet fibres beside Phoebe's body. We've taken DNA from that hair and matched it to the national DNA database. Would it surprise you if I said that hair's DNA is your DNA, Stu?'

Stu's eyes narrowed. 'Eh? I don't understand. Why the hell would you think I killed her?'

'We believe that Phoebe Evans was spreading rumours about Cath and Vince's affair. In the pub and to anyone else who would listen. Did you go down to Phoebe's house to confront her about that, Stu?'

'No, of course not,' he replied.

'You just told us that you've never been to Phoebe Evans' house but we found a trace of your hair, on the carpet, beside her body. How can you explain that to us?'

'I can't,' Stu said trembling.

'You were there, weren't you, Stu?'

'No, I wasn't. I promise.'

'For the purposes of the tape, I'm going to show the suspect item reference 393Y.' Ruth pulled out a document. 'This is a statement from Mel Evans, Phoebe's mother.

Would it surprise you if I told you that she saw your van driving up her road at 10pm?'

Stu shrugged and looked at the floor.

'When we asked you yesterday where you were on the night Phoebe was murdered, you told us that you were in your shop all night until 11pm,' Nick remarked. 'And you gave us the CCTV tape to prove it, didn't you?'

Stu nodded but said nothing.

'We've looked at that tape, Stu,' Nick continued, 'and you turned it off at 9.30pm. Can you explain why you did that?'

Stu shook his head. He was shaking like a leaf.

'It seems to us that you must have closed up the shop early,' Ruth stated, 'and then you went out in your van. Is that right?'

Stu shook his head.

'Did you drive your van round to Phoebe Evans' house and then murder her, Stu?'

Stu's face was white as he looked up helplessly at the duty solicitor. 'I think I'm gonna be sick. I can't do this anymore.'

The duty solicitor looked over. 'I think my client really does need a short break now.'

Having executed a Section 18 Search Warrant, Georgie and Garrow were now dressed in forensic suits and working their way through Stu and Cath Morton's flat. SOCOs had arrived at the same time and were scouring the flat for forensic evidence.

Garrow and Georgie made their way into the Mortons' tiny kitchen.

Georgie pulled a face. 'Smell of condoms, don't they?'

Garrow frowned. 'This kitchen?'

'No, you plank,' she laughed. 'These bloody forensic suits.'

Garrow shrugged. 'I think it's just the gloves.'

'Okay,' Georgie rolled her eyes. 'These gloves smell of condoms, don't they?'

Garrow gave her a withering look. 'I don't know, do they?'

'Jim?' Georgie said with a wry smile. 'I take it you have used a condom before?'

Garrow shook his head. 'Piss off, Georgie. I just don't

particularly want to be discussing the smell of a condom at a crime scene.'

'You're such a prude,' Georgie teased.

Garrow shrugged and grinned. 'Maybe it's just that you've had more experience with condoms than me?'

Georgie gave him a playful shove. 'Hey, I'm gonna pretend you didn't say that.'

Garrow smiled as he started to open cupboards and search them.

Spotting peanut butter, Georgie moved a few tins and jars. 'You like peanut butter?'

'Not really,' Garrow replied.

'Me neither,' Georgie said. 'Gets stuck to the roof of your mouth, doesn't it?'

'I can't remember.'

'I think it's an American thing isn't it?' Georgie asked. 'Except they have it with jelly in sandwiches which I could never get my head round. Bit of a faff having to make jelly for a sandwich.'

Garrow gave her a look.

'What?' Georgie asked defensively.

'Jelly in America means jam,' Garrow sighed. 'It's just a peanut butter and jam sandwich.'

'Yeah, I knew that,' Georgie joked.

'No, you didn't,' Garrow teased her.

'Found anything?' she asked him.

'Nothing obvious,' he replied.

Georgie crouched down and opened the cupboard below the sink. She moved bottles of detergent and bleach.

Nothing.

'Let's try the living room,' Georgie suggested. 'Or do you say *drawing room*, Jim?'

'That's very funny,' Garrow stated. 'We called it the *sitting room*, which is very middle-class.'

'Yeah, well we called it the *front room* which is classic working class.'

They entered the 'living room'. There was a large sofa and a matching armchair in a beige checked material. A couple of newspapers and a magazine were arranged neatly on a low coffee table. The room was dominated by a huge plasma HD television and sound system.

Glancing through the window, Georgie could see that the SOCOs were now starting to search the wheelie bins at the back of the property. She wondered how the interviews with Stu and Cath Morton were progressing.

Then something caught her eye.

There was an old electric fire attached to the wall where the fireplace should have been. It had to be decades old and she wasn't sure if they were even legal anymore.

On the black stone hearth were flakes of plaster that had fallen from the wall. Crouching down, she looked at the wall where it joined the fire. There were flakes of paint and plaster missing from the edge as if someone had recently moved the electric fire away from the wall before pushing it back.

'Got something?' Garrow asked as he approached.

'Yeah, I think so,' Georgie said feeling a little buzz of excitement. Then she pointed to what she was looking at. 'I think someone has moved this fire away from the wall. And given the plaster down here, I think they've done it very recently.'

Garrow gestured. 'Shall we have a look?'

'Yeah.' Georgie held the metal grill that covered the face of the fire. She pulled it slowly and could see that its edge was coming away from the wall. She manoeuvred it gently until there was a six-inch gap between the fire and the wall.

Taking her phone torch, she clicked it on and shone it through the gap.

She turned and looked at Garrow. 'Yeah, there's a cavity at the back here.'

Garrow reached across and they both pulled the fire from the wall steadily. It crunched as the plaster split and it came completely away from the wall, except for the electric cord.

There was a green Asda supermarket plastic bag sitting in the cavity.

What the hell is in that?

Opening the bag tentatively, Georgie pulled out a dark green plaid shirt. It was large and clearly belonged to a man.

As she unfolded it, they could see dark blood stains on the arms and front of the shirt.

'Bingo,' Garrow said under his breath.

Georgie nodded slowly. 'Got you!'

Chapter 51

'Interview conducted with Catherine Morton, Llancastell Police Station. Present are Catherine Morton, Detective Sergeant Evans, Duty Solicitor Cliff Patrick and myself, Detective Inspector Ruth Hunter.' Ruth then glanced over at Cath who looked angry. 'Cath, do you understand you are still under caution?'

Cath was staring at her across the table but said nothing.

'Cath?' Ruth asked again. 'Do you understand what I just said to you?'

'Yes.'

'Can you tell me your whereabouts on Monday night?' Ruth enquired.

'I've told you this already,' Cath groaned. 'I was sleeping next to Stu. Jesus!'

Ruth fished out an image from a folder and turned it to show Cath. 'For the purposes of the tape, I am showing the suspect item reference 361T. As you can see, this is a photograph of the tyres on Stu's van. And here is a mould made from the tyre tracks of a vehicle that we found at the place where Vince Thompson was murdered.'

Cath glared at her. 'I've just told you, he wasn't there.'

'The mould of the tyres is a match for the same make of tyres on Stu's van,' Ruth stated.

'Yeah, well that doesn't prove anything,' Cath scoffed. 'Having the same make of tyre doesn't prove he was there does it?'

'We have an eyewitness that saw a man and a woman,' Nick explained. 'The man was wearing a black baseball cap.'

Cath laughed. 'Jesus. Is that all you've got? You'll get laughed out of court.'

She's starting to get right up my nose.

'Where was Stu on Wednesday night?' Ruth enquired.

'He was the in the shop,' Cath replied.

'All night?' Nick asked.

'As far as I know,' Cath shrugged.

'And as your shop closes at 11pm, that would mean Stu would have been there until then?'

'Yes,' Cath snorted. 'Of· course.'

Nick narrowed his eyes. 'That's funny. Because Stu gave us the CCTV from that night and he turned it off at 9.30pm.'

Cath pulled a face. 'What?'

'Yeah,' Ruth said. 'And then someone saw him driving up Klea Avenue at 10pm. Is there anything you can tell us about that?'

'No.' Cath shook her head. 'As far I knew, he was in the shop until 11pm and then came up to the flat at about 11.30pm.'

'Did you tell Stu that Phoebe had been telling people that you were having an affair with Vince Thompson?'

'I don't think so,' Cath replied uncertainly.

'You don't *think* so?' Ruth asked in a tone of disbelief.

Cath shrugged. 'I might have mentioned it in passing.'

'Come on, Cath,' Ruth snapped loudly. 'You told Stu that Phoebe Evans was spreading rumours in the pub and elsewhere that you and Vince were having an affair. And Stu went over to her house to warn her off. It got out of hand and he ended up killing her, didn't he?'

Cath looked rattled for the first time. 'I've no idea what you're talking about.'

There was a knock at the door and Georgie poked her head in.

'Boss, I need to show you something,' she said under her breath. 'It's urgent.'

Ruth nodded. 'For the purposes of the tape, DI Hunter is leaving the interview room.'

Going to the door, Ruth came out into the corridor and saw Georgie and Garrow standing waiting. From their expressions, she could tell they had found something.

'What is it?' Ruth asked.

Georgie got her phone and showed her a photograph. 'We found this shirt hidden in the wall behind an electric fire in the Mortons' flat. It's got blood all over it.'

'Jesus,' Ruth sighed, realising they now had the evidence they needed. 'Great work, guys.'

Opening the door, Ruth went back into the room. 'For the purposes of the tape, DI Hunter has re-entered the room.'

Ruth composed herself and then looked over at Cath. 'My officers have just found a blood-stained shirt hidden in a wall in your flat. Is there anything you can tell us about that?'

The blood drained from Cath's face. 'I'm not saying anything else.'

'I'm assuming that the blood on that shirt is Phoebe Evans'?' Ruth enquired.

Cath stared at the floor. 'No comment.'

Ruth looked across the table at her. 'Cath, you need to help yourself here. You need to tell us where Stu was on Wednesday night.'

'No comment.'

Ruth sat forward. 'Cath Morton, I am arresting you on suspicion of perverting the course of justice. You do not have to say anything, but it may harm your defence if you do not mention, when questioned, something that you later rely on in court.'

Cath didn't respond.

Nick looked up and gave Ruth a wink.

Chapter 52

R uth had left Stu in the holding cells for an hour before re-interviewing him and confronting him with the evidence they had found in the flat. By the end of the last interview, Stu was broken. Ruth knew that if they left him alone to think about what they had accused him of, he might just break and confess. She'd seen it many times before and her instincts told her that Stu was at that point. What she really needed was a confession for both murders.

Having repeated Stu's rights, Ruth looked across the table at him. His breathing was shallow and fast. The tension mounted as they sat in silence for a while.

'Stu,' Ruth said quite suddenly. It seemed to startle him. 'I'm going to take you back to the evidence we found at Phoebe Evans' home. If I can remind you, we found a follicle of your hair on the carpet beside Phoebe's body. You told us earlier that you had never been to Phoebe's home. Can you tell us how you think a follicle of your hair got into her carpet?'

Stu shook his head but he was staring at the floor. His right foot was jigging nervously.

'Come on, Stu,' Nick said. 'We know you were there, mate.'

'Stu, we've been into your flat this afternoon,' Ruth stated very gently. 'We found the shirt you hid in the wall.'

Stu immediately put his face in his hands and let out a low moan.

'There's blood on the shirt, Stu,' Ruth explained softly. 'Is that Phoebe Evans' blood on your shirt?'

Stu nodded slowly and then he started to weep into his hands. His shoulders juddered as he tried to get his breath.

'For the purposes of the tape, the suspect has nodded to confirm that the blood found on item reference 822F is Phoebe Evans',' Ruth stated. She then waited for a few seconds as Stu tried to compose himself.

'Stu?' Ruth whispered. 'It's okay.'

Stu looked up. His face was red and wet from where he had been crying. He was shaking all over.

'You can tell us,' Ruth said with an empathetic look. 'Did you kill Phoebe?'

Stu nodded almost imperceptibly. 'I ... I shouldn't have gone over there,' he stammered. 'But she was saying all these things about ... Cath. And that bloke Vince.'

'And that made you angry?'

'Yeah.' Stu nodded and wiped his face. 'People were laughing at me in the pub. Then these kids were saying stuff in the shop.'

'So, you went to tell her to stop?' Nick asked.

'Yeah, it wasn't true what she was saying ... I didn't know why she was lying.'

Ruth looked at him. 'What happened when you went over?'

'Phoebe started saying all these horrible things,' Stu said. 'Saying that Vince had been doing things to Cath.'

'Did you tell her that you'd killed Vince?' Nick enquired.

Stu frowned. 'No. But she said she knew it was me that done it.'

'And then what happened?'

'I told her to stop saying stuff about Cath or else. I got up to leave. Then she started calling me names. She called me a retard. She said I probably had a small cock 'cos I'm fat … There was a hockey stick behind the dresser. I grabbed it and told her to shut up. But she wouldn't. So … I hit her.'

Stu dissolved into tears.

'Stu,' Ruth said. 'I need you to tell us what happened on Monday night when you followed Vince.'

Stu put his head in hands and sobbed.

'Did you kill Vince Thompson, Stu?' Nick asked.

Stu nodded and whispered, 'Yeah.'

The duty solicitor looked over. 'I think my client needs some kind of break.'

Ruth nodded. It didn't look like Stu was in a fit state to say anything else for a while. Their questions about Vince's murder would have to wait.

She looked over at him. 'Stuart Morton, I'm charging you with the unlawful murder of Phoebe Evans and Vince Thompson.'

Chapter 53

Thirty minutes later, Ruth and Nick walked into Llancastell CID to a huge round of applause and cheers.

'Nice work, boss.' Georgie wandered over and handed her a plastic cup half-filled with Prosecco.

'Cheers.' Ruth smiled. 'Let's not get ahead of ourselves yet. As far as I'm concerned, he only confessed to Phoebe's murder.'

French, who was swigging from a can of beer, frowned. 'You don't think he killed Vince Thompson as well?'

Ruth pulled a face. 'Yeah, I do think he did. But until I hear Stu explain what happened and why, I'm going to have to keep an open mind.'

Nick frowned. 'But I asked him. And he confirmed that he did kill Vince Thompson.'

'I know that,' Ruth stated. 'But I don't think he knew what he was admitting to at that point in the interview. I'm sure when we interview him again in an hour or two, he'll give us the details of what happened the night of Vince's murder too.'

Garrow came over and handed Nick a can of Coke Zero. 'Here you go, Sarge.' Everyone was aware that he was in recovery.

'Aw, you shouldn't have.' Nick gave a wry smile. 'At least it's cold.'

Georgie smiled. 'I love the fact that Lord Jim drinks Prosecco even though there're beers in the fridge.'

Garrow shrugged. 'I just don't like beer.'

'And I guess Prosecco is the closest thing in here to Champagne,' Georgie teased.

Garrow shook his head as he smiled at Georgie. 'You are aware that both my parents were teachers?'

Georgie raised an eyebrow. 'Where was that? Eton?'

Garrow gave Georgie 'the finger' and everyone laughed.

'Thanks for the drink, guys,' Ruth said, raising her cup. The Prosecco was just this side of room temperature. 'And thanks for all your hard work. We're nearly there on this.'

French looked over. 'When are you talking to the CPS, boss?'

'After lunch.' She began to walk back to her office. 'I'll keep you posted. I need everyone to check and recheck everything you've got on Stu Morton. We need something more than what we have already, I'm afraid. And can we just have a dig around Graham Wheeler. I'm still not convinced that he's not involved somewhere along the line.'

Walking into her office, Ruth slumped down into her office chair. She clicked on the BBC News App on her phone, wondering if the police in Semley, Wiltshire had discovered any remains connected to Sarah's case. As far as she could see, there was nothing.

Nick poked his head in. 'Have you got a minute?'

She gestured to a chair. 'Take a pew.'

'Something I need to run past you,' Nick said.

The way he said it made her feel uneasy.

'What's wrong?' she enquired.

'I followed that Paul Thurrock last night,' Nick admitted.

'Jesus,' Ruth sighed. 'What did you do that for?'

Nick shrugged. 'He accused me of beating him up. I can't exactly go and have a chat with him, can I?'

'No, you can't,' Ruth stated.

'I just thought I'd see what he was up to and if there was anything dodgy going on,' Nick explained.

'And?'

'I followed him to the top of the multi-storey in town,' Nick said. 'He parked up on the roof next to a black Range Rover. He then exchanged packages with someone sitting in the back of the car. And then he drove away.'

Ruth raised an eyebrow. 'Really?'

'I ran a check on the licence plate,' Nick explained. 'Turns out the car is registered to Curtis Blake.'

Ruth felt tense at just hearing that name. Blake was a vicious drug dealer who had been responsible for the death of a DS in Llancastell CID a few years earlier. He also had a long history with Nick going back two decades.

'Bloody hell, Nick!' she exclaimed.

Nick rolled his eyes. 'I know.'

'Isn't Blake in Rhoswen, serving a sentence for conspiracy to supply?'

'That's what I thought,' Nick agreed. 'But I haven't had a chance to check on the PNC yet.'

Ruth pointed to her computer. 'Want me to check now?'

'Yeah, please.'

Ruth logged into the Police National Computer Database and began to search for details on Curtis Blake.

After a few seconds, the information came up on the screen.

She read it and then gave Nick a dark look.

'His conviction was quashed on appeal two weeks ago,' she said. 'He came out of Rhoswen last week.'

The blood visibly drained from Nick's face.

Chapter 54

L ooking at the paperwork in front of her, Ruth gave a sigh. There was still nothing on the news about the police search in Wiltshire. It wasn't surprising. It could take days, even weeks, before the SOCOs had combed every inch of the site.

Grabbing her bottle of water, Ruth stood up and decided to stretch her legs and wander out into IR1. Most of the CID team were at their desks, tapping at computers or on the phone.

She strolled over to the scene boards. Her copper's instinct told her something wasn't right about Stu Morton's admission to Vince's murder. The same make of tyres and a black baseball cap wasn't enough. They still had Daniel's account of that night and his claim that there was a woman in the car. It couldn't have been Cath Morton. Stu's motive for killing Vince Thompson was revenge for their affair. That just didn't make sense. Had Stu been with another woman?

Looking up at the boards, her eyes rested on the photo-graph of Graham Wheeler. Maybe Nick was right. What if

Vince had refused to hand over the photographic negatives in return for the £2,000? That would give Wheeler motive to go after Vince and gun him down. Maybe the negatives had simply been inside his jacket or a pocket in his jeans? Once he had shot Vince, Wheeler searched him, found what he was looking for and fled the scene. The woman in the car could have been Liv Wheeler.

'What if these two murders aren't connected?' Ruth said out loud, to no one in particular.

She turned around and looked at the CID team who were giving her a confused look.

'Sorry, boss?' French asked.

'What if these two murders just aren't connected?' she repeated.

Nick scratched his beard and frowned at her. 'I thought we always went on the assumption that there are no such things as coincidences? Two murders in one week in a place like this is very unlikely. So, our natural assumption is that they have to be linked.'

'But we could have got it wrong,' Ruth admitted with a shrug. '*I* could have got it wrong.'

'You think Kevin Parks killed Vince?' Garrow asked.

Ruth just didn't know. She looked around the room. 'Anyone found anything on Graham Wheeler?'

Georgie looked over and pointed to her computer. 'Nothing, boss. I'm just looking at his social media pages. He's making a song and dance about the fact that he's running the London Marathon next year. He's raising money for his daughter.'

Ruth nodded. She'd seen Daisy being taken away in an ambulance. 'Does it say what's wrong with her?'

Georgie shrugged. 'Some genetic disorder. Alport Syndrome.'

What?

'Let me have a look,' Ruth said, rushing over and looking.

On the screen was a *Just Giving* page, a photo of Daisy Wheeler and an explanation of Alport Syndrome.'

Shit!

Nick looked at her. 'Something wrong?'

'We need to go.' She hurried to her office and grabbed her jacket.

Nick frowned. 'What's going on, boss?'

She gave him a dark look. 'Daisy Wheeler is Vince Thompson's daughter.'

Chapter 55

Ruth and Nick sped across Llancastell, sirens and lights going as they zipped through the traffic.

'How can Daisy Wheeler be Vince Thompson's daughter?' Nick ran a red light and nearly hit a cyclist.

'Careful.' Ruth winced. She then looked over at Nick. 'Alport Syndrome is a rare genetic disorder. Amis told me that Vince Thompson suffered from it and that's why he had a kidney transplant. Daniel has it too.'

Nick raised an eyebrow. 'And so does Daisy Wheeler.'

'Exactly,' Ruth said. 'Graham Wheeler and Vince weren't fighting about old photos. They were fighting because Vince must have found out that Daisy was his biological daughter.'

'Did the Wheelers adopt her then?' Nick asked.

'I don't know,' Ruth said as her head whirred. 'That's where they were going the night Vince was killed.'

'How do you mean?'

'Daniel said Vince told him they were going to pick *someone* up before leaving Llancastell. They were on their way to the Wheeler's house to get Daisy. Somehow Wheeler must have got wind of what Vince was going to do, ran him off the road and shot him.'

'How does Daniel's mother fit into all this?' Nick enquired.

'Jesus,' Ruth said as something else dawned on her. 'Daniel was always told that his mother died in childbirth, along with his sister. Charlotte Taylor died in 2013. That's eight years ago.'

'So, Charlotte died in childbirth, but the daughter survived. And that's Daisy Wheeler,' Nick said, piecing things together.

Ten minutes later, they careened around the corner and sped up the driveway to the Wheelers' home. The gravel crunched noisily under the tyres as they parked up.

Ruth looked out. 'All the cars have gone.'

Nick gave her a look as he jumped out and went over to the door. He knocked aggressively and then moved to a ground floor window where he cupped his hands and peered inside. Ruth got out and went in the opposite direction peering into the windows.

Jogging over to the front door, Nick put his ear to it.

'Anything?' she asked.

'Not a peep,' he replied.

'They're all out,' Ruth said as they went back to the car.

Her phone rang. She recognised the number. It was Charlie from *Clear View Children's Home*.

'Charlie?' she said, hoping there was nothing wrong.

'Someone's taken Daniel,' Charlie gasped, his voice full of anxiety.

Ruth's stomach tightened.

'What? Are you sure?' she asked. 'He hasn't wandered off again?'

'No,' he trembled. 'I took them to the local park. I didn't think anything would happen if I was there. A car stopped by us and a man got out and dragged him in.'

'Did you get a look at the car?' she enquired, feeling sick with fear.

'Yes. It was a navy-coloured Volvo 4x4. I don't know what they're called.'

Graham Wheeler.

'Okay, don't worry,' Ruth said. 'I know who that is. I'll call you as soon as we have anything.'

She ended the call and looked at Nick. 'Wheeler has taken Daniel.'

Chapter 56

As Ruth and Nick sped away from Wheeler's house, Ruth was frantically trying to work out where Wheeler might be heading with Daniel. She also didn't know whether Liv and Daisy Wheeler were in the car.

'What does Wheeler want with Daniel?' Nick asked as he pushed down the accelerator and the engine roared.

'Daniel is the only eyewitness to Vince's murder,' Ruth said.

Nick frowned. 'But Daniel didn't see the person who shot his father. And Wheeler must know that or we would have arrested him straight away.'

'Maybe he just doesn't want to take any chances,' Ruth suggested. 'He can't be certain that Daniel won't put two and two together and realise who he actually saw that night.'

'You think he's actually going to kill Daniel?' Nick asked, shaking his head.

'I just don't know,' Ruth said. 'He's desperate.'

Nick looked at her. 'We showed Wheeler those photographs yesterday, didn't we?'

'Yes.' Ruth wondered quite where Nick was going with this.

'And we asked him if Daniel had ever lived there,' Nick continued. 'Wheeler must know that at some point we're going to find out Daisy's real identity.'

'Okay,' Ruth shrugged.

'Wheeler knows they've got to go into hiding. Otherwise, Daisy is going to be taken away from them.'

'So, where are they going?' Ruth enquired.

Then Nick thought of something. 'Maybe they're going to take her out of the country?'

'Holyhead?' Ruth suggested.

Nick shook his head. 'Wheeler knew as soon as he snatched Daniel, we would have an all-ports warning out. He'd never get onto a ferry.'

Ruth glanced over, her eyes widening. 'The airfield. Wheeler has a plane at the airfield.'

With that, Nick pulled the handbrake and spun the steering wheel so that they skidded around and faced the opposite direction.

Ruth winced as the car came to a stop.

'The airfield is that way,' Nick said pointing.

'Yeah, well you could have just done a U-turn, boy racer,' Ruth groaned. 'My stomach is all over the place as it is.'

Grabbing the Tetra radio, Ruth said, 'Control from three six, over.'

'Three six, Control receiving, go ahead, over,' replied the voice of the CAD operator.

'We have a suspect, a Graham Wheeler. We believe he has kidnapped a Daniel Thompson and is heading for the Rednal Airfield, south of Oswestry, over. Wheeler is driving a navy Volvo XC90. I'm gonna need a DVLA check on that plate, over.'

'Three six, received. Stand by please, over.'

Nick swung the car hard right and then left as he manoeuvred the back lanes to join the main road out to the airfield.

'Three six from Control. We have a Volvo XC90 registered to a Graham Wheeler. Licence plate, Yankee Alpha one nine, Charlie Bravo Charlie, over.'

'Three six to Control, received,' Ruth said. 'I need an all-units notice on that vehicle and suspects. All units to proceed with caution, over.'

'Three six, received. Over and out.'

A few seconds later, Nick hammered around a bend and came to a main road. Without stopping, he turned left.

'Airfield is about four miles up here.' Nick changed down a gear and took the Astra up to 70mph.

Ruth peered ahead through the windscreen. Her mind turned to Daniel. As if he hadn't been through enough in the past few days.

Nick saw something and pointed. There was a car up ahead and they were making up ground on it.

It was a navy-coloured Volvo XC90.

Bingo.

'Found you, you fucker,' Nick growled as he revved the engine.

Ruth clicked her radio again. 'Control from three six, over.'

'Three six from Control. Go ahead, over.'

'We are now in pursuit of suspect, Graham Wheeler and suspect vehicle. Heading south on the A495, over.'

'Received. Stand by, over.'

Nick went hammering up the hill and over the crest. Wheeler's Volvo was now only about half a mile ahead, and they were gaining. Nick pulled out to overtake a car towing a caravan and shot past it at speed.

'Wheeler's never going to stop,' Ruth said, as her anxiety grew. 'He's got too much to lose.'

Nick looked at her. 'He can see we're behind him. How does he think he's going to get on a plane and leave the country?'

Ruth grabbed the radio. 'Control from three six. Suspect still heading south on the A495. One mile north of Whittington. Over.'

A moment later, they screamed through the tiny village of Whittington. The village green and church went past in a blur.

Just up ahead, a transit van pulled out of a turning in front of them. Nick swung the car onto the opposite side of the road, missing it by a few feet, and throwing Ruth hard against the passenger door.

'Dickhead!' Nick bellowed at the driver.

'White van drivers for you.'

Wheeler's Volvo was now only five hundred yards away. It pulled out to overtake, and whizzed past two cars. However, as Nick pulled out to do the same, there was an enormous tractor coming the other way.

Ruth's eyes widened. It wasn't the first time Nick had done a manoeuvre like this but she did wonder if his luck was going to run out.

Oh shit. We're never going to make it!

Nick slammed the car down into third gear and gunned the engine. Ruth felt herself being pushed back into her chair as they zipped through the gap with inches to spare.

'Nice one,' Nick said, still focussed on the road ahead.

As they approached a pub, three middle-aged cyclists came out of the car park and into the middle of the road.

'Jesus!' she gasped through gritted teeth as Nick slammed on the brakes.

Ruth felt the Astra's tyres skidding as she was thrown forward. The seatbelt dug hard into her shoulder and chest.

The cyclists looked up as they skidded towards them, almost in slow motion.

They looked terrified.

Oh my God, we're going to go ploughing into them!

Ruth screwed her eyes closed instinctively. She waited for the hideous sound of impact.

The car stopped.

Opening her eyes, she saw the petrified cyclists looking at them, bracing themselves for impact.

They had stopped with inches to spare.

Thank God!

'You all right?' Nick asked.

'Yeah, I think so,' Ruth gasped, getting her breath back.

They both looked at the road ahead – Wheeler's Volvo was out of sight.

Shit!

Chapter 57

I t was ten minutes later by the time Ruth and Nick arrived at Rednal Airfield. Wheeler's Volvo was parked on the right-hand side of the car park.

Okay, they're definitely here then.

She just prayed that they weren't too late. A dozen or so private planes were lined up on the far side of the runway. To the left was a two-storey building that housed offices and the airfield's café and bar.

Getting out of the car, Ruth frantically scanned the area for signs of Daniel or Wheeler's car. She then spotted a mechanic who was wearing an orange high-vis vest and carrying a clipboard. He was inspecting a red and white Piper 32A six-seater plane.

Jogging over, she pulled out her warrant card. 'Afternoon. DI Hunter, Llancastell CID.'

'Right you are,' the mechanic nodded – he was eager to help.

'I'm looking for Graham Wheeler,' she explained with a sense of urgency.

The mechanic pointed to the plane and smiled. 'I'm

just getting this plane ready for Mr Wheeler and his family.'

Ruth looked at him. 'I'm afraid this plane can't go anywhere today. Can you tell me where Graham Wheeler and his family are?'

The mechanic looked confused and then pointed over to the two-storey building. 'They said they were getting a coffee in there. But Mr Wheeler said he needed to fly as soon as possible so he was going to log his flight plan in the office.'

'Any idea where they were going?' Nick asked.

'I think he said they were going to Northern France.'

'Thanks,' Ruth said. 'And no one is to leave this airfield until they talk to me first.'

The mechanic nodded with a serious expression. 'Okay. Understood.'

Ruth and Nick turned and moved quickly towards the building.

They went inside and saw offices and a small cafeteria to the right.

Nick pointed to the offices. 'I'll try in here.'

Entering the café, Ruth could see there were three or four pilots at a table, drinking coffee and chatting. But there was no sign of the Wheeler family or Daniel anywhere.

Where the hell are they?

Out of the corner of her eye, Ruth spotted a man through a window outside the back of the building.

Wheeler!

He then moved out of sight.

'Out there,' Ruth said loudly to Nick as he joined her.

'Where?

She pointed and pulled at his coat. There was no time

to explain. 'They're out the back. Come on!' she shouted as she ran.

Ruth and Nick both broke into a sprint as they crashed through the main doors.

They hammered around the building and headed to the back.

Nothing.

A few old beer crates and some cardboard boxes.

Shit!

Wheeler had disappeared.

Where is he? And where the hell is Daniel? Ruth wondered anxiously. She wanted to beat the living daylights out of Wheeler for taking Daniel.

Nick pointed to the fire exit doors that were half open. 'Through there.'

They broke into a run and Ruth smashed through the exit doors with Nick just behind her.

They looked left and then right. Just dark empty corridors.

Nothing.

'Where the hell are they?' Ruth growled to herself.

They could hear the sound of running feet above them on the fire escape staircase.

'Up this way!' she yelled.

Leaping up the steps, two by two, Ruth felt the muscles in her thighs begin to burn.

Jesus, this really hurts.

Reaching the next floor, she glanced both ways.

Nothing.

The sound of running feet came again from above.

'Come on,' Nick urged, as he took over the lead.

Dragging in air, they arrived at a doorway that led out onto the roof of the airfield building. It gave them a bird's eye view of the runway and the fields beyond. But they didn't have time to take in the view today.

The wind whipped around their faces as they spotted Graham Wheeler, with Daniel, Liv and Daisy in tow, running for the other side of the roof where there appeared to be another doorway.

'STAY THERE! POLICE!' Nick yelled.

'What the hell does he think he's doing?' Ruth muttered angrily.

The fugitives had now reached another door. However, as Ruth and Nick sprinted after them, they could see the door was locked. Wheeler frantically pulled at the door handle but it was no use.

Right! Now they're trapped!

Wheeler grabbed Daniel and climbed rather awkwardly over the safety rail and onto the perimeter wall. Nothing now protected them from a hundred feet drop onto the concrete below.

Jesus!

Liv had her arms around Daisy as they watched on – they looked petrified.

'Graham! What are you doing?' Liv shouted.

Ruth and Nick stopped at the rail, panting and trying to catch their breath.

Wheeler stood behind Daniel with his arm around his neck and chest.

'Ruth!' Daniel shouted as he looked at her in desperation. He sounded scared.

'It's okay, Daniel. I'm here now,' Ruth reassured him as she then glared at Wheeler.

'What are you doing, Graham?' she hissed at him.

Wheeler didn't answer – he looked desperate. Maybe he didn't know quite what he was trying to achieve.

'Don't do anything stupid,' Ruth said calmly, before climbing over the rail.

'Stay where you are!' Graham shouted, before moving backwards towards the edge of the wall.

Oh God, if he slips now, they're both going to die.

'You need to let Daniel go,' Ruth said, raising her voice over the noise of the wind.

Graham shook his head. 'No.' His eyes were roaming around wildly – he wasn't thinking straight, and that was dangerous.

Daisy looked over in floods of tears. 'Daddy! What are you doing?'

Ruth looked at him and then gestured to Daisy. 'Come on, Graham. You need to give this up and come down from there.'

'No.' Wheeler shook his head. 'You don't understand.'

'I do understand, Graham,' Ruth stated, taking a more conciliatory tone. 'I know about Daisy. I know about Charlotte. And we can sort that out if you let Daniel go and come down.'

Wheeler glanced backwards - the heels of his shoes were now only a foot from the edge. The battering wind made it feel even more precarious.

Ruth took a nervous gulp. A sudden blast of wind could send them both hurtling to the ground. 'Please, Graham. You don't want to do this.'

'I'm going to lose everything,' Wheeler shouted desperately.

'No, you're not,' Ruth said. 'Look at your wife and your daughter. You've put them through enough. You need to let Daniel go, come down and we can sort out this mess.'

Daisy broke free from her mother's arms and ran over to the railing. 'Daddy, I'm scared. I don't understand what you're doing.'

Wheeler looked at Ruth and closed his eyes for a second. It was over. He then slowly took his arm from around Daniel and let him go.

Daniel thought for a moment, jumped down and sprinted into Ruth's arms.

'It's all right. You're safe now,' she reassured him.

Wheeler threw his leg over the rail as Nick grabbed him roughly and put him in cuffs.

Chapter 58

It was 7pm by the time Ruth and Nick walked down the corridor to interview Graham Wheeler at Llancastell Police Station. Ruth felt exhausted and her body ached all over. She was getting way too old to be charging around airfields chasing people.

Nick looked at her. 'You okay, boss?'

'Yeah,' Ruth replied. 'Why, don't I seem okay?'

'Not really,' Nick admitted. 'You haven't said more than two words since we got back.'

'I watched Social Services picking up Daniel earlier,' she said. 'He looked at me as he went and it broke my heart.'

'I'm sure you can see him again,' Nick reassured her.

'Yeah, I know,' Ruth nodded. 'To be honest, I'm absolutely shattered. When I first took this job, I thought it was going to be sitting at a desk, boring paperwork and the odd tractor theft.'

'Yeah, it's not really like that up here, is it?'

Ruth rolled her eyes. 'No, not really,' she said dryly.

They entered Interview Room 2 and sat down.

Wheeler's solicitor, James Barker, had arrived and had been briefed on his arrest. Wheeler was now dressed in a regulation grey tracksuit as his clothes had been taken away for forensics.

Ruth and Nick settled themselves and put their files down on the interview table. Nick leant across the table to start the recording machine. A long electronic beep sounded as Ruth opened her files and gave Nick a quick look of acknowledgement.

'Interview conducted with Graham Wheeler, Llancastell Police Station. Present are Detective Sergeant Nick Evans, Solicitor James Barker and myself, Detective Inspector Ruth Hunter.' Ruth then glanced over at Wheeler. 'Graham, do you understand that you are still under arrest?'

'Yes,' he mumbled almost inaudibly.

'Can you tell us why you kidnapped Daniel Thompson and took him to Rednal Airfield?' Ruth asked.

'No comment.'

James Barker had clearly instructed Wheeler to conduct a *no comment* interview.

Ruth looked over at him. 'Is Daisy your biological daughter, Graham?'

'No comment.'

'We know that Daisy is the biological daughter of Vince Thompson and Charlotte Taylor,' Nick stated. 'We just don't know how you ended up bringing her up as your daughter.'

'No comment.'

'Can you tell us where you were on Monday night?' Ruth asked.

Wheeler shrugged. 'No comment.'

'Did you shoot and kill Vince Thompson on Monday night?'

'No comment.'

Ruth looked at Nick in frustration. Wheeler was clearly going to put the burden of proof onto the police and the CPS. She wondered if Liv Wheeler was going to go down the same route.

Chapter 59

I t was thirty minutes later and Ruth and Nick had finished interviewing Wheeler and returned him to a holding cell in Llancastell nick. He wasn't going to give anything up.

Having cautioned Liv Wheeler, Ruth and Nick now sat opposite her in Interview Room 2. Her solicitor, James Barker, sat next to her.

'Liv,' Ruth said quietly. 'Can you tell us why you and your husband took Daniel today?'

Liv looked at them. Her face was streaked from where she had been crying. She looked totally broken and a far cry from the snooty woman they had interviewed a couple of days ago.

'I don't know. It was Graham's idea,' she whispered.

Right, so she's not going for a 'no comment' interview. Interesting, Ruth thought.

Ruth pulled over a file. 'Maybe we should start at the beginning?'

'Yes,' Liv replied, but she was looking at the floor.

Unlike her husband, Ruth already got the feeling that she was ashamed of what they had done.

'For the purposes of the tape, I am showing the suspect item reference 290R,' Ruth stated. 'Liv, we have a birth certificate for Daisy that my officers found at your home,' Ruth explained. 'On this birth certificate, you and Graham are registered as Daisy's parents. My officers suspect the document is a fake. Is there anything you can tell us about that?'

Barker leaned in and whispered something into Liv's ear. Ruth assumed he was advising her not to answer the question and say *no comment*.

Liv shook her head at him. 'No, I want to talk about this now. We did a terrible thing.' She began to cry and put her hands to her face.

Ruth waited for a few seconds so she could compose herself. She handed Liv a tissue. 'Here you go.'

'Thanks.' Liv sniffed, taking the tissue and wiping her face.

'Why don't you tell us what happened?' Ruth asked gently.

Liv nodded as if somehow the thought of getting it off her chest was a massive relief.

'Charlotte came to work for us about nine years ago,' Liv explained.

'Charlotte Taylor?' Nick asked to clarify.

Liv nodded. 'Yes.'

'When you say *work for us*, what do you mean by that?' Ruth asked.

'Graham and I were expanding our wedding business at the hall and we needed someone to take the bookings, run the diary. There's a small apartment at the top of the hall, so she and Daniel lived in there. It was part of the deal we did.'

'Where was Vince Thompson at this time?' Nick asked.

'He'd been sent to prison for dealing drugs three months earlier,' Liv replied. 'A few weeks after Charlotte moved in, she discovered she was pregnant with his child. That wasn't ideal but we'd signed a contract with her.'

Ruth frowned. 'Was Daniel attending school?'

'Yes. He went to the nursery down the road,' Liv replied. 'I think he was about two.'

'So, Charlotte lived with you at the hall the whole time she was pregnant?' Nick asked.

'Yes … I found it particularly difficult because Graham and I couldn't have children.'

'Okay. Can you talk us through what happened at the birth?' Ruth enquired.

'Charlotte collapsed in our hallway and went into labour one night. It was only a few days before her due date. We could see that she was getting into difficulties, so we called an ambulance,' Liv said as another tear came down her face. 'I think Charlotte must have haemorrhaged because there was lots of blood quite suddenly. And then Graham could see a baby's head. Somehow he managed to deliver the baby but Charlotte was slipping in and out of consciousness. We cut the cord and I took the baby away to clean her up. And then Graham realised there was another baby coming.'

Ruth's eyes widened in astonishment. 'Twins?'

'Yes. She never told us,' Liv replied. 'And this time the baby that came out was blue. It was cold and it wasn't breathing. Graham tried to revive her while I took the first baby upstairs to get a blanket. A few minutes later, the paramedics arrived. They tried to revive both Charlotte and the second baby. Then they rushed them to Llancastell University Hospital. But they were both dead on arrival.'

Liv burst into tears at the thought of what had

happened. She dabbed at her bloodshot eyes with the tissue and took a deep breath to steady herself.

Ruth looked at her. 'And this happened while you were upstairs?'

Liv nodded and whispered. 'Yes.'

'With the baby?'

'Yes. It all happened so quickly.'

'And Graham never said anything to the paramedics?' Nick asked.

'He was covered from head to toe in blood,' Liv stammered. 'I mean, he'd just delivered a stillborn baby and watched Charlotte die in front of his eyes. I don't think he was in a fit state to say anything to anyone.'

Ruth narrowed her eyes and asked, 'So you just kept hold of the baby?'

Liv nodded as she blinked away more tears. She was visibly shaking.

'And no one ever put two and two together and realised there was a missing baby?' Ruth asked, almost unable to believe the story Liv had told them.

Liv shook her head. 'No. And we told ourselves that had we given up Daisy, she would have been taken into care. We were going to bring her up as our own. We didn't see the harm in it.'

'What about Charlotte's midwife? She would have known she was pregnant with twins?' Ruth asked in disbelief.

'Charlotte had been assigned about three or four different midwives during her pregnancy. Her notes went missing once. It was shambolic,' Liv explained. 'I guess no one checked her pregnancy records after she died. Or if they did, they didn't check them thoroughly.'

'What about Vince?' Nick asked.

'We spoke to Vince at Charlotte's funeral,' Liv

explained. 'He'd been given compassionate leave from the prison for the day. When he'd been convicted of drug dealing, Charlotte told him she wanted nothing to do with him. He didn't even know she'd been pregnant, and certainly didn't know it had been with twins.'

'But he did eventually find out that Daisy was his biological daughter?' Ruth asked. 'How?'

'About a year ago, Vince saw the charity fundraising that Graham had been doing for Daisy and Alport Syndrome in a local paper,' Liv said. 'He came up here one afternoon with Daniel to talk to us. He knew that Alport was incredibly rare. And when he saw Daisy, he said he knew that she was Charlotte's daughter. We denied it so he asked us to prove that one of us suffered from Alport. He knew we were lying. And he just put it all together.'

'And then he blackmailed you?' Nick asked.

'Yes,' Liv nodded. 'First money. Then the free house in Llancastell. Then more money. He promised every time that he would leave us alone. He rang us last Monday night and said that he was coming to pick up Daisy whether we liked it or not. Graham and I jumped in the car to intercept him. I didn't know Graham had a shotgun in the boot. When we found him driving towards our house, we chased him for a bit and then ran him off the road down in Chirk. He came for us with a baseball bat, so Graham shot him.'

There were a few seconds' silence as Ruth looked over at Nick. She couldn't remember working on any case like it before in all her thirty years of policing.

'And now we're going to lose everything,' Liv wept and shook her head.

Ruth looked over at her. 'Liv Wheeler, I'm charging you with conspiracy to kidnap and murder.'

Chapter 60

That evening, Ruth, Sarah, Doreen and Ruth's daughter Ella were sitting in Ruth's living room in her house in Bangor-on-Dee. Ruth had drunk a little too much wine as she was feeling relieved after a rollercoaster of a week.

Ella jumped up from the sofa. 'I'll get more wine, shall I?'

Ruth smiled. 'Yeah, keep it coming, darling.'

Sarah gave her a wry smile. 'Ruth Hunter, I do believe you're a bit drunk.'

'Me? No?' Ruth laughed.

Ella turned back from the door. 'Mum, you're hammered.'

Ruth shrugged as she drained her glass. 'I don't care. This week has been completely mental.'

'Well, I've had a glass,' Doreen stated. 'And I'm pissed as a fart.'

Everyone laughed.

Sarah rolled her eyes. 'That's because you're not meant

to be drinking, Mum. I don't think chemotherapy and wine are a good combo.'

'Well, it's the best I've felt for ages.' Doreen raised an eyebrow and then looked at Ruth. 'And if we're having a party, Ruth, can we have some music?'

Ruth smiled. 'What are we having? *The Searchers*? Or *Billy Fury*?'

Doreen winked at her. 'I thought that was our little secret?'

Ruth was now standing at the stereo, wondering what music to put on. 'So, it's either Deep New York House or Nosebleed Belgian Techno?'

'I like The Everly Brothers,' Doreen said.

More laughter.

Ruth linked her phone to the Bluetooth on the stereo and soon found *Sealed With a Kiss* by *The Everly Brothers*.

There was a knock at the door.

'I'll get it.' Ruth made her way out to the hallway and over to the front door.

She saw a tall figure behind the door that she recognised.

'Expecting someone?' Ella called from the kitchen.

Ruth smiled as she began to open the door. 'I am actually.'

Charlie was standing on the doorstep. Beside him stood Daniel with his rucksack.

'Special delivery,' Charlie joked, gesturing to Daniel.

Ruth leant down and smiled. 'Hello, Daniel. Do you want to come in?'

He nodded. 'Yes, please.'

Charlie looked at her. 'I'll leave you two to it then. Any problems, you know where I am.'

Ruth ushered Daniel into the hallway.

'Why don't you take off your rucksack, eh?' Ruth suggested.

'Chelsea are playing in the FA Cup tonight,' he said. His eyes bright and full of life. 'Can we watch the high-lights later?'

'I'm sure we can.' Ruth nodded. 'Why don't you come through?'

Daniel stood close to her as they walked down the hallway and into the living room.

'Everyone, this is Daniel,' Ruth said with a beaming smile. 'He's going to be staying with me for a while.'

'Hello, Daniel,' everyone said.

Chapter 61

Megan's pink light threw a beautiful hue over her tidy bedroom. A pink chiffon sheet hung like a canopy over her bed. Nick was reading her a bedtime story but struggling to keep his eyes open.

'Daddy?' she asked with a frown. 'Are you falling asleep?'

Nick grinned and then raised his eyebrows dramatically. 'Me? No. Of course not.'

'Yes, you are,' she giggled.

'Okay.' Nick pointed to the picture book which featured a witty caterpillar. 'Last page for tonight. *So Cyril said, 'Why are you looking so sad? And Stan the squirrel replied, 'Someone has stolen all my acorns again. I don't know who's doing it.' Cyril gave him a look. 'I think I do.'*

'So do I,' Megan exclaimed excitedly.

Nick then closed the book and kissed her forehead. 'And we'll find that out tomorrow.'

'Do you know who it is, Daddy?' Megan asked.

Nick smiled. 'Mmm, I've got a few suspects in mind.'

'Suspects? What's *suspects?*'

Nick laughed. 'I'll tell you tomorrow, okay. Now go to sleep poppet.'

As he padded over her soft carpet, he glanced back at Megan as she shifted her pillows and settled down.

He opened the door quietly, went down the landing and the stairs. There was a suitcase by the door. Fran's parents were back from holiday the following day, so she was returning home. He hoped that eventually she would be able to move on from the assault by Thurrock. He wondered if he'd helped or made it worse.

At that moment, Fran appeared at the top of the stairs holding a few more things that she wanted to pop in her case.

'All set?' Nick asked her.

Fran nodded. 'Yeah.'

'It's been nice to have you here, despite the circumstances,' Nick said with a half-smile.

'Yeah,' Fran said quietly. 'You and Amanda have been amazing this last week. I don't know what I'd have done without you.'

Nick pulled a face. 'I think I just made things worse.'

'No.' Fran shook her head. 'You didn't. And I'm sorry if I was angry with you about going to talk to … him.'

'You don't need to apologise about anything,' Nick stated, reaching out and putting a reassuring hand on her shoulder. 'I just didn't want him thinking that he'd got away with it, that's all.'

'Yeah. When I thought about it after, I was glad you did that. It felt like at least someone was standing up for me,' Fran admitted. 'Does anyone know who did attack him?'

Nick shrugged. 'No. I've no idea.'

For a second, Nick remembered watching Thurrock in

the car park and his meeting with whoever was sitting in Curtis Blake's car. And then the thought that Blake was out of prison.

'He came in for a day,' Fran explained. 'But he was off sick again today.'

Amanda came out and smiled. 'Is anyone going to help me lay the table or are you two just going to stay out here chattering?'

Nick shrugged. 'Sorry. Mum.'

Fran put her hand to her mouth and laughed.

Amanda gave him a playful hit. 'Don't be weird, Nick. Just come and help me.'

Nick gave her a salute and looked at Fran. 'We'd better go.'

Just as they turned to go into the kitchen, there was a loud knock at the door.

Nick looked at Amanda and frowned. 'Expecting anyone?'

She shook her head. 'No.'

Opening the front door, Nick saw two men in suits standing on his doorstep.

He didn't recognise them.

The older man had a greying beard. He pulled out a warrant card. 'DS Carter, St Asaph CID.'

Nick was none the wiser. He didn't recognise either of them but then again, he'd never had much to do with the CID at St Asaph.

'How can I help?' Nick asked, starting to feel a little uneasy about their presence on his doorstep.

'We're looking for a Nicholas Evans,' Carter explained.

Nick frowned. 'Yes. That's me. Is there a problem?'

Carter took a step forward and looked at him. 'Nicholas Evans, I am arresting you on suspicion of the murder of Paul Thurrock. You do not have to say

277

anything, but it may harm your defence if you do not mention when questioned something which you later rely on in court. Anything you do say may be used as evidence in a court of law,' Carter said. 'Do you understand your rights, sir?'

Enjoy this book?
Get the next book in the series
'The Portmeirion Killings' #Book 13
on pre-order on Amazon
Publication date September 2022
www.amazon.co.uk/dp/B0B4X2SMCG
www.amazon.com/dp/B0B4X2SMCG

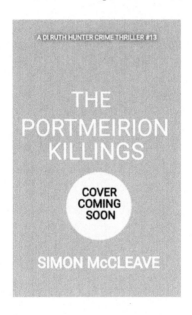

The Portmeirion Killings
A Ruth Hunter Crime Thriller #Book 13

Your FREE book is waiting for you now

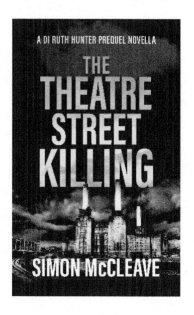

Get your FREE copy of the prequel to
the DI Ruth Hunter Series NOW
http://www.simonmccleave.com/vip-email-club
and join my VIP Email Club

RUTH HUNTER SERIES

London, 1997. A series of baffling murders. A web of political corruption. DC Ruth Hunter thinks she has the brutal killer in her sights, but there's one problem. He's a Serbian War criminal who died five years earlier and lies buried in Bosnia.

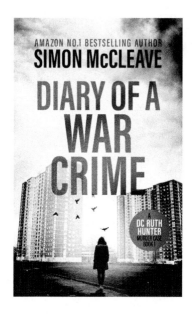

My Book
My Book

AUTHOR'S NOTE

Although this book is very much a work of fiction, it is located in Snowdonia, a spectacular area of North Wales. It is steeped in history and folklore that spans over two thousand years. It is worth mentioning that Llancastell is a fictional town on the eastern edges of Snowdonia. I have made liberal use of artistic licence, names and places have been changed to enhance the pace and substance of the story.

Acknowledgments

I will always be indebted to the people who have made this novel possible.

My mum, Pam, and my stronger half, Nicola, whose initial reaction, ideas and notes on my work I trust implicitly. And Dad, for his overwhelming enthusiasm.

Carole Kendal for her meticulous proofreading. My excellent publicists, Emma Draude and Emma Dowson at EDPR. My designer Stuart Bache for yet another incredible cover design. My superb agent, Millie Hoskins at United Agents, and Dave Gaughran and Nick Erik for invaluable support and advice.

Printed in Great Britain
by Amazon